The Crimson Wing

BY

H. C. CHATFIELD-TAYLOR

*Author of "Two Women and a Fool," "The Idle Born."
etc., etc.*

HERBERT S. STONE & COMPANY
CHICAGO AND NEW YORK
MCMII

CONTENTS

I

I

"Conquest's Crimson Wing."—GRAY.

The Crimson Wing

I

THE ONE

"Will you play or would you rather make love to Marguerite Clairon?"

She said it with a smile that displayed two rows of perfect teeth,—Clotilde Berthon, of the *Bouffes Parisiens*, a little confection of pink and white flesh, who might have stepped from a *fête galante* by Watteau.

He stood by the door of her salon at Ems; he smiled, but for a moment he did not answer.

He saw the flare of candles in a crystal chandelier, the dull yellow of gold against a green cloth, the untamed look of men and women watching the turning of a card, like hungry animals when the keeper approaches with a tumbril of raw meat. He saw his friend, Guy Egerton, hurrying towards the table; and then, sitting apart, with her back turned towards the players, he also saw a slender girl with a face, white and beautiful, against the tumbled masses of reddish hair.

"In either case I shall probably lose," he said in answer to the question, "but at present I value my pocketbook more highly than my heart."

"You are wise to keep the pocketbook," said the actress, "without it you would have a poor chance with love," and she led the way towards Marguerite Clairon.

The girl looked up as they approached. At sight of the Prussian uniform she frowned.

"War is not declared," laughed Clotilde Berthon. "Let me introduce the Count von Leun-Walram, who speaks French like a *Boulevardier*."

He clicked his heels together and bent at the waist.

"At last," he said, "I meet *la belle Clairon* of the *Palais Royal*. From admiration to adoration is, I fear, but a step."

"*Tiens!*" she answered, "very prettily said."

For a moment the young actress looked at him. A strong face, she thought, with its glow of health and clear blue eyes, its high cheek bones and resolute mouth. He was almost handsome, too, in his light blue *attila* braided in white.

"I don't like Prussians," she continued, "but I like blondes. Won't you sit down?"

The young soldier laughed and drew a chair beside her.

"Take care," whispered Clotilde Berthon, as she turned away, "Paul D'Arblay is very jealous—he is watching you already."

The soldier followed her eyes. At the table, beside his friend, Guy Egerton, he saw a man looking at him stealthily from behind his cards. The face was certainly not pleasing—sly black eyes under shaggy brows which grew together on the forehead; a skin of ashy whiteness, thick, bestial lips, partly covered by a slight moustache with a cynical droop to the ends; and a retreating chin on which a pointed black beard grew in patches. In the man's buttonhole was the red and black ribbon of some unimportant order—he might be anything suspicious,—a political spy, a *chevalier d'industrie*.

"You do not like him," said Marguerite Clairon when her friend had gone. "You think that he has a bad face."

"To dislike the friend of a queen is treason,' he said, evading the question.

The girl looked at her pretty shoulders and arranged a rumpled ribbon.

"*Fichtre!* he is no friend of mine," she answered with evident dislike.

"And yet, our hostess——"

"Said he was jealous," she interrupted, taking the words from his lips. "That proves that I do not love him."

"A strange idea," he laughed; "cannot a man be jealous of the woman who loves him?"

"Not if he is sure of her—and, alas, a woman who really loves cannot dissemble. Indifference and deception make men jealous—devotion only makes them conceited and bored."

For a moment he watched her intently, not thinking of what she said. The wavy folds of Titian hair, the delicate skin with its mystery of tints, the arched brows, the curling lashes, the dreamy blue eyes with a look of longing for the unattainable,—the face was beautiful, but he could not help thinking it was pathetic. She saw him watching her and her expression quickly changed to the hunted look which women have when they have had to fight with the world.

"What did Clotilde say your name was," she asked suddenly; "the Count von Leun-Wal— Wal—?"

"The Count von Leun-Walram," he answered, smiling at her attempt to pronounce the German.

She looked at the blue *attila* with the white

corded frogs and silver buttons and the braided *husarenschärpe* about the waist.

"You are a Hussar," she said.

"Yes."

"Lieutenant?"

"No," he answered, with a touch of pride, "Captain in the 13th Hessian Hussars."

" *Mon Dieu*," she laughed, "'Captain the Count von Leun-Walram, 13th Hessian Hussars—I can't call you all that. What is your Christian name?"

"Ludwig," he laughed.

"That is better. I shall call you Ludwig. That means Louis, doesn't it?—the same as our Emperor."

"Yes, and I'm afraid that I shall forget the pretty name of Clairon, because Marguerite is so beautiful."

"How well you speak French," she exclaimed, and she gave him an inquisitive look.

"You wish to know?— Well, my mother was an American, and my father a distant relative of the Duke of Nassau, and because he was a liberal in '48 he was banished; so I grew up in France. I might have been a painter if the Duke hadn't forgiven my father— but in consequence I am a soldier. Since the Duke lost his duchy I have been a Prussian in a Hessian regiment—all kinds of a mixture,

you see.   Now let's talk about the weather.'
Then for a moment he watched the players.

They were women of the half world and men
of the whole world, French mostly, for in '70
Ems was a smart resort for Parisians, although
a Russian and a torpid Spaniard were seated at
the table, the one with money heaped before
him and the other with a gaunt, solicitous look
in his motionless face. The man, D'Arblay, held
the bank, and Ludwig's friend, Guy Egerton,
was flushed and excited with a meagre stake
before him.   It worried Ludwig, for Egerton
had been of the Coldstream Guards till cards
went against him, and being forced to ex-
patriate himself and his sword he fought with
Prince Charles of Bavaria in '66.   He had
managed to keep his billet in the Bavarian
service because he had proved himself brave
and a good fellow withal; but gambling was
his besetting vice and the German knew that
he could not afford to lose.   It was to keep an
eye on his friend that he had come to Clotilde
Berthon's salon that night.

"Even if you are a Prussian," said the girl
beside him, "I'm glad you're not French." The
voice was deep and soft, like the tolling of a
bell afar off.   It made him forget the players.

"A curious sentiment," he answered.

She shrugged her shoulders.

"A woman must love. Sometimes it is a degenerate, sometimes a savage. I prefer a savage, and you Prussians are savages."

"Yet, I repeat it is a curious sentiment for a Frenchwoman, for one with the great name of Clairon, for one who is herself on the stage."

The girl's eyes flashed.

"Because my namesake, the great Claire Clairon, dared to love as she chose, she was libelled and insulted ; because she had the courage to uphold the dignity of her profession she was imprisoned and driven from the stage, and all by Frenchmen."

"Yet it was a Frenchman who said of her, "*Tout jusqu' à l'art chez elle, a de la vérité!*"

She looked at him long and curiously. "So you are not a savage, after all," she said with disdain; "so you dabble in poetry, you who are so full of blood and vigour. Alas!—I once knew a poet,—fair and worthless as an apple of Sodom."

The soldier laughed.

"You remind me of an ostrich," he said. "You cover your thoughts with cynicism, and imagine no one can read your heart."

"My heart!" scoffed the girl. "I defy you to read it."

"Opinion is merely experience. Your views and the look in your eyes tell me the story."

"Well?" she exclaimed.

He drew his chair nearer, so that he could look into her face. His lowered voice was soft, and to her it had the rare touch of sympathy.

"He was a poet," he said, "a French poet, shall we say, with slender, blue-veined hands and dreamy eyes, and when he touched his lyre your soul was thrilled as it had never been before; and so you drifted on, happy in the consciousness of a great love,—until the end came, and you fell, a sacrifice to his vanity and conceit. You managed finally to pick yourself up, stunned and bruised from the fall,—but your soul is somewhere up there in the clouds. There, am I right?"

"I believe you are the devil," she said, with a look that startled him. "No one else could read a woman's heart like that."

Her look told him plainly of an awakening desire hardly to be dignified by the name of love, because of the suddenness with which it was aroused.

"It is easy to understand a woman," he answered carelessly, in an endeavor to misconstrue her meaning, "unless you happen to be in love with her. Then she surpasses all understanding."

"What if you should bring back my soul from up there in the clouds?" she asked.

Her eyes had a look which made the blood thrill in him; and he was conscious of her meaning,—but he left the seat beside her suddenly.

"I shall not try," he said.

"*Mon Dieu*, but you are cold," and with a glance full of resentment she turned away.

He saw a middle-aged banker come towards her; one of the great financiers of Europe. He was fat and bald and the lids of his little piggy eyes were swollen and red. As he laid his hand upon her shoulder she shuddered and drew back, and the look she gave him was of loathing and horror.

"Not playing, my dear," the officer heard him say. And her glance quickly changed into a smile, while the banker's face beamed with the same self-satisfaction with which he would have viewed his superb hotel in the Avenue des Champs Élysées, or his race horses.

The soldier turned away. He had beheld a woman beneath the mask, while the banker saw only the smile of an actress—and his heart cried out against the injustice of a world which condemns the woman while it honours the brute who drags her down.

As he started towards the baccarat players he saw Guy Egerton push his last bank-note over to D'Arblay. Then, leaving the table hurriedly, his friend came where he was standing.

"No luck, Ludwig," he muttered, breathing deep and excited. "It beats the devil how the cards run." He took out his eyeglass and wiped it, and when he had screwed it in his eye again he stroked his curling red moustache and tried to calm his nerves.

"Guy, you are a fool," said the German.

"I know it," answered Egerton with a nervous little laugh.

Ludwig's glance wandered towards the table. D'Arblay still dealt and he heard the Spaniard sitting next him say "*banco*"—so he kept his eyes fixed on the hands which held the cards, for the stake was now the capital of the bank. To right and left *tableau* the cards were dealt, then D'Arblay whispered something which made the players laugh; but the soldier's quick eye caught a movement of his fingers, the white glint of a card.

"Nine," said the man, as he turned over his cards, and reached for the Spaniard's money. A moment later he sold the bank to the Russian and left the table.

"Come, Guy," said Ludwig with a hand on his friend's shoulder, "when luck's against you—quit."

"I've got to," said the Englishman, sadly, "unless you stake me."

"Not to-night, Guy—luck's against you. To-morrow if you insist, I will,—and play myself."

"That'll be worth coming to see," laughed the Englishman, and with the swagger of the British guardsman he strode towards the hostess to say good-night.

Marguerite Clairon still sat beside the banker. As Ludwig passed her he stopped.

"Good-bye," he said, pressing her little white hand to his lips.

"Savage," she whispered.

The soldier laughed and walked away. The girl followed him with her eyes until he had gone—then she left the banker suddenly and ran towards the door.

"Marguerite! Where are you going?" cried D'Arblay as she brushed past him.

"*N'importe!*" she said, jerking back the arm he had caught.

As she passed through the door she closed it. The Englishman was already on the stairs, the German but half way down the hall.

"Ludwig!" she called.

He turned at the sound of his name. It was almost dark in the hallway, but he heard the rustle of a skirt and caught the delicate, sen-

suous odor of *Chypre*—then the door opened
softly and in the flood of light beyond the girl
he saw a brutal face.

She caught both his hands. He saw her
half closed eyes, her curving lips.

"I shall see you again, Ludwig," she said,
"you will come back."

She was so near, so beautiful, so dangerous.

"If I dare," he whispered hoarsely.

When she looked he had gone, and while
she listened to the tinkling of his little silver
spurs upon the stairs her breath came quick
and fluttering.

"Love," she sighed, "love, there is nothing
else."

"Very pretty," said a man behind her.

"You followed, Paul D'Arblay," she cried
in a voice of anger. "You played the spy!"

He had the look of a crouching animal,
cowed by the keeper's lash, but still untamed.

"Because I love you," he said.

The girl shrugged her shoulders and
laughed.

"Well!—what is that to me?"

He bent his head to her and stretched out
his hands.

"You are cruel, Marguerite,—why are you so
cruel?"

She looked up—a pair of steely eyes in a white face.

"I have my hotel and my carriage. I want but one thing else—you cannot give it."

He was close and he tried to take her hand. She drew away.

"Sometime," he said, "one year, ten years, it matters not—you will belong to me."

"*Tiens!*" she answered, "we shall see."

II

THE OTHER

"I hate these Prussians and I hope there will be war."

And having said it, Marcelle de Lembach turned her back upon a group of officers passing in the Cur-Garten. A young Hussar had looked up suddenly and caught her eye; she was conscious of a quick glance of admiration, and for some reason the color had mounted to her cheek.

Her father, General the Marquis de Lembach, moved his chair away from the table where they had been dining, and laughed.

"War," he chuckled. "Bismarck is too clever to risk having the old King's throne tumbled into the Spree."

He was a retired French officer of nearly seventy, tawny and wrinkled, with snow-white hair and a tuft of beard under the waxed moustache which bristled on his upper lip.

The other person at the table on the Cursaal terrace was Guy Egerton.

"I'm afraid, General," he answered, "that the blood in Germany has been growing thicker than water—even in the South."

14

"Then Bavaria, Württemberg and Baden are ingrates, Captain Egerton," cried the old soldier, "for Napoleon made them what they are."

Egerton thought it wise not to answer, and Marcelle turned to watch the crowd passing in the Cur-Garten—people with time to kill, people with ills to cure.

Along the river front the lights of Ems were reflected in the black waters of the Lahn. The July air was close and hot, like the sultry calm that precedes a storm; typical, too, of the times, for already war clouds were gathering beyond the Rhine. When the band ceased playing the girl turned towards her father suddenly.

"Isn't it silly to quarrel about an old tottering throne which nobody wants? What would be the harm if an unknown German prince should be king of Spain?"

"The cause lies deeper than that, my dear," said her father. Sadowa and the snub to our country at the peace of Prague—Frenchmen do not forget."

"And Waterloo," said the girl thoughtfully.

The Englishman laughed.

"By Jove, you might add Jena to the list," he said, stroking his red moustache.

The General started—an angry flush crossed his face.

"No, father dear," said the girl, with a hand

upon his arm. "No more politics. It's bad for your heart." The véteran frowned but did not speak.

Marcelle listened for a while to the grating of the feet upon the gravel walks and thought of many things—war, her father's crotchety ills, her own loneliness, and the future which promised so little. Then she became suddenly conscious that some one behind her was watch-. ing her intently. An impulse forced her to turn her head. At the next table sat the young Hussar whom she had seen passing in the Cur-Garten. He was gazing at her too fixedly and she turned her head away.

At the same moment Egerton looked up and smiled. The Hussar saluted and the Englishman, being in mufti, lifted his hat.

"Who is that man who has just bowed?" she asked.

"That?" laughed Egerton; "why, that is Boul' Mich'—the best fellow I know."

"Boul' Mich'!" she repeated, "surely that is not his name."

"Oh, dear, no. His brother officers call him that because he lived in France and paints and sings French songs and is at heart a Bohemian."

"Well!" she said, "his name?"

"In the Almanach de Gotha he is the Hereditary Count Ludwig - Siegfried - Hermann - Friedrich-Maximilian von Leun-Walram. Is that name enough?"

"Von Leun-Walram!" exclaimed the girl excitedly. "Why, father, it must be cousin Ludwig."

"Possibly," assented the General, without enthusiasm.

It was now Egerton's turn to be curious.

"Your cousin?" he asked, looking at the girl in surprise.

"Yes, my mother was an American, and her own cousin married the Count von Leun-Walram. He was a relative of the Duke of Nassau, who refused to recognize the marriage because the countess was an American. So for years the Count lived in France. Ludwig, their son, was older than I, but we used to play together nevertheless. My mother died when I was twelve, and after that I lost touch with him, except that I knew that his mother died too, some time afterwards. You see, my father and the old Count never got along well."

"A man of his birth," growled the General, "who joins the revolutionists—I should say we did not get along well."

"Boul' Mich' is certainly your cousin," said the Englishman, wiping his monocle and then screwing it carefully in his eye. "He told

me the story one night when we were fighting
the campaign of '66. It was not until Ludwig's
mother died that the old Count was pardoned.
Very romantic, isn't it?"

Marcelle did not answer, for the idea of a
harmless adventure came to her. Turning
quickly she caught the Hussar's eye and gave
him a smile of recognition.

It was now the soldier's turn to blush. As
soon as he could recover from his astonishment he jumped to his feet, clicked his heels
together and saluted. Seeing that both the
girl and Egerton were laughing he came
towards them.

"Don't tell him who I am," whispered Marcelle. Her father started to object, but Egerton begged him not to spoil the sport.

As the soldier came towards the table he
tried to recollect where he had met the girl.
She was one of the most beautiful women he
had ever seen. Her keen brown eyes, set
wide apart, had a look of honesty and courage.
Her skin was clear and white, and the dark
chestnut hair fell upon her shoulders in two
graceful curls. He saw that she was tall and
slight and her head well poised. Her face
had lighted up when she smiled, but in repose
it was calm and spiritual and it appealed to
him strangely. He knew that he had seen

her somewhere, but it must have been long ago.

"Won't you join us, Count?" she said sweetly.

He bowed and drew a chair beside her. In the awkward moment which followed he looked appealingly at Egerton, but his friend merely laughed at his confusion.

"Surely you have not forgotten your old friends of the Boul' Mich'?" she said.

It was a bold remark for a young French girl, and she was ashamed of having made it.

He glanced at her curiously—something in the voice, something in the look,—yes, he remembered at last, but he was tempted to lead her on.

"Mademoiselle," he answered, "there are no angels in the Latin quarter."

"Bravo, Boul' Mich'!" exclaimed Egerton.

But the girl felt the rebuke more keenly than the compliment.

"I did not know that Prussian soldiers were familiar with the place where angels live," she said, with attempted sarcasm.

"Not yet," he answered, with meaning. "But the fortunes of war may lead us there."

"*Sacré!*" thundered General de Lembach. "You will never get beyond the Rhine."

The young soldier looked up quietly and met the eye of the veteran.

"You must admit, sir," he said, good naturedly, "that even a Prussian may die for his country. Whether he may reach heaven is a matter for the theologians, not for soldiers to discuss."

"*Sapristi!* I like your spirit," answered the General, pounding on the table. "Kellner, another glass!" Being an Alsatian, he spoke German, but he was French to his fingers' tips.

"I'll be glad to get where they talk God's language," he said, by way of apology for his German blood of centuries back.

"Ah!" said the young officer, turning to the girl. "You see, I was right. The place where they speak God's language must be where the angels live."

Marcelle burst into laughter.

"You haven't the slightest idea who I am. Why do you play hide-and-seek behind silly speeches?"

He looked at her fixedly for a moment.

"Hide-and-seek," he said. "It is a children's game."

"And you are a full-grown man."

"But I remember a little maid of twelve with deep brown eyes and lips that were always smiling."

She looked up suddenly.

"Ah! you do remember!" she exclaimed.

"A boy's first love is not easily forgotten," he answered.

Again the colour swept across her face. "Father dear," she said, turning away quickly, "surely you remember cousin Ludwig?"

"By name," growled the General. "I was campaigning in Italy when your relatives were at Lembach. Malcontents are not much to my taste."

The German drew himself up with dignity.

"My father, sir, was in advance of his time. The man with the courage to stem the popular tide is a scapegoat, or, at best, a martyr; the man with the cleverness to rise on the crest of a popular wave is a patriot. To-day all Germany holds my father's views."

Filial loyalty appeals to a Frenchman, and besides, the General saw his attack had been uncalled for.

"Ludwig, my boy," he said, "you are right to defend your father," and pouring some wine into the glass the waiter brought him, he added, "Come, join us in a glass of *tisane;* Marcelle, a toast."

"To the soldiers of France and Germany," said the girl, raising her glass. "May they always be friends!"

"I drink to that," growled the veteran, "because the soldiers of Germany are not all Prussians."

The young officer's eyes flashed.

"There are many German States," he cried, "there is but one German People." Then he saw the look of consternation in the face of his cousin. "Marcelle, I drink your toast," he added, raising his glass to his lips.

"I say," said Egerton, wishing to avert hostilities, "as an Anglo-Bavarian I am the natural arbiter to whom American relatives should refer their Franco-Prussian disputes; and to open negotiations, all parties are invited to picnic with me to-morrow at a bully place I know—just beyond Frücht. On the way back we will make a peace offering at Baron Stein's tomb."

"Oh, how lovely !" exclaimed Marcelle with enthusiasm.

The General glowered but acquiesced; it was hard to divert his mind from politics.

"The picnic is all very well," he muttered, "but there is no need for peace negotiations, for there'll be no war and Prince Leopold of Hohenzollern will not ascend the Spanish throne."

A reply was on Ludwig's lips, but a look from his cousin restrained him.

"Bismarck, where is he?" the General rambled on. "At Varzin with a bilious attack. And the French ambassador, Count Benedetti, where is he? Why, here at Ems, where the King of Prussia takes his annual cure. There is no foreign office here and no Chancellor to put in his oar. I tell you Benedetti has taken the bull by the horns—watch the events of the next few hours—watch them, I say."

The General looked at the young officer, but his challenge to an argument remained unaccepted, so reluctantly he raised his glass and drained it.

"Speaking of angels," said Marcelle, "there goes the Ambassador now."

Ludwig turned and saw a small, elderly man, with bowed head and stooping shoulders, pass near the terrace. The light shone full on his features, and he thought the face looked drawn and careworn. His nose was straight and thin, and the lips smooth-shaven; the hollow cheeks were partly covered with grey side whiskers. In answer to the General's salute he raised his hat with a courtly gesture, displaying a conically shaped head that was bald and shiny.

"The French Ambassador," mused Ludwig, "I'd hate to ·be in his shoes. Two nations growling in leash—one false step and they spring at each other's throats."

But the band drowned his words, and for a time they listened to the music. As the last strains died away the girl noticed two people seating themselves at the next table.

"What a stunning creature!" she exclaimed, then suddenly turned away and tried to hide her confusion, for she saw her mistake.

But Ludwig followed her glance.

"Marguerite Clairon!" he almost exclaimed, and he tried to hold back the blood he felt rising to his temples. Egerton could not suppress a smile, but luckily Marcelle's eyes were turned away.

Then the lights in the band pavilion were turned out, and the blue-coated bandsmen of an infantry regiment tramped past the Cursaal.

"Let us go," said Marcelle, rising from her seat; "see, even the band has stopped playing."

As Marcelle passed the actress her impulse was to turn.

For an instant their eyes met: defiance on the one part—on the other curiosity and contempt,—for between them was the barrier of caste, insurmountable, inexorable. The glance was momentary, yet the heart of each was strangely thrilled.

Marcelle walked on, and as she descended the terrace and entered the shadowy park, Ludwig, who had not dared to look at Marguerite Clairon, breathed more freely.

Near the band pavilion General de Lembach met Count Benedetti, so the Ambassador and the soldier strolled on. Meantime, Egerton, mumbling some excuse, disappeared in the darkness.

Ludwig and Marcelle walked on together. Both were thinking of a grey château among the hills of Alsace, with slant roofs shining in the sunlight and pointed turrets piercing the clear blue overhead. They could see the white avenues wind among the beeches and firs, and hear the murmur of the water as it gushed from the lips of stone-hewn nymphs in the fountain before the terrace. He remembered a moment when she stood among the lilacs, smiling beneath an aureole of chestnut hair, a moment when the air was languorous and the dying sunlight plashed golden in her face, and he stooped and plucked her a flower. She meantime, was thinking of a blue-eyed, sunburnt boy, and the words he had whispered: "Marcelle, I shall love you always."

She made a sudden effort to break the silence. "Are you stationed at Ems ?" she asked.

"No, my squadron is at Coblentz, but I have

just been detached, and as I have a two weeks' furlough, I am on the way to Leun to see my father. I stopped off here to have a day or two with Egerton. We were sword brothers in '66, when we were both fighting Prussia.

"And where do you go from Leun?"

"To Berlin; I have just been gazetted to the staff of the Crown Prince Frederick because —because I know France."

Then he was sorry he had said it, for he caught her troubled look.

"Tell me of yourself, Marcelle," he went on quickly. "My life is nothing but barracks and drills—and memories of France," he added in a lower tone.

"My life since my mother died," she answered, with a touch of sadness in her voice, "six years in a hateful convent, and three in Algeria among the Kabyle tribes with father, then two more—at nearly every watering place in Europe."

"Algeria," he repeated, "you must be half a soldier."

"I love it," she said, with enthusiasm. "I learned to ride like an Arab, and shoot, and I was free. Oh, Ludwig, I hate the way a young girl must act in France,—eyelids on the droop, lips that must never smile, and never speak above a whisper."

Her cousin laughed. "With a soldier father and a Yankee mother you could not be a convent novice," he said; "but whatever they think in France, I like you better for it."

"Isn't it strange that we should meet again?" she suddenly said. "But when you stared at me to-night, I thought I had never seen a ruder man."

He turned and looked at her, superb beside him, in a night of wonderful brilliancy. "When I saw you on the terrace," he said, "I stared because I had never thought a face could be so beautiful."

"I may forgive you," she whispered softly.

"I can never forget those days at Lembach," he answered in a low, thrilled tone—"never—so long as I live."

He felt her tremble on his arm, and when he dared look, he saw her tall and pliant in a white, thin gown, and more radiant, he thought, than the star-shine in the blue vault above.

"Marcelle," he whispered, "there is nothing that I would not do for you."

She looked at this splendid cousin who had come into her life again at a moment when she so yearned for some one who could understand her, some one who would sympathise.

"Thank you, Ludwig," she said; "it means a great deal to me."

"Then you will let me be your friend?" he asked.

She did not answer, for she heard her father's voice calling through the darkness and she hastened her steps. At the door of the hotel Ludwig stopped to say good-night.

"Until to-morrow," he whispered, touching her hand to his lips. The moment was ended, but not the memory of it, for she stood by the door alone—listening to his steps. Faintly, faintly through the night came the rattle of a sabre on the flagstones, and as she turned away she shuddered, for she had remembered the words she had spoken that night in anger:

"I hate these Prussians. I hope there will be war."

III

THE TURN OF A CARD

Between the old bath house of the *Vier-Thürme* and the Roman church a bridge spans the Lahn. When Ludwig left the hotel he wandered towards the river, and as he crossed he stopped midway between the shores.

Gazing at the tedious black river flowing unceasingly towards the Rhineland and the sea, he thought of his cousin Marcelle. Honesty, courage, womanliness—he had seen them in her face that night. Strange she had come back so suddenly into his life, at a moment when she had faded to a vague and distant memory of his boyhood. Then he thought of the pretty, red-haired actress who had startled him with a look, and he wondered, as he had often wondered, whether it were worth while to fight out in his heart a mere question of right and wrong.

Two men sauntered across the bridge, and one of them turned as he passed, and, looking at him curiously, took a step towards him.

"I say, Ludwig, is that you?"

The soldier started from his reverie.

"Hallo, Guy," he exclaimed, as he recognized the voice.

"By Jove," said the Englishman, seeing his friend alone in the darkness, gazing at the river; "are you contemplating suicide?"

"No, merely killing time."

"You'd much better come with me to Clotilde's."

Ludwig saw the man D'Arblay waiting in the shadow beyond.

"All right," he said suddenly, "I promised to play to-night, if you did," and he stepped out beside his friend. On being introduced to D'Arblay he treated him with studied civility. When the three men left the bridge they turned into the shady walk by the river bank, and a moment later rang the bell at the door of an apartment house.

On the stairs Ludwig heard the sound of music and laughter, and as he stepped on the threshold of her salon, he felt the pressure of Clotilde Berthon's little hand. Beyond her he saw lights and flowers and beautiful women, and beneath the crystal chandelier Marguerite Clairon, with her white arms akimbo and her pretty head swinging to the rhythm of the daring song she sang. When suddenly through the flare of the candles he met her glance, a quick, numbing sensation darted through him, and he fought to keep back the thoughts that crowded to his brain.

"*La belle Clairon, brava! brava!*" rang through the room as the last notes of the song died away, and he saw her flushed and smiling amid the hand claps and the shouts. The Russian and the Spaniard and other men in black coats and white bosoms, crowded round her, crying, "*Encore! bis! bis!*" and when she shook her head they fell on their knees at her feet, but to no avail.

"Let Clotilde sing," she cried. "Come, Clotilde—*Voici le sabre de mon père!*" Then she ran, laughing, towards the hostess and pushed her under the crystal chandelier, and meanwhile the slender, dreamy-eyed youth at the piano ran his fingers over the keys to the notes of *La Grande Duchesse.*

"*Brava, Clotilde. 'Le sabre de mon père,'* " shouted the black-coated men, until the pink and white diva of the *Bouffes Parisiens* smiled and began the music of Offenbach.

The queen of the moment was dead—long live the queen—but the manœuvre had left Marguerite Clairon by Ludwig's side as she had intended it should.

"I knew that you would come," she whispered, pressing his hand.

He looked away and tried not to meet her glance.

"It would be worth crossing a desert to hear you sing," he said with an effort, "and I only had to cross a river."

"Why do you act as though you were afraid of me?" she asked, glancing up at him queerly.

"It is a long story, Marguerite, and I fear that it would not interest you."

"A long story!" she repeated. "Why you have only known me since last night."

"That gives me the chance to say it seems like a lifetime since then." His laugh was cold, and she knew he was keeping something back.

"Why did you come here to-night?" she asked suddenly.

"To play baccarat," he answered.

His brusqueness startled her. What sort of a man was this tall, blue-eyed Prussian, whose glance had thrilled her, who was so subtle and yet seemingly so frank, whom twice she had seen colour at her look, but who would not talk to her except in flippant compliments or brutal candour, or words about herself but not of him nor of love.

"I see you have your war-paint on," she said, with an impatient shrug. "Take care, you may be vulnerable to modern weapons," and she turned and walked away.

For a moment the soldier stood looking after her. Those soft, mysterious eyes—so deep, so pathetic,—was he right in believing there was a woman underneath? He thought of another face, less striking, less dazzling, but with a frank, sweet look that to him was far more beautiful; then he wondered why all his life he had fought with his desires because of an ideal.

The applause for Clotilde Berthon died away.

"Cards!" called D'Arblay, rattling a stack of counters between his fingers. "Come, ladies and gentlemen, baccarat," and soon the green table was girdled by faces, with Ludwig's among them.

D'Arblay bought the bank, but Ludwig to try him forced the bidding, and when they drew for places he had the luck to be next him at the right *tableau*, with Egerton opposite.

"Chance makes me sit by you," whispered Marguerite Clairon at his elbow, "not choice."

"It may be *banal* to say it," he answered, "but life is merely a game of chance."

"Yes," she scoffed, "with luck all on the side of the man."

"Not when he plays fair," he said.

"How can he play fair when the world gives

him all the cards, and the woman can only follow suit?"

"He might throw down his hand," he
laughed, "and call for a new deal."

"The game men play in Utopia, perhaps, but
not in Europe."

For a minute he fingered his counters.

"Perhaps some day we may revise the rules,"
he said quietly.

"There is but one rule," she replied, with a
touch of bitterness in her voice, "and because
men made it it will never be revised."

He looked at her long and searchingly, and
a faint little smile trembled to her lip.

"The arrows of savages are poisoned, are
they not?" she whispered, under her breath.

D'Arblay saw the look she gave him.

"Come, make your bets," he interrupted,
gruffly.

Ludwig pushed his stake upon the line and
left it *à cheval*, and when the deal was finished
he picked up his cards; but he was thinking
about all she had said, and wondering, so
D'Arblay was forced to ask him twice if he
wished to draw a card.

He lost the first *coup*, and the cards went to
Marguerite Clairon—but it brought him back
from dreaming, and when he saw Guy Egerton
challenge the limit of the bank and lose, he

remembered the purpose which had brought
him there.

The play went on, and the faces grew eager
and flushed or deadly white.   After each turning of the cards the counters clicked on the
green baize cloth, and there were little sighs
half suppressed, and mutterings, and eyes that
glared, and fingers that clutched; but when the
cards were being dealt he could have heard a
pin drop.   There were glances too, slanting
and stealthy, and when the *coup* was big and
the winner careless, he sometimes saw a coun-
ter or two find its way under a little white hand
to a pile to which it did not belong.   But
should Clotilde, the hostess, not have her per-
centage?   So he merely smiled to himself, and
glanced at the hands of the banker each time
the cards were dealt, and in the end his
patience was rewarded.

Three times when the green cloth before
Guy Egerton had been swept clean, Ludwig
had seen D'Arblay take a roll of bank-notes
from his pocket and push them across the
table, making each time an entry in his
note book.   Again he repeated the transac-
tion.

"Four thousand, is that correct?" he said,
as he replaced a little gold pencil in his pocket
and took up the cards to deal.

"Yes," muttered the Englishman, counting the notes; and Ludwig noticed the trembling of his hands as he placed the full thousand before him.

The capital of the bank had now at least quadrupled, but though no one went "*banco*," the Russian brought up the stakes of the left *tableau* to near the limit, while at the right there was little on.   With a quick glance D'Arblay took in the situation and dealt.   On the right the cards had passed down the table and back to Ludwig; on the left they had stopped at the Russian.   To Ludwig, to the Russian, and to the bank a card was dealt, and slowly again to right and left *tableau;* but before he gave himself the second card D'Arblay said jokingly: "Your hand is smaller than your stake, Clotilde, and that I call a compliment."

Meantime his hands made a gesture towards the little actress, and while the other women snickered, he dealt himself a card.

"Nine," he said, when the cards were turned, but as he reached for the stakes of the players he happened to glance up suddenly and catch Ludwig's eye upon him.   The soldier's look forced him to turn away, and for a *coup* or two he played and lost, then he turned to a girl who stood behind him, saying:

"Take the bank for awhile, Yvonne. I have a headache."

Then as he hurriedly counted the money before him, he murmured close to her face:

"If you win—well, there's a pretty bracelet of diamonds and pearls in the bazaar by the Curhaus."

"Luck's against me," whispered Ludwig to Marguerite Clairon. "See if you can't change it"—and he swept his few remaining thalers towards her and pushed back his chair.

As he walked towards D'Arblay, the French-man tried to slip quietly past him.

"Surely you are not leaving us," he said, stepping between him and the door.

"Only for a little air," answered the man impatiently. "I have a bad headache."

"The air on the balcony is delightful," said Ludwig, pleasantly, "and there is a buffet in the next room. Can I not have the honour of touching glasses with you?"

The extreme politeness of the invitation increased D'Arblay's suspicions, but finding no reasonable excuse he was forced to bow coldly and follow the soldier towards the dining-room. Ludwig stepped aside at the door to let the Frenchman precede him, and as he did so he picked up a pack of cards which lay on a marble-topped console.

Marguerite Clairon had been watching them from behind her cards. She had seen D'Arblay glance quickly from side to side like a caught animal, and also the cold, sharp look the soldier gave him. When the two men entered the dining-room and the door closed after them, she gave her place to a youth behind her, and, waiting until she was unobserved, stole quietly out on the balcony and went towards the dining-room window.

The two men had the room to themselves. The casement windows were both open, and between them stood a buffet on which was an array of decanters and glassware.

"No wonder you have a headache," said Ludwig. "The air in there was close."

"Yes, it is much cooler here," answered the Frenchman, for something to say, but eyeing the soldier furtively.

"I'm sure a little refreshment will help your head," continued Ludwig, stepping up to the buffet and putting down his pack of cards, which meantime had caught the Frenchman's eye. "A little *sirop de groseilles* and water?" he added.

"No, cognac," said the man.

Ludwig quietly filled two little glasses from a decanter.

"Prosit!" he said, raising his own to his lips.

The Frenchman drained his glass and put it down without a word, then Ludwig took up the pack of cards.

"You seem to be fond of play," he said.

"It is a distraction," shrugged D'Arblay.

The soldier began to shuffle the cards, and he did it with a deftness that astonished the Frenchman.

"You are an expert," the man muttered.

Ludwig caught his eye and smiled.

"Yes," he answered, "would you like to see a new method of making the pass? It is better than yours."

D'Arblay's face changed colour and his glance travelled from side to side.

"The pass—what is that?" he asked in a dry, unsteady voice.

"The pass," Ludwig continued, running the cards gracefully up his arm and letting them drop back into his hand again like the opening and closing of a fan, "is for the purpose of reversing the cut without detection. Your method of inserting the second and third fingers above the cards to be brought to the top is effectual but clumsy. It is much simpler to do it with the little finger. Shall I show you?"

Tense as two wrestlers the men glared at each other, Ludwig cool and impassive, D'Ar-

blay with his hands twitching together to beat
back the anger rising in his blood.

"When I decide to become a 'Greek,' " the
Frenchman sneered, "I shall come to you for
instruction.   At present I prefer to play an
honest game."

Ludwig merely raised his eyebrows. Taking
a card lightly between his fingers, he threw it
across the room with a quick twist of the wrist.
The card sailed up almost to the ceiling, hovered for a moment and came back.   He caught
it deftly in the pack.

"Did you ever hear of a certain Robert
Houdin?" he asked, "the man who used to
give *soirées fantastiques* in the Palais Royal?"

"I believe that I have heard the name," the
man answered curtly, showing the whites of
his narrowed eyes.

"He once went to Algeria," Ludwig continued, "in the service of the French government, to work miracles in competition with
the Marabouts and expose those clever im-
posters.   When he returned to France he went
to live at Blois.   I believe he is still there."

"I suppose this edifying story has a point,"
muttered D'Arblay, with a quick glance at the
door.

"All in due time. You see, my father was
once a political exile, and for purposes of

economy, as well as retirement, he also went to live at Blois."

"So I am to have the history of your father," snarled the man, edging away from the buffet.

Again Ludwig quietly stepped between him and the door.

"I was a lad at the time," he went on, "and I used to meet the famous conjuror sunning himself in the public square. One day we scraped up an acquaintance and as Houdin took a fancy to me I used to go frequently to his house, so in time I managed to pick up a few interesting tricks,—among them the various methods of making the pass."

He stepped towards D'Arblay quickly and looked him straight between the eyes.

"The next time you pass a nine to the top of the pack be careful that Robert Houdin or one of his pupils is not in the room."

He saw the man's angry flush, the knitting of his dark brows, and he kept his eyes fixed upon him.

"You have no proof," the fellow muttered; "my word is as good as yours."

"I want redress, not proof."

D'Arblay tried to put on a bold front, but he was cowed by the soldier's glance. It was not the look of a weakling nor of a braggart. He knew that he had a man to deal with—and at heart he was a coward.

"Well," he said, with a shrug, "what do you propose?"

"That you return to Captain Egerton and to myself every thaler of which you have robbed us, and that you leave Ems within twenty-four hours; as for your friends—that is their look-out. I have no desire to create a scandal."

The Frenchman took two or three turns across the room; his eye roved like a falcon's, and his breath came quick and panting.

" *Eh, bien*" he growled at last. "I accept."

Ludwig stood for a moment thinking, then in a low, sober, measured voice, he said:

"I forgot to say that I include Mademoiselle Clairon in the stipulation; every thaler you have taken from her must be returned as well."

At the sound of her name the man's face grew livid, his hands clenched and he sprang towards Ludwig.

"Then, by God, I refuse," he cried.

"Then the alternative is this——" And Ludwig hurled the pack of cards squarely in D'Arblay's face.

Dazed by the suddenness of the affront, the man staggered back and brushed against the buffet. His eyes were almost blinded by rage, but he saw the shining glassware, and clutching wildly at a decanter he drew back his arm to hurl it. With the trained instinct of a soldier Ludwig rushed towards him, but the man's arm had been seized suddenly from behind, and in the window beyond Ludwig saw a woman's face—white and trembling.

"Don't be a fool," he cried, gripping the fellow's arms and pushing him back against the casement.

D'Arblay struggled to free himself, but the German only held the tighter, and while he kept him pinioned, Marguerite Clairon wrenched the decanter from his grasp. At sight of her the man's rage knew no bounds.

"Since women fight your battles——" he hissed in the soldier's face.

"When you are willing to act like a man," said Ludwig quietly, "and not like a coward, I shall release you."

The fellow fought with all his strength to free himself, but his flabby muscles were powerless in the German's grasp.

"You have me at a disadvantage," he whined at last; "I am forced to accept your terms."

"If you ·wish satisfaction," said Ludwig, slowly releasing him, "you may have it— though honour does not compel me to meet a card sharper."

"I have too much respect for our hostess,"
sneered the man, as he smoothed out the wrin-
kles in his coat sleeves, "to create scandal in
her house."

"So you admit that I was right in calling
you a coward," said Ludwig quietly.

For a moment D'Arblay stood glaring at
Marguerite Clairon, who waited in the open
window—white and rigid as a thing of marble;
then, with a shrug he turned towards the
soldier. There was a hard glitter in his eyes
and his smile seemed frozen on his face.

"I am content to wait," he said; "my time
will come."

"As you wish," answered Ludwig, opening
the door quietly and holding it for him to pass.
When he had gone he turned to the actress.

"I thank you," he said, "but why did you do
it?"

"Because I saw that he intended to kill you,"
she answered in a thrilled voice.

"Men quarrel best alone, Marguerite," he
said gently, "but I understand," and he turned
towards the door.

She seized his hand suddenly and drew him
back.

"Don't, Ludwig," she cried, "don't go away
from me like that"

IV

THE TURN OF A LIFE

Marguerite closed the door. Ludwig watched her dumbly for a moment as she came towards him. He saw her white hands as she clasped them together, and under a glow of reddish hair he saw her face—flushed, beautiful, human. She looked up strangely at him and spoke in a low, tremulous voice.

"Could you be so cruel as not to forgive my following?"

"I have nothing to forgive," he faltered.

She played with the scarf about her shoulders, knotting and unknotting it several times.

"I followed, Ludwig," she said at last, "because I know Paul D'Arblay—because you were with him."

"Don't think that I am ungrateful," he answered in a deep breath.

Suddenly she caught both his hands and looked into his face. Her eyes burnt through him.

"My savage," she cried.

She was very close,—she waited. He pressed her two hands to his lips, but did not speak.

45

"And you would have fought for me," she murmured.

"Yes," he answered in a hoarse whisper.

"Come," she said softly; then smiling radiantly, she led him away, and he followed, not knowing where, not daring to ask, for within his heart he fought like a drowning man borne down by furious eddies.

Then he heard the faint creaking of a hinge, and from the light he went into a shadowy room, where through an open window he saw the stars. Before a mirror two candles flickered in tall brass holders, and he caught a glimpse of silver brushes and cut-glass bottles amid soft, pink silk and fluffy lace, and as the door closed gently behind him he breathed a whiff of delicately scented air.

She lighted a cluster of tapers on the chiffonnier. The shadowy walls and cornices of gilt, the damask curtains and the brocade chairs became a harmony of green and gold, and as he followed, trembling, his feet touched the white softness of fur.

He saw her go to the window and stand for a moment leaning against the casement.

She held a curtain tightly in her hands, with head rested against white arm in a way to show the beautiful profile of her face against the green damask. The breeze from the open window ruffled a wavy *"repentir"* of reddish hair, and the light of the candles was tempered by the night beyond. A faint sigh came from her lips, and he knew that she waited, but he dared not go.

"I thought you were brave," she said, with a touch of anger in her rich soft voice; and as he did not answer she came back into the room, and saw him gazing at her with his motionless eyes.

"I'm not a coward, Marguerite," he said suddenly, "I'm only a fool."

Not understanding, she shrugged her pretty shoulders and went to the dressing table. He saw the shining hair which waved and curled about her neck, the white gauze gown with square cut bodice and ruched *"tablier"* of olive-colored silk, the scarf of flowers with silver foliage slanting from one shoulder across the slender waist; and when she sat before the mirror and picked up a brush to smooth her rumpled hair, he went and stood behind her and gazed at her face in the glass beyond. For a time he looked entranced into the dreamy eyes with their curling lashes and arching brows. When he met her glance in the glistening mirror she laughed with a little trembling laugh, quietly drew the silver stopper from a crystal bottle, and as he drank in the fumes of the luxurious perfume, she whispered softly, "Have I no charm to calm thy heart?"

"Yes, Marguerite, yes," and he closed his eyes. For a moment all resistance seemed to be dead in him, and he felt helpless as one engulfed in a flame. His lips all but touched her soft, fragrant hair—but with a courage born of despair he beat back the wild torrent rising in his veins, and with cold, clenched hands turned away.

In the mirror she saw him bending towards her, flushed and trembling, and then in a brief moment his face grow white, and she had seen the look of an inward struggle; and when he turned away she sat staring into the glass before her, dazed by both anger and wonderment. Then he went to the window and stepped upon the balcony. A quick impulse seized her and she followed.

He was leaning upon the railing, staring into the night beyond. Too mystified to understand, she crept beside him and waited for him to speak. For a time he seemed not to notice her, so she moved a little nearer, and he felt her hand stealing into his. Suddenly she looked up into his face.

"You have brought back my soul from up there in the clouds," she said impulsively. "Do you wish it?"

He saw her lustrous eyes, her parted lips, and faith in himself seemed afar off. For a moment he dared not speak, lest the desire within him be not conquered.

"I'm afraid I could not be like the poet," he said.

She drew her hand back quickly. "At least you are a man," she answered with impatience.

"I am afraid you would never understand my position," he continued after a moment.

"All men think alike about women. That is, about women like me," she added, with a touch of sadness in her voice.

"If it were not for the selfishness of men," he said, with much feeling, "the world would be a very different place for women."

She pressed his hand again in a way that sent the warm blood flushing through him. "You cannot change the world," she murmured. "Why not take all it has to offer?"

He gazed for a moment at this temptress with the eyes of a Magdalene and the touch of an odalisque, and wondered again if it were worth while to fight out an abstract question of right and wrong, when all the world seemed arrayed against him. Then he turned away and looked far over the sleeping city and the rugged forms of the mountains into the fathomless night, where a single star shone brighter than all the rest.

"Because I am waiting for the best the world can offer," he said finally, in answer to her question.

"Surely that is love."

"Yes, it is love," he answered hoarsely.

For a moment she was silent. When she spoke there was bitterness in her voice.

"I understand. Because it was so easily won, you do not consider it worth while."

He turned and looked at her.

"You are very beautiful," he said. "It would be very easy to care for you, if—if I dared."

"If you dared!" she exclaimed in surprise. "You are a soldier. Surely you are not afraid?"

"Yes," he answered, "I am afraid. I dare not destroy a belief which has become a part of myself."

She shrugged her white shoulders and laughed. "You talk as though it were a question of religion."

"It is a question of faith, which is much the same thing. I believe that some day I shall meet the one for whom I have been waiting. When I do, I wish to have nothing to regret. I shall ask a great deal, and I believe it is wrong to ask more than I am prepared to give."

She gazed thoughtfully at the street below. She had never heard a man talk in this strange way, and she was trying to understand his meaning.

"If you were a priest," she said finally, "it would be different,—but a Prussian officer—"

"I told you at first you would not understand," he said.

"But I do understand. It is the way a woman feels,—until—until it is too late."

Tears filled her eyes, and she tried to laugh them away.

"Don't take what I say to heart," he said sympathetically. "After all, I doubt if I am responsible for being a fanatic. Did you ever hear of the strange sect they called the Puritans, pioneers in the wilderness of an unknown land and all because of an ideal? My mother was of that race; their blood is in my veins. You see, I can't help being peculiar—it is a question of atavism."

She looked at him reproachfully. "Don't," she said, "don't scoff at yourself. A moment ago I thought you were sincere. Do you wish me to doubt?"

He took her hand and held it while he spoke. "Dear," he said tenderly, "I have made a confession to you that has never been made to a living soul, and I did it because of something you said to me to-night at the card table. I have tried to take the world just as it is, and keep my thoughts to myself. If my comrades were to know my life has been different from theirs, that I believed a man should be judged by the same standard as a woman, I should be laughed out of the regiment. Why I have told you this I cannot say; but, in spite of what you said just now, I felt somehow that you would understand—that you would sympathise.''

She placed her hand upon his shoulder and stood looking at him with eyes that were full of tenderness and admiration.

''I do understand,'' she said. ''Ah ! believe me, there is not a woman living so bad that her heart would not thrill to know that a man could feel like that.''

He touched her hand to his lips; then they turned away in silence and walked slowly back into the scented room.

She drew out a chair and sank back upon the cushions, thinking. In the light of the candles he seemed so tall and handsome, and as she breathed the fragrant air, the hateful beast within her awoke again, and with it the wish to drag him down. No, he should not be so far above her. She had won his confidence and she would wait, and when the moment came again—— Suddenly she met the gaze of his eyes; afraid that he might read her thoughts, she sprang from the chair and ran to the window, and as the night air fanned her temples, she closed her eyes and stood for a moment with the temptation within her arms. Then she heard a voice from afar off—whispering— and it came nearer and clearer and true—and it spoke not of passion, but love,—and when she looked again he stood beside her.

"I am going, Marguerite," he said.

"So soon?" she answered, trembling; then suddenly she cried impulsively, "Yes, Ludwig, go!"

But in the moment as she walked beside him towards the door, again without and within her there was a strange unquiet, a feverish activity in the air and in her heart. She looked up and saw his face; he was near her—his breath almost mingled with her breath. "No," the voice of the breast cried out, "it is not true; he did it to tantalise you—and he will whisper the tale to another and she will laugh, and together they will mock you."

"Marguerite," he said, "last night I saw a look in your face which made me believe you would understand; to-night I know."

Then in the burning of her blood a feeling of shame swept through her—and suddenly she caught his face between her trembling hands. The look into his eyes was long and penetrating, but she saw only honesty and clear courage.

"And I doubted," she cried. "Ah! please forgive me."

"Forgive you, dear?" he said. "I am not on the house tops."

His hand was on the door. She thought of the wild flushed faces in the other room—the painted women.

"No, no," she cried, "not that way," and she led him quickly towards the door which opened to the hall. On the threshold she stopped, and looking up into his face suddenly, said in a voice that trembled:

"Let this be the end. Let me keep the memory of to-night."

"As you wish, Marguerite," he answered. And as he moved away the sweet mystery of his nature seemed to float around her and a subtle, beautiful love lay still like a child between her breasts—and she stood afraid to move lest it awake.

V

VIVE LA BAGATELLE

It was the day of Egerton's picnic; they had visited the tomb of the great Prussian statesman Baron Stein, and their faces were turned towards home. General de Lembach patted the neck of his donkey and looked along the direct road to Ems. Marcelle and Ludwig gazed at the longer route through the valley of the Schweizer. The sun was at least an hour high, and as they had been compelled to jog their horses to the slow pace of the General's donkey, they persuaded themselves that they longed for a gallop—but in reality it was to prolong the day to its utmost.

The General shook his head. "Too much Crimea, too much Algeria, too much good food between campaigns. I'm afraid my liver is no longer young enough even for an ambling donkey."

"Father," said Marcelle, with a wistful glance towards the shady green valley, "even if you and Captain Egerton do take the short road, Ludwig and I might ride the other way and get to the hotel as soon as you—if not before."

Egerton knew the rôle of a friend thoroughly. "Yes, General, and to make sure of it, I know a capital inn where you and I can stop for a glass of Marcobrunner."

"There's too much acid in those Rhenish wines," mused the veteran doubtfully. But his old eyes rested on Marcelle, so graceful, so to the saddle born. How like her mother she looked; and he thought of the day when Lieutenant Colonel de Lembach, the blunt chasseur, fresh from Algeria, with his cross, just won under the Duc d'Aumale, glittering on his breast, rode to the hounds at St. Germain and yielded to the glance of the fair Miss Lord, the American beauty of Louis Phillipe's court. Twenty years her senior, he had not given his age a thought, and he had won the tourney for her hand from all the youths and dandies of the court, perhaps because he was so very blunt and different. The thought of that day brought a lump to his dry old throat, and when he saw the pleading look of Marcelle's frank brown eyes, he forgot that the young Hussar beside her wore a Prussian tunic.

"Well, well," he muttered; "I suppose I mustn't forget—I was young once myself; but be sure you gallop."

"Yes, father," laughed Marcelle, and Egerton, the watchful friend, saw the faint reddening of her cheeks. Perhaps Ludwig saw it as well, for he could not keep his eyes from her.

When the General and the Englishman had disappeared beyond the hill crest, Marcelle and Ludwig turned their horses to the left and walked them quietly along the shady road towards Miellen.

It was cool in the valley of the Schweizer, and the shadows of the rocks were lengthening. The water purled, and the sunlight trickled through the leaves, and there were glades and woodland lanes to tempt, so they loitered and thought not of galloping.

Ludwig looked long at the girl beside him— so sincere, so womanly she seemed—"And the little actress," he thought, "ah, how thankful I am—and yet!'

It is often the case that when two people are suddenly linked in secret sympathy, the power of speech is lacking, and each finds in silence the expression of vague desires but newly born. It is then that the many sounds of nature strike chords in unison with the heart. Whether the rustling of the leaves, or the ripple of the water over the pebbles was in harmony with their thoughts matters little, but, for a time, they walked their horses in silence, each realising in a dim, indefinite way that the other possessed what a great poet has called "sympathy in years, beauties, and manners."

When Ludwig spoke, his words were inspired by the moment.

"I was thinking of Alsace, Marcelle," he said, "and the rides we used to take through the Hochwald. I can see you now, on your little piebald pony speeding through the forest, with your brown curls streaming in the wind —and I by your side when I could keep there, and Hans, the fat Alsatian groom, pounding along on his cob, breathless and worried out of his mind lest you break your neck."

"Oh, how terrible it is to grow old," she cried.

"Old!" he laughed; "old at twenty-three?"

"Perhaps it is wicked to think so," she said after a moment, "but sometimes it seems as though I have cares enough to make me feel old. Poor, dear father, he does not realise how hard it is for a young girl to be an old man's sole companion, and—and I would not let him realise it for the world."

"Persuade him to adopt me," he said eagerly; "I should be your big brother then and take all the cares from your shoulders."

"But big brothers always sympathise with other men's sisters," she protested

"Then let me be your champion, and fight for you."

She looked up impulsively. "Yes, I like that better," she said, and snatching a bow of scarlet ribbon from her ivory handled riding whip, she fastened it on his sleeve with a pin taken from her dress. "My colours—champion!" she added, laughing.

"And if it were only the days of chivalry," he sighed. "How I long for war so that I may do battle for you!"

They had stopped unconsciously. The horses were leisurely nibbling the grass by the wayside.

"I wish you would not talk of war," she said. "It makes me remember that yesterday I hated all Prussians. I forgot how terrible war is—how unnecessary!"

"War is not unnecessary," he answered quietly. "It is only through wars that nations fulfil their destinies."

"And this war which may break forth to-morrow," she said, with bitterness, "a mere dog-in-the-manger quarrel about a tottering throne, which nobody really wants—is that destiny?"

"Yes," answered Ludwig, earnestly; "every war my country has fought since the Elector of Brandenburg became King of Prussia has brought the German people closer together; brought us nearer the ideal of the great statesman whose tomb we have just visited."

He hesitated a moment. "Alas, I fear another and a bloodier war must be fought before the unification of Germany is realised. But if it is destiny—"

"Destiny!" she answered with contempt. "Yes, and perhaps another unnatural boundary will be wiped out, and the French frontier will be the Rhine!"

"Perhaps," he continued thoughtfully. "But the natural boundaries of a nation are not mountains or rivers, but its own flesh and blood."

He turned and looked towards the South. "There are people speaking German there," he said.

Her eyes flashed. "Yes, we Alsatians have German blood in our veins, but our hearts are French to the core. Don't think it is our German blood which makes your Moltke and your Roon work night and day to get your troops in readiness and your Bismarck keep his spies in every court in Europe and break his word as often as he makes it. No, it is your German cupidity."

Ludwig dropped his reins upon his horse's neck and let him browse upon the bank.

"No, Marcelle, it is not cupidity," he said
finally, "and Bismarck is merely a means to
an end. There was a greater man than he, who
foresaw the events that are coming to pass.
That man was Baron Stein. I say a greater
man, because, in the darkest hour of our history he conceived the idea of a united Germany. Unlike our Bismarck, as you call him, he
believed that if a deep national sentiment were
to be aroused, the people must be free. His
work was not done for the King of Prussia, but
for the German nation. He had the power of
a Napoleon against him; so has Bismarck—but
it is not the same Napoleon."

Marcelle's thoughts turned to the Emperor
as she remembered him on his visit to Algeria,
and she saw a vision of a silent, pale-faced
man, with lustreless, watery eyes—so gentle,
so wanting in the look of energy! It was the
face of a dreamer—good-hearted, courageous
even, as a fatalist is courageous, because of a
belief in destiny.

She wondered if Ludwig were right.

"You have not said one word of the glory of
war," she said, "only of the necessity of it. I
am afraid that deep down in your heart you are
not a soldier."

His face grew thoughtful. "I understand
your meaning," he said, "and I think you are

right. I am a soldier, but only by force of circumstances, as my ancestors were before me."

Marcelle smiled.

"Those are scarcely the feelings of a soldier," she said.

"No, you are right. I would gladly change this uniform for the paint-stained jacket of the raggedest *rapin* in Paris."

"Ah, but the world expects certain things from certain men."

"Yes," he answered, thoughtfully.

She drew up her reins, and, speaking to her horse, started slowly down the road. In a moment he was by her side.

"Ludwig," she said, "we have a common ancestry,—let us forget that we are French and German."

"Gladly, fair cousin, but, unfortunately, an ancestor of mine surrendered with the Hessians at Trenton."

"Ah," she said, her eyes sparkling with pride, "I can tell a better story. My grandfather was with Rochambeau. You see, I am all on the side of right."

"The side of right," he repeated. "Yes— but in the war which is to come, where is the right?"

He asked the question more to himself than to her.

"Do you realise what that war means?" she asked. "You and I shall be enemies."

"Yes, Marcelle," he answered gravely, "I realise it. Yesterday I prayed for war—not from a soldier's love of it, but because it seemed a necessary evil out of which much good might come. Don't ask me what I feel to-day. I hardly dare confess it to myself."

"Yesterday—to-day?" she said, meditatively. "Time has no conscience, or one day would not seem as though it were always."

She was gazing into the deep, sunless forest. Perhaps it was the burning of his eyes which forced her to look towards him.

"Does not 'always' begin," he said, "when love begins?"

"Don't," she answered, in bewilderment, "don't spoil the memory of to-day."

He tightened his bridle reins. The horses stopped together without the word of command.

"Nothing could make me forget to-day," he said in a low voice,—"nothing."

She turned towards the west, where the ponderous, sullen clouds, banked high against the sky, were flushed with crimson.

"Yes, Ludwig," she answered, with a frightened look—"war!"

He tore the bow of ribbon from his sleeve and touched it to his lips. "War!" he exclaimed, "war proves a soldier's loyalty to his colours. '

"But not to the colours of an enemy."

"You are right," he said, after a painful pause. "A soldier's duty is to his country. God grant that mine may not be put to the test."

Marcelle shivered. It was the rush of damp air from the forest after the sunlight had gone.

"It is getting very late," she said, gathering up her reins and urging her horse to a gallop.

The clack of the iron shoes, the wind against her face, was keen delight. She gladly gave herself up to the exhilarating motion.

"Oh, Ludwig !" she called, "what joy to breathe !"

"Go slow," he laughed, "or your joy will be short-lived."

He was thinking of the pace and the sudden turn in the road ahead.

"Nonsense," she cried; "don't talk of fear."

Her whip stung the horse's flank. He bounded forward; loose stones rattled down the valley-side. On she dashed, a glow of pleasure in her cheeks, her hair tossed by the wind; she was lithe and easy in the saddle as an Arab of the desert, and always before him—provokingly before him as he thumped along behind with the stiff, methodical seat of a Prussian *Reit-Schule*.

At the turn in the road she threw her horse on his haunches and he drew up standing, with panting sides and his nostrils sniffing the air. She had given the plodding, hired beast a new lease of youth.

"I'm glad the French cavalry are not all Amazons," he said, as he halted beside her.

"Wait till you face the white-cloaked Spahis," she cried exultantly.

By the road-side, a hundred yards ahead, a stream rushed whirling over a bed of stones. On a bank before it lay the felled trunk of a tree.

"Let me show you the way we Arabs ride," she laughed.

With a weird cry learned in the desert, she was off, and he was following. Through the dust which curled behind her, he saw the wild leap through the air, the tree clean taken, the water cleared, the horse on the bank with heels well under—then, a girth broke, and she fell and was dragged along the bank while his heart stopped.

No chance to take off clean. A jerk at the rein pulled his horse to the right and he avoided the tree; then a dash through the seething stream and a scramble up a bank of slipping earth, which near unhorsed him—then a clutch at her bridle reins.

Deep gashes in his horse's flank proved the fury with which he had ridden, but he never knew how it happened—or anything, until he held her in his arms and was dashing the water of the stream upon her colourless face.

He had stopped the horse somehow, and leapt clear of the saddle. When he had dragged her from under the hoofs, his own mount was galloping, riderless, towards Ems.

Cold and trembling he knelt over her. Ah! the terror of those moments until he saw that she had only been stunned. At last the persistent dashing of the water on her temples caused her faint eyes to open, and he exulted in the luxury of that moment.

She lay white and motionless in his arms, until the impetuous tune his heart beat out sent the colour rushing to her face as suddenly as it had gone. Frightened, she drew away, and looked bewildered from side to side, not daring to meet his eyes.

He had thrown the reins of her horse over the branches of a bush by the roadside. The animal was leisurely nibbling the turf, and trampling the girth which had done the mischief under his feet. The saddle, which had turned, perched upon one flank and was kept from falling by the one girth that remained intact.

"It was the girth," she finally spoke. "I felt it give."

"Thank Heaven, you are alive!" he exclaimed.

She started to move and gave a little cry of pain. Her shoulder was bruised.

"It is nothing," she said, in answer to his anxious look. "The worst of it, you will think me such a bad horsewoman — after all my boasting."

"I think you are the pluckiest girl in the world. You had presence of mind and kept your head from the ground. You didn't faint until all was over."

"And you had the presence of mind to stop my horse. I shall never insult the Prussian cavalry again."

"Part of our training is to catch runaway horses," he laughed.

"You evidently expect the enemy will run away."

"To see you smile again," he said eagerly, "is enough to make me forgive even that."

A flash of lightning illumined the sombre forest, and there was a loud clap of thunder. They had not noticed the storm that had been

gathering, nor that it was rapidly growing dark
—but now raindrops began to fall.

Marcelle sat up with an effort that wrenched
her injured shoulder, and looked about her anxiously.   "Why,   what   has   become of   your
horse?"

"After my futile attempt to keep up with you
on horseback, I thought I could do better on
foot."

"Well!" she said, bursting into laughter;
"one horse, two people, and at least three kilomètres to anywhere—not to mention the rain.
Vive la bagatelle!"

"What a girl you are!" he said admiringly.
"Most women would cry."

" 'Tears, idle tears, I know not what they
mean,' "   she   answered   in   English,   with   a
bewitching French accent.

He looked up at the streaming clouds and
laughed.

"I should certainly call this rain 'tears from
the depth of some divine despair,' " he added.

"Poetry is all   very well," she exclaimed,
"but the sensible thing is to go home."

In brushing the tumbled hair from her forehead, she made the discovery that her hat was
gone.   She looked around in dismay.

"You must join the Prussian cavalry," he
laughed, placing his forage cap upon her head

at a rakish angle. The light blue and red were becoming.

"Oh, for a mirror, that you might see how well you look in my colours !"

She held out her hand pleadingly.

"Stop being silly, and help me up,—that is, if you can have any thoughts of getting me home. Do you realise the seriousness of the situation? It is not a usual thing for a young girl to be out in the forest, with night coming on—even if her companion happens to be a cousin."

A downpour of rain, in the nature of a miniature cloudburst, drowned his reply. In the hurry in which she scampered to the nearest tree, she forgot her aching shoulder.

It was a bedraggled little caravan which wended its way into the village of Miellen. Ludwig, muddy and hatless, trudged beside a steaming, dripping horse, on which Marcelle rode, drenched to the skin.

They were cold and comfortless, but managed to secure some brandy at a wayside inn, and after much gesticulating and parleying on the part of the inhabitants of Miellen, they succeeded in unearthing a rickety carry-all and were eventually rumbling on their way as fast as a decrepit horse could speed them.

They spoke but little, however, for their thoughts were mostly of dry clothes and other material comforts, and finally the lights of Ems began to flicker through the mist. Just before they reached Marcelle's hotel a carriage came rattling across the bridge and a fortuitous flash of lightning showed the tawny face of the General under the low hood.

They met at the hotel door. Marcelle wore her soldier's cap, Ludwig was soaked and hatless, and the porter hastened to tell of the horse which had galloped home riderless, so they were forced to make a clean breast of the whole adventure. But when the General's face grew glum the girl silenced him by saying:

"Remember, father, you told us to gallop— and a soldier's daughter always obeys orders."

"And some day you will break your neck," he cried, but his anger was quelled.

"I should like to know, sir,"—Ludwig diverted the subject,—"what sort of a magician turned your donkey into a victoria and pair?"

"Common sense," laughed the General. "A comfortable room at Lindenbach, a capital dinner and the best carriage obtainable. Better than getting wet, I call it."

"Rather," drawled Egerton, "only donkeys stay out in the wet."

"So it seems," answered Ludwig, with a

glance at his bedraggled regimentals; then he turned towards Marcelle. He said something about quinine and steaming draughts and colds, and when he thought the General was not listening he whispered something more about meeting her in the Cur-Garten in the morning at the hour when the band played. There was an exchange of glances which meant much, and a formal "good-night" which meant little; for love is whimsical, and when two people are aware of his presence they are likely to postpone acknowledging it until the confession can no longer be withheld.

When Egerton and Ludwig left the hotel the German went bareheaded, for though his friend had seen the forage cap on Marcelle's pretty head he kept the joke to himself, at least for the time. The rain had ceased, and they walked together until they reached the bridge across the Lahn.

"Go to the Cursaal, Guy," said Ludwig, "and when I have changed my wet things I'll join you."

As he crossed the bridge alone he walked with a light step and hummed a merry tune, and many times he repeated to himself, "Time has no conscience, or one day would not seem as though it were always." When he left the bridge he passed beneath a balcony, and from the lighted windows above came the sound of music and laughter. "Poor little Marguerite Clairon," he thought—but love has no conscience either; so it was hard to realise that only yesterday he had stood upon that balcony at the parting of the ways

VI

CASUS BELLI

When Ludwig joined Egerton at breakfast the following morning, the Englishman had finished his coffee and rolls, and the waiter was handing him a copy of the special edition of the Cologne *Gazette*, which had just reached Ems.

"Mornin', Ludwig," he said, as he unfolded the newspaper and smoothed it out upon his lap.

"Good-morning, Guy—any war news?" the German answered, drawing back a chair and seating himself.

"Don't know, see in a minute."

As Ludwig poured out a cup of coffee for himself, his eye fell upon the date-line of the paper. "Wednesday, 13 July," he read and he wondered what that day would bring forth, for he had an inborn superstition about the number 13.

"Well, I'm blowed!" said the Englishman, suddenly putting down the paper. "What do you think the King of Prussia has done?"

"Give it up," answered Ludwig, as he buttered his roll. "He is a kind-hearted old gen-

73

tleman, and is likely to do anything well intentioned, when let alone.''

"Well, he's done it this time," growled Egerton. "That slippery Corsican, Benedetti, gets hold of him off here at Ems, while Bismarck is ill and cannot interfere, and makes him tip the word to Prince Leopold of Hohenzollern to withdraw his candidature for the Spanish throne.''

"The devil you say !" cried Ludwig, dropping his roll with a start.

"Yes, old fellow, the King backs down completely; Prince Leopold withdraws; France gets what she wants—and there'll be no war. Here, read it for yourself,'' and he passed the paper across the table.

Ludwig seized it eagerly and ran his eye along the news item, which startled not only him that morning but all Europe with him.

"Of course there's a lot of diplomatic rot,'' the Englishman went on, ''about its only being a family affair of the Hohenzollerns and not an international question. So the little court at Sigmaringen, where Prince Leopold hails from, informs Madrid that he withdraws, and Madrid informs the Spanish Embassy at Paris, and thus the Prussian Foreign Office keeps a clean set of books; but in plain English, Benedetti has trumped the king here at Ems, while Bis-

marck—the ace—is off at Varzin, so we soldiers
may as well hang up our swords."

"Mine—yes," answered Ludwig dryly, "but
yours wasn't even taken off the hook."

"Why, man, Bavaria couldn't have kept out
of the mess. I'd have had a fight on one
side or the other—and it didn't much matter
which; though I'd rather have been with you
than with the Frenchies."

"Well," said Ludwig, laying down the paper
and quietly resuming his breakfast, "if that
news is true you needn't worry about fighting.
for the present at least. And for my part, I
can't say I'm sorry," he added, after a minute.

The Englishman glanced at his friend in
amazement.

"By Jove !" he exclaimed, "if I were a Prussian and my King had just shown the white
feather"—then a sudden thought struck him
and he began to laugh. "Ah, I see—it is no
longer treason for a pretty French girl to wear
a Prussian forage cap."

Ludwig's face grew the colour of the band
upon the cap, but fortunately for Prussian
and Anglo-Bavarian peace relations a servant
approached and handed Egerton a little pink
letter. The note was unmistakably in a feminine hand and looked very plump,—so it was
the Englishman's turn to look embarrassed.

"She's up bright and early," said Ludwig, glad of the opportunity to turn the tables. "She must have been awake all night thinking about you."

"By Jove!" mused Egerton, looking at the writing quizzically, "I haven't the remotest idea whom it is from." Then to assuage his curiosity he tore open the envelope—when to his amazement a bundle of bank-notes fell into his lap.

"She seems to love you a good deal," laughed Ludwig.

"I say," answered the Englishman, tossing the letter across the table, "read that."

As Ludwig read he smiled to himself. "One who loves you deeply," the note ran, "and saw you lose more than you could afford, takes the liberty of sending the enclosed with the hope that you will grow wise in your day and generation."

"How much was 'the enclosed,'" he asked.

"Five notes of a thousand each," answered his friend, after counting the bills. "It would be insulting if it were not so extraordinary."

"Perhaps it was Clotilde," suggested Ludwig slyly, for he thought it unwise to betray D'Arblay's ruse for cancelling his pilferings without detection.

"I can't keep money sent me by a woman,"

mused Egerton. "What the deuce am I to do with it?"

"Guy," answered his friend, after a moment's reflection, "if I should play baccarat with you to-night and turn up 'nine' for myself twenty times in succession, and you couldn't see anything wrong about it except the fact that I did it, would you keep those notes, ask no questions, and acknowledge you're too big a duffer ever to play cards?"

"So you know something about it, eh?" exclaimed the Englishman, with a suspicious glance at Ludwig.

"I have nothing to say," the latter answered, "beyond the proposition I have just made. Do you accept or not?"

The Englishman pondered for a moment, took out his glass, wiped it carefully, and adjusted it in his eye.

"You say you'll turn up 'nine' twenty times and I won't see you do it. By Jove, you can't!"

"I made the proposition," said Ludwig quietly. "Do you accept?"

"Yes," grunted Egerton, after a moment's thought, "and I will lay you a 'pony' you don't do it."

"Done," answered Ludwig, picking up the Cologne *Gazette* again and glancing at the news that meant peace.

But his thoughts were elsewhere, and after a moment he dropped the paper into his lap and gazed wistfully across the river. He saw the row of white hotels glistening in the morning sunlight, and his eye rested on a window which he knew was Marcelle's. A few fashionables were already strolling among the trees of the Cur-Garten, and when strains of music floated across the water he left his seat so suddenly that the Englishman looked up and smiled.

"Hope you'll have a pleasant walk, Ludwig," he said.

"Aren't you coming, too?" Ludwig asked to hide his embarrassment.

"Two's company and three's a crowd. Meet me at the Cursaal for luncheon. By the way, when are you going to Leun to see your father?"

"That's my affair," said the German curtly, for his friend's chaff had begun to annoy him; so buckling on the sabre he had laid across a chair, he picked up his cap and strode clanking from the room.

Crossing the river he entered the Cur-Garten and mingled with the throng of idlers promenading to the music of the band, or sipping the waters of the various springs. Tall blonde officers, broad in the shoulder, slight in the waist, with clicking spurs and peering eyes, strolled by in groups, to whom he mechanically touched the visor of his cap; civilians as well, of many nations, in short-tailed coats and baggy trousers, passed and repassed, while women with rustling overskirts of many flounces and absurd little feathered hats perched high on wavy puffs of hair, ogled and prattled; but he sought in vain for the face of Marcelle.

As he sauntered along the shady walks he heard heated words of argument on the lips of the passers-by; all were discussing the news which had just reached Ems in that special edition of the Cologne *Gazette*, and "Peace" was the almost universal verdict. But while his brother-officers ground their teeth in rage, his heart beat faster at the thought of war deferred.

He met a little man in a brown suit of clothes. The straight thin nose, the smooth-shaven lips, the hollow cheeks, partly covered by grey side-whiskers—he had seen the face but once, yet he remembered it well—Count Benedetti, the French Ambassador. Ludwig wondered as he passed him why he still looked drawn and careworn after the diplomatic triumph he had won.

Though the band played and the people around him strutted in their finery and talked

of peace, the French Ambassador walked on
with a heavy heart, for he had been ordered to
make a new demand upon the King of Prussia,
with but one intelligible outcome—War.
While the presses of the Cologne *Gazette* had
been grinding monotonously through the
night, stamping white pages with news of
peace, a dispatch had been flashed across the
wires from Paris to Ems in the cipher of the
French Foreign Office. It was signed by the
Duc de Gramont, Minister of Foreign Affairs,
and read:

"We have received from the Spanish Ambassador the renunciation handed in by Prince
Anton in the name of his son, Prince Leopold,
but we cannot regard it as adequate. To have
its full effect, it is indispensable that the King
of Prussia should join with it the assurance
that he will not again, at any further time
approve this candidature. The excitement
here is intense."

Could any sane man expect that a monarch
with a million soldiers under arms or at his
call, should humble himself again, after he had
already humiliated his country in the eyes of
Europe?

Probably de Gramont did not expect it nor
wish it, for there was in France an Emperor
too physically weak from a chronic illness to

take the reins of government himself, and an
Empress who had risen from the ranks and
was, like the Minister, intoxicated with glory
and power. A diplomatic victory had been
won—but Prussia as a government, or William
the First as a king, had not been humbled;
and besides the chassepot had a greater range
than the needle-gun and the mysterious mitrail-
leuse was yet untried. When the chauvins of
the boulevards, with Sadowa rankling in their
hearts, raised the shout that France had been
dishonoured because Prince Leopold had withdrawn his candidacy for the Spanish throne
without the official cognisance of Prussia—de
Gramont and the Empress thought it was the
voice of France. The one fancied himself a
Talleyrand and sent the dispatch to Benedetti,
—the other acclaimed it her war; but they
counted without their hosts. Although there
was in Prussia a peace-loving king, who
granted all that had been asked in the only
way in which he could retain his self-respect,
there was also a crafty Chancellor fuming and
fretting at far-off Varzin who read the hand-
writing on the wall, and only awaited the
moment when he could juggle the cards.

In de Gramont's mind there was the Roman
Catholic Germany of the South, Austria, Italy,
—"more allies," as he said, "than could be

used,'' to march with the Imperial troops after the first victory; and there was no longer a Frederick the Great at Potsdam to beat off Europe. Brilliant game, and possible of being played —but for the crafty statesman of the North. Russia coached to watch Austria,—red-legged soldiers still in the Holy City,—England watching the main chance,—which was munitions,— and the ultramontane South Germans caught between two fires, with a vivid memory of '66, and blood that had been growing thicker than water ever since the days of Stein. Checkmate! But this time the king was an emperor.

While the French Ambassador strolled along the gravel walks at Ems, hoping against hope, not daring to ask a formal audience of the king but resolved to make de Gramont's demand first as a friendly plea, then as a threat, Ludwig hastened on, thinking not of politics, but of Marcelle.

He met the King taking his morning promenade, and he drew his heels together and stood at salute. King William had a kindly, satisfied look in his gentle eyes, and his stately grey head was held erect. Perhaps the tears of his wife or the humiliation his mother had endured at the hands of the first Napoleon had prompted him to whisper the word ''withdraw'' to his kinsman candidate for the Spanish

throne—but whatever the truth might be he
felt the incident was closed. So with a light
heart he answered the salutations of the throng
and strolled beneath the trees, breathing the
fresh morning air.

Ludwig, having reached the end of the
promenade without meeting Marcelle, wheeled
to the right about and walked in the direction
taken by the King. At last he saw her coming towards him. The trim straw hat with the
white ostrich plume, the rose-coloured gown
with its flounces and bows, the little yellow
gloves, the tips of the pale grey boots—he saw
them all; though with his gaze fixed upon her
clear brown eyes; and his heart was a-tremble.

"I have been looking for you everywhere,
Marcelle," he whispered, as he saluted her
father, and wished him anywhere but at her
side. General de Lembach, however, had
begun to think him a fine, soldierly young fellow. Perhaps, as now peace seemed assured,
he had begun deep down in his sere old heart
to think that a mediatised lord of Prussia was
not a bad *parti* for even a de Lembach, for he
had the tact to mumble something about weary
legs and a seat, with an accompanying sug-
gestion that the young people should do the
walking.

So Marcelle and Ludwig strolled on through

the park. People came and went along the gravelled walks, the sunlight filtered through the leaves and brightened the finery; the band played a waltz by Strauss.

Perhaps the music and the humming of the voices were in harmony with their feelings, for the world seemed bright and roseate, and for the moment happiness was triumphant. He was thinking again of the day when she was standing among the lilacs in far-off Alsace, and she of the words he had whispered then, for since that night on the Cursaal terrace they had been constantly in her mind. She felt the burning of his glance and looked away.

In the passing throng she saw a beautiful face beneath a glow of reddish hair. The eyes that had been gazing at her turned away; they were sweet and pathetic, and she wondered at the change. But Ludwig did not notice the little actress, for Marcelle's sweet fragrance was about him. He saw only the burning of her cheek against the dark masses of her hair; and his heart was attuned to a joy so great that it made him afraid to speak lest it take wing.

"Peace, Marcelle," he said. "Isn't it glorious news?"

The girl turned towards him smiling.

"I knew that deep down in your heart you were not a soldier," she answered.

"Ah, Marcelle," he cried, "I fear there is room there for only one thought—and it is far from soldiering."

She glanced up at him from under her brows and in the bright sunlight her eyes sparkled tormentingly.

"What a tiny little heart!" she laughed.

They had stopped near the pavilion of the band. The last strains of the waltz died softly on the morning air.

"It is all there is of myself, Marcelle," he said, "and the thought is all about you."

"Don't, Ludwig, don't talk like that," she said.

"Yesterday I should not have dared," he murmured close to her face, "but to-day when the war clouds have gone and the sun is shining, when the soft air whispers peace, and the colours I wear next my heart are undimmed by that hateful word 'enemy'—may I not say, 'Marcelle, I shall love you always'?"

Her eyes told him better than any words, though he dared not believe the love he had awakened.

"Marcelle!" he cried, impulsively.

She heard a step on the gravel walk and drew back startled. A dignified old gentleman with the bearing of a soldier was coming towards them, and by his side was a pompous little man

talking and gesticulating excitedly. Following
at a respectful distance was an officer in uniform. The crowd had stepped aside and she
and Ludwig were standing alone in the centre
of the walk. She drew him hurriedly away.

"The King!" she whispered.

With his heart still fluttering at her glance,
Ludwig sprang to attention and touched the
visor of his cap with his white-gloved hand;
but the King of Prussia was too absorbed in·
what his companion was saying to notice the
salute. A troubled look crossed his face, and
he stopped suddenly near the place where they
were standing. Dazed by this sudden interruption to their dream, Marcelle and Ludwig
stepped quietly back among the trees.

The little man in the brown suit of clothes
who was talking so animatedly was Count
Benedetti, the French Ambassador. They saw
the look of displeasure on the King's face—the
Corsican's excited manner—and they waited,
not daring to move.

King William held a newspaper in his hand
—the special edition of the Cologne *Gazette*
which had created the flutter of excitement
along the promenade. When Benedetti finished speaking, he handed him the paper, with
a manner in marked contrast to the high-
wrought diplomat.

"Prince Leopold has withdrawn his candidature," he said, in a quiet tone. "The news is already printed."

The Ambassador took the paper without glancing at it.

"Your Majesty," he protested, "Prince Leopold's desistance will not appease the excitement which has been aroused in France."

The King looked at him in surprise.

"The courier dispatched from Sigmaringen should arrive to-day. I shall then send for you and make the communications as already arranged."

Ludwig stared in amazement at the little Corsican. An ambassador waylaying a Monarch in a public park, in times like these, to transact business of state! It seemed incomprehensible; and when he listened to Benedetti's reply, rolling from his lips with Latin volubility, he was appalled by the insolence of the request.

"In order to calm the anxiety," he heard him say, "and strengthen the good understanding between the two countries, it is desirable to guarantee the future as soundly as the past, and in that view, I beg to be authorised to transmit to my government the assurance that Your Majesty would, if necessary, exert your authority to prevent any attempt to

resume the candidature that has been aban-
doned."

Could the peace-loving King but see one idea
in that flow of words—Ludwig wondered. He
had humbled himself already that war might
be averted, and he was asked to bind his country's actions for all time. Was not this more
than pride could bear?—and the young officer
waited breathlessly for the reply. Marcelle,
too, understood enough to make her tremble at
the outcome.

"You are asking me," they heard him say,
"for an undertaking without limit and embrac-
ing all contingencies. I could not bind myself
à tout jamais."

Ludwig had seen the effort the King had
made to control his temper. Ah, how proud
he was of his sovereign! He was the gentleman even in anger.

He saw the Corsican's eyes flash, and he
heard him say insistently, "I have been
urgently instructed by my government to present this request."

Still the King's manner was dignified and
courteous.

"I cannot alienate my liberty of resolution,"
he answered, "I have no hidden designs. This
affair has cost me too much serious thought
not to wish it to be irrevocably set aside."

Such forbearance, such generosity! Ludwig glanced at Marcelle, but her eyes were fixed upon the King, and she saw only an enemy to her country. Even Benedetti seemed to realise that to succeed he must conciliate.

"It will be possible in this regard," he said, in milder tones, "to meet on the ground Your Majesty has chosen. I am addressing the head of the Hohenzollern family, and in that capacity Your Majesty can assuredly accede to the request I am instructed to make."

Again the colour mounted to the King's face. "It is impossible to go so far," he said curtly; "you ask too much. I am unable to make this new and unexpected concession."

Ludwig saw the Ambassador grow more vehement, his face flushed and his arms waving excitedly.

"Again I must ask your Majesty to authorise me to assure my government that this candidature will never be resumed with your consent."

Such disrespect to his Sovereign! The hot blood rushed to Ludwig's temples; he could have struck the man for his insolence, and instinctively he fingered his long cavalry sword.

Struggling to control his temper, the King

turned to the adjutant who stood a few steps away, and said in a voice of command:

"Be kind enough to inform Count Benedetti that there is no reply, and that I cannot receive him again."

Then with the courtly salute of an old-school gentleman, he quietly resumed his promenade.

VII

NOBLESSE OBLIGE

Ludwig had seen the King pass by on his way to Berlin and had started to follow with the cheering crowd, but turning back, he stopped before the Cursaal, and now stood leaning on the iron parapet along the river bank, gazing at the brown, sluggish water.

A King had insulted a Nation, a Nation had insulted a King. A crafty statesman had "edited" a telegram to suit his ends: two armies were unleashed.

In Ludwig's pocket was a telegram summoning him to join the staff of the Crown Prince. Because he had lingered on at Ems, he must go to the front without taking leave of his father, and the thought of it filled his heart with black despair. He tried hard to look upon war as a soldier should, but could not. He did not think he was a coward, for he had been under fire in '66 and was no more afraid than the men about him, and he knew he should do his duty because of the family name; so he might as well be frank with himself and acknowledge that it was Marcelle and the thought that he would be fighting her people which made the idea of war seem so terrible.

No, not that alone, for as she had said, deep down in his heart he was not a soldier.

He smiled to himself when he thought what a strange combination he was of artist, feudal knight, and Puritan. He knew that he had the painter's love for the beautiful, and he tried to believe that he was chivalrous. Of one thing he was certain. His American mother's life had taught him the ideality of love, and because of a promise he had made her he had gone through life a fanatic to his own heart, but a man of the world to his comrades. Oh, what bitter fights he had had with himself, how many moments when his faith had almost failed him! The Latin Quarter was certainly a strange cloister, but he could not help thinking that the very boldness of his attack upon the world had made it easier. The lowest dens of Paris, the sight of vice in its most loathsome forms, had been his safeguard; for these had convinced him that he was right and the men about him wrong.

The cheering for the King grew louder and made him realise he was rambling far from the thought of war, but he liked to think of the past. That year in Paris—at the atelier! How

he longed for it again; that year in the realm
of sympathy, when he had striven to produce
with paints and brushes the unattainable long-
ings of his soul. To think that destiny had
placed a sword in his hands when he sighed for
a maul-stick!

A commission in the little army of the Duke
of Nassau which duty forced him to accept,
and then the Prussianising of a captive prov-
ince—events over which he had no control, but
which forced him now to draw his sword
against the very land he loved. Did he have
two natures, he wondered, each distinct in
itself? For only the other day his heart had
thrilled in anger at the insult to his King and
the thought of war had seemed glorious.

No, it was all Marcelle, he said to himself,
Marcelle, as unlike the convent demoiselle as
the rose is unlike the violet. To form the
purple in her veins, the blue of ancestors had
blended with the vigorous red from *Outre-mer;*
in her eyes was the fire of the pioneer, in her
cheeks were the lilies of France. So it
pleased him to dream. All his life he had
waited for her coming, and she was to be torn
from him by that terrible, terrible thing,
Destiny!

Then, somehow in very contrast, he thought
of Marguerite Clairon. She had overwhelmed

him for a moment and passed from his life
—like those others who had tempted him.
No, not quite: for in her sweet, pathetic eyes
he had seen the awakening of a soul. "Poor
little Marguerite Clairon!" he sighed again
as he had that night beneath her balcony, and
then she went from his mind—for the brown
eyes of his cousin watched over him and made
him ashamed that he had given the other even
a thought.

"With God, for King and Fatherland!"

Again the echoes of the cheers floated across
the river, and he wondered if he had the courage to go to Marcelle's hotel for the farewell
he had been dreading. And only a week
before he had been praying for war—but time
has no conscience. Then with a sudden effort
he summoned all his forces, and pulling himself together, he left the river bank and walked
erect and soldier-like towards the colonnade
connecting the Cursaal with the Curhaus. "No
more day-dreaming," he said to himself; "no
more trying to swim against the current which
sweeps me on. There is but one word—duty
—and it is clear and well defined."

A street urchin passed him whistling a tune
of the day—unconsciously he hummed the lines.

"Lieb Vaterland, magst ruhig sein
Fest steht und treu die Wacht am Rhein."

It made the warm blood tingle in his veins. He was a soldier once more.

He had taken a roundabout way because there was a florist's booth in the colonnade bazaar. An hour remained or more before his train left, but the flowers must not reach her until he had gone, he thought. A pretty white-aproned girl, with bright pink cheeks and braids of flaxen hair waited on him at the florist's stall, and when she saw his gay uniform and the rank of his *achselstücke* she beamed and blushed like the roses in her hand as she told him with downcast eyes that her betrothed was a trooper in his regiment.

"This war is terrible, *Herr Rittmeister*," she murmured; "my heart is breaking at the thought that Rudolph must go."

"But when he comes back with his *Wacht-meister* stripes and his Cross, how proud you will be," Ludwig said cheerfully.

"If the *Herr Rittmeister* would be so kind as to keep an eye on Rudolph and see that no harm comes to him," whispered the girl, trembling at her daring.

"I would gladly, pretty one, but I will not be with the regiment, because I'm a staff officer," and he began to search the shop for the flowers he wished. She brought garish bouquets of many colours, wrapped round with stiff white paper, perforated in lace work patterns, and when he shook his head she pouted and looked injured because they were her handiwork. But he was thinking of a book of Balzac's which he had read—*Le lys dans la Vallée*—and a passage he had always remembered:

"And I sought the flowers to make her a bouquet, and as I gathered them one by one and cut off the stems, I thought as I admired them that the colours and the leaves formed a harmony which, in charming the eye, created a poetry in the mind, just as music awakens a thousand memories in the hearts of those who love."

"My love shall be told her in Jacqueminot roses," he thought, "and lilies,—the crimson of the pioneer, the white of the cavalier; it will be herself, and that is my only thought." Then with his own hand, he bound together a loose bunch of the flowers he had chosen. The little flower girl looked on curiously while he made his own bouquet and pricked his hands with the thorns, thinking how dearly he must love some one to take such trouble. But when he gave her the directions for sending the flowers and she read the French name, she pitied the fine young captain whose sweetheart was an enemy. Choosing the finest red rose she could find, she came towards him blushing and pinned it on the breast of his *attila*.

"For the handsome *Herr Rittmeister*," she said, making him a pretty curtsey.

"Thank you, my dear," he answered. "I'm sorry that I can't keep an eye on Rudolph."

And smiling he drew on his white gloves and left the flower-stand, wearing the crimson rose. He knew it did not look soldierly, but he had not the heart to throw it way until he was well out of sight, so he strolled through the colonnade towards the Curhaus. Suddenly he saw a pale, sweet face under a shining mass of Titian hair. A queer little tremor shot through him, and his impulse was to turn his eyes away and pretend not to see her; but the thought that he could be so needlessly unkind made him ashamed, so hastening his steps he walked straight towards the little actress.

"I'm glad of the chance to say good-bye, Marguerite," he said, as she looked up startled and saw him standing by her side.

"How glad I am to see you again," she cried impulsively; then she checked herself suddenly—"I'm off for Paris to-morrow you know. The trains are too crowded to-day."

"And I'm off to join the Crown Prince," he answered. "A king and an ambassador meet in the park—and the whole course of our lives is changed.   But that is life, Marguerite."

Her eyes met his glance, then turned away slowly, growing sad and thoughtful as she spoke.

"I can't bear to think that you will be an enemy."

"I love France too well to wish it," he said.

She thought of the pretty brown-haired girl she had seen in the Cur-Garten.

"Yes, Ludwig, I understand," she said, "and I wish you the best luck in the world—honours in this hateful war, and—and happiness when peace comes again."   Then she tried to smile.   "That is more than a French girl ought to wish," she added quickly.

"Thank you, Marguerite," he said, taking her little gloved hand, and as he did so he saw the crimson rose the flower girl had pinned upon his jacket.   In the impulse of the moment he tore it off and gave it to her.

"Until we meet again," he said, with a flutter of shame in his heart, for he thought of Marcelle.

"I shall keep it always," she whispered, not daring to meet his glance.   She heard the click of his spurs as he turned away, and with misty eyes watched him until he entered the

Cur-Garten,—then, with a heavy heart, she walked on, pressing his rose to her lips.

"And because I would make him like the others," she thought, "I dare not try to win his love. *Mon Dieu*, but the penalty is hard!"

When Ludwig reached Marcelle's hotel omnibuses stood before the door and sweating porters were piling them high with luggage. French guests were hurrying away to reach the train connecting with the Cologne express for Paris, and as he entered the hallway and picked his way among valets with bags and maids with hat-boxes, the gesturing, chattering travellers drew aside as though he were tainted with contagion. The men glowered as he passed, and the women in pretty Paris gowns shot glances filled with hate for the Prussian tunic.

In the glass-covered courtyard, beyond the desk of the concierge, he found Marcelle and her father deep in the study of a time-table. The General looked up at the sound of the clanking sabre, and while his tawny face grew red his eyes sparkled with hostility. Marcelle, too, coloured and turned away, and it was a depressing, awkward moment for the young soldier, for in his cousin's efforts to conceal her emotion he saw only enmity to him.

"I hope you will pardon me, General de

Lembach," he said, with trepidation, "for the liberty I take in calling to pay my respects."

The old soldier drew himself up with all the dignity of a veteran of Malakoff and Solferino.

"There is no apology necessary, sir," he answered in tones of studied politeness. "I quite understand the motive which prompts your visit and I appreciate the civility because of its well intentioned purpose. I, however, regret extremely that recent events should interrupt our agreeable relations."

The young officer felt the blood tingle in his cheeks.

"I thank you, sir," he answered stiffly, "for your consideration, and I deplore the untimeliness of my visit." Then his hand flew to the visor of his cap, and he wheeled with military precision towards Marcelle.

"Mademoiselle," he said curtly, "my compliments."

And Marcelle knew that another heart was being tortured.

"Nonsense, Ludwig !" she cried impulsively; "you are my cousin, and I can't let you leave without telling you of the pleasure it has given me to meet you again—and thank you for all your kindness to us here at Ems."

It was a glad tune Ludwig's heart beat out.

"Thank you, Marcelle," he cried.

"My child," the veteran muttered, "remember France has declared war——"

"I understand," said Marcelle, quietly, "and should Ludwig and I meet again we will not forget our duty. We ask only the privilege of saying good-bye."

Her voice quivered as she spoke, but she made a brave fight and kept back the tears.

The General shrugged and walked a few steps away. He realised he had been over-harsh, so he made this silent capitulation to Marcelle's wish.

"You go to Paris to-morrow?" Ludwig said hurriedly, to keep back the words he did not dare speak.

"No," she answered, "we go direct to Alsace by the Rhine and the Palatinate."

"To Alsace?" he exclaimed, in amazement, "why, it will be the seat of war."

A proud flush spread across her face.

"You forget, Ludwig, that Alsace is France," she answered quietly.

"Forgive me, Marcelle," he muttered, with bowed head.

For a moment they stood together in silence, and patriotism and love fought hard for the mastery. He was a soldier and there should be but one choice; but with her, duty was less clear and well defined, and foremost of all the arguments tormenting her was love itself.

When he heard her father's voice calling "Marcelle!" he refused to believe it was the end, and a wild rebellious thought filled his heart. To resign in the face of the enemy would be disgrace in the eyes of the world, but to make an enemy of her people would be torture.

"Marcelle!" he cried; "Is it good-bye? I cannot——"

But the words died on his lips.

"*Noblesse oblige,*" she murmured, and it was the answer to his thoughts.

For one long moment they looked deep into each other's eyes, then he took her hand and kissed it.

His flowers were brought at nightfall. Crowds were passing beneath her window, singing *Die Wacht am Rhein*, and she seemed to hear the echo of the Paris mob singing the Marseillaise.

II

I

EN' AVANT!

Sunshine was on the woods and the white villages, and the air was bred of the mountains. Marcelle let her horse jog leisurely beside her father's barouche as her eyes wandered from the wrinkled old soldier, propped up by the carriage cushions, to the hazy sky-line of forested hills.

Stretched out before her was the bright countryside with vineyards and orchards and fields of flax, while in the valley below a sleepy river coiled amid the green meadows and glistening villages of Alsace. Where the stretch of white road ahead met the highway from Hagenau, she saw the head of a crawling line of red-legged soldiers.

"Look, father!" she exclaimed. "A column is marching towards the north. Can't we reach the cross-roads in time to see it pass?"

General de Lembach, keen as his daughter for the sight of *culottes rouges*, gave a word of command to old Hans the coachman, and the carriage went rolling towards the valley, with Marcelle galloping ahead, her cheeks aglow,

her hair ruffled by the wind. She felt content
to breathe that clear air of Alsace forever, if
only Ludwig—but the thought was treason.
So her whip curled round the horse's withers,
and in the childish enthusiasm of hers for the
day, and the glorious ride down the mountain
side past the wooded glades and the little white
farm-houses and the fresh green heaths, she
tried to forget those days at Ems.

What a joy it had been, she thought, to
reach their grey château among the firs and
beeches, with the dogs to bark and the servants to beam a welcome, after the bitter, trying journey back to France.

They should have taken the Cologne' express, but her father refused to beat a hasty
retreat; perhaps deep in his soldier's heart he
hoped to see something of the mobilisation of
the enemy. So they had jogged slowly by the
Rhine to Bingen, and thence by carriage
across the Palatinate to the frontier. The
trains had all been requisitioned for the
mobilisation, and in the tedious trip by road,
they, being French, had been treated almost
as spies, for whenever they approached the
cantonments of troops they were guarded and
watched, and subjected to delay and annoyance
by every officious subaltern and pettifogging
mayor who saw fit to question them. At last

they had entered France at the border town of Wissembourg, and but a few miles beyond was Lembach and the grey château.

The French army was being massed upon the frontier, and in the neighboring town of Hagenau was Abel Douay's Division of Mac-Mahon's Corps. When General de Lembach heard the French drumbeats he stiffed his back and looked straight to the front, keen as any subaltern to see the insolent Prussians get the sound trouncing they deserved. But during his almost daily drives to the cantonments at Hagenau, his old soldier's heart began to worry and he shook his head many times. He had seen the fair-haired Germans quietly mobilising in barracks beyond the Rhine, while about him was disorder and chaos, unequipped and unprovisioned regiments with half-filled ranks, and reserves Heaven alone knew where. There was bound to be a battle soon—the Prussians surely would not wait to be attacked, so he feared they might take the offensive and cross the frontier. Now when he saw that French division in the valley below he breathed a sigh of relief, for at last troops were moving to the front.

At the cross-roads the carriage stopped and Marcelle drew rein, while a regiment went swinging by. It was a regiment of Turcos from Africa, bearded and brown, with baggy legs and Arab caps aslant. The flicker of steel, the swaying heads with their red checchias, the trembling green banner with the open red hand and spread fingers upon its field—a sight to make the warm blood tingle through her.

"*Vive les Turcos!*" she cried, in her enthusiasm,—and the Kabyles grinned under their crimson head dresses, while the old veteran in the barouche looked on and smiled, for the First Arab Tirailleurs had been "his children" under the African sun.

Tramp, tramp along the highroad went the sinewy Turcos, with canteens rattling and sword bayonets clicking against their canvas breeches, and in their rear came the Fiftieth of the line, red-trousered and sunburnt. But the General's practised eye was not to be dazzled by mere glittering panoply, and again he shook his head while his wrinkled face grew thoughtful.

A pitiless rain had fallen in the morning and the highway was covered with grey, soft mud, though the sun shone warm and bright upon the fields. Down upon the road towards Hagenau were caissons locked together, artillery men lashing their horses, wagons stuck in the ditches, laggards panting by the roadside, horse chasseurs with rain-soaked shakos tangled amid the infantry, aides-de-camp shouting oaths, soldiers in the cottage doors begging for food and drink, and when the old veteran saw the confused and half-filled ranks he thought with sadness of those fair-haired, blue-eyed Prussians, so quietly mobilising beyond the Rhine.

But Marcelle's heart thrilled to the notes of the bugles, the tramping battalions. The jaded fantassins and weary horses stumbling through the mire, the heavy wagons rumbling in the ruts, the jolting caissons, were to her but the concomitants of war, and surely French valour was invincible.

The General and his staff came clattering towards her, with aiglets glittering in the sunshine and the headquarters guidon fluttering in the wind. Under the gold-leaved képi of the commander she saw a pale turgid face with dreamy eyes and waxed moustaches. A battery of mitrailleuses had blocked the road, and while the artillerymen lashed their panting beasts and swore, the General drew rein near where she sat her horse.

"Vive General Douay!" she cried, waving her handkerchief. *"Vive l'armée!"*

The General glanced up at the sound of his name and saw her smiling face, so he threw a kiss and then in the barouche beyond he recognized his old friend De Lembach, who had fought side by side with him at Malakoff. He sidled his horse towards the carriage, and dismounting threw the reins to an orderly. He was tired and hot, and as the road was blocked he was glad of a moment's respite from the trying march.

Marcelle gazed at him admiringly. General Abel Douay—the *beau sabreur*—with his képi rakishly aslant upon his grey head, his braided tunic glittering with epaulettes and orders,— General Abel Douay, brave, ignorant soldier of the empire—with Duty for his watch-word, and his only belief the Invincibility of France.

"Sweet and pretty as ever, eh?" he whispered to Marcelle as he shook her father's fulvous old hand in the way that sword-brothers understand. "*Mon Dieu*, if I were only a lieutenant!" And the girl's face flushed with pleasure and pride.

"If our antagonists were only girls, my General," she laughed, "France would need no other champion than yourself."

"*Fichtre!* but I call that a doubtful compliment," and a young aide-de-camp waiting near had difficulty to suppress a smile.

"I'm glad to see movement at last," growled General de Lembach, by way of interruption, "and I call it high time."

"Come," laughed General Douay, "don't look so glum, Lembach. It's always this way at the beginning."

"I suppose you're moving on Wissembourg," answered Marcelle's father, with a glance towards the north.

"Yes, and it will be late when I go into camp," said General Douay, looking up at the slanting rays of the sun.

"Ducrot and Raoult are at Reichshoffen, aren't they?" General de Lembach continued.

"Yes."

"And Lartigue is at Hagenau——"

"Yes."

"Humph," mused the old veteran. "One division at Wissembourg, twenty odd kilomètres from supports, a prey for the first corps of Prussians with the energy to cross the Lauter. I don't envy you, Douay, egad, I don't."

General Douay laughed.

"Prussians crossing the Lauter into France! That's rich! Professional jealousy, Lembach; you wish you were with us, eh? *Mon Dieu!* but I'm sorry you're not."

General de Lembach was gazing at a gun-carriage stuck in a ditch, with artillerymen lashing and staff officers threatening, then his eye wandered to a cottage by the roadside.

A group of stragglers came pouring through the door, waving long loaves of bread and bottles of red wine.

"I wish some one were with you," he said finally, "who knew how to untangle knots. It isn't the way it was in my day."

"All old soldiers have the liver complaint," thought Douay.

"You remember only the glory of old days," he said cheerily. "You forget the gloom."

"Possibly," answered the veteran, shaking his head dubiously; "but the transport wagons are at Vernon and Chateauroux, the camp outfits are at Versailles, and even you, the first on the ground, haven t got all your reserves. Is that the sort of army ready to the last gaiter button Le Boeuf promised us? Is that the sort of army to beat the victors of Sadowa?"

"Ha, ha, ha!" laughed the commander of MacMahon's Second Division; "why, man, at Gallipoli Saint Arnaud was tearing around like a mad hatter because the War Office hadn't sent him any tents and ambulances; why, man, in Italy the troops were grubbing for roots while the Emperor was shouting that the Ministers at home were skalawags and robbers. Well, we won in '54, we won in '59, and we'll win in '70—for the very simple reason that you can't conquer French valour, my General."

Marcelle had been listening to every word, her lips tense and eager, her eyes brown and troubled as the waters of a winter stream.

"No, no, no!" she cried; "it can not be! Prussian precision a match for the dash and valour of our soldiers!" But her enthusiasm was checked by the thought that there might be more Prussians as brave as the one she knew among the enemy.

"Ah, my child," answered the veteran sadly, "I thought as you three weeks ago—a battle, a rout, then on to Berlin! But I saw them mobilising there beyond the Rhine—such order, such method, and every one so terribly in earnest."

"Treason!" cried Douay. "Treason! and you a soldier of France! For shame!"

The old General turned on him with flashing eyes.

"Then tell me why eight army corps are huddled along the frontier, partly in scattered positions, partly in close concentration? Why is two-thirds of the army crowded along the line of Metz-Saarbrücken, with MacMahon and your brother Félix Douay both out of touch and exposed?"

The General shrugged his shoulders after the manner of a Frenchman perplexed.

"Ask MacMahon at corps headquarters, or

the Emperor at Metz. I only command the Second Division of the First Army Corps. It is trouble enough. Let my superiors untangle the knots."

"Yes, '*débrouillez vous*,'—what you all say from field marshal to corporal. But why in the name of common sense, when our army was hurried pell-mell to the frontier, didn't we make a dash into the Palatinate, and cut off South Germany from Prussia? Two weeks lost, while the enemy mobilises in barracks, and now you go ambling on to Wissembourg to sit down twenty kilomètres from supports and wait till the Prussians are ready to pick you up."

"Come, Lembach, your liver is bad," laughed General Douay. "When I'm picked up it'll be time to talk. Think of Saarbrücken; all we had to do was to cross the frontier and they ran like sheep."

General de Lembach did not answer. He sat quietly in his carriage with sad, lustreless eyes turned towards the north. Beyond those hills sombre hordes were swarming, alert and eager, as he had seen them there across the Rhine. This over-confidence, this disorder, what could it portend but disaster?

General Douay's attention had meanwhile been arrested by an aide-de-camp who, edging his horse through the ranks of a regiment of foot chasseurs, had dismounted and saluted.

"The way is clear, my General," said the officer. "The artillery that blocked the road is on the march." So the commander wheeled towards his old comrade's carriage.

"I must be off, Lembach," he said. "You'll change your tune before we meet again."

"With all my heart, I hope so," answered the veteran sadly, as Abel Douay pressed his hand.

"When I get back from Berlin we'll have it out," the soldier laughed, and turned towards Marcelle.

"We are not croakers, you and I," he said, looking up at her admiringly and patting her horse's neck. "Death to every enemy of France—eh, my pretty one?"

But the girl's look grew suddenly pensive, and General Douay noticed a blush crimson her face to her hair.

"What! has my little sweetheart left her heart beyond the Rhine?" he laughed. "How do you like that, my General?" he asked, with a glance towards the old soldier in the carriage.

"My daughter knows her duty,' answered General de Lembach coldly, and his face assumed a quiet hardness. Marcelle shuddered—for happiness seemed very far away.

Then General Douay's sword clattered against his red trouser leg, and his little spurs tinkled like chiming bells as he swung into the saddle. A nod to his old comrade, a kiss thrown to Marcelle, and as he rode away he called, "*Au revoir*, my friends!" in a cheerful voice, while a little pet spaniel yelped and frolicked about the heels of his horse.

Marcelle watched the General and his staff pick their way along the troop-choked highway, with epaulettes glinting, and the silk guidon fluttering in the wind. The road beyond was dense with marching men far as her eye could see—masses of blue and red pushing their way along in an eddying column towards the land of the foe, and in the slanting sun-rays the tangled rifles flickered and a sea of crimson képis rose and fell.

"To fight for France" she sighed. "Oh, if I were only a man !" And she turned her eyes away to hide the tears she could not keep back.

But the grey, wrinkled veteran, propped up against the carriage cushions, saw only the stragglers panting by the roadside, the swearing teamsters, the cumbersome horde of sutlers and camp followers, swarming at the rear.

Again he shook his head, and as his old, watery eyes gazed towards the Rhineland he seemed to hear the chanting of strange war songs and the rumble of slim black guns, seemed to see grim Uhlans on the sunny slopes of Alsace, with pennons fluttering at their lance heads. Was reason leaving him, he wondered, or was that thought a prophecy?

When the last cart had rumbled by and the rear guard had slouched towards the north, he mumbled the word "home" to his coachman, and the carriage rolled away towards Lembach.

Marcelle rode in silence beside her father. The sun was still shining, but grey-black clouds loomed above the forest to the south, and the wind had fallen away until it scarcely ruffled the leaves. She saw the villages, whose red roofed houses dotted the valley side, and she heard the distant tolling of bells; she passed harvesters toiling by the roadside, and hale, pink-cheeked peasant women driving in rumbling carts; and everywhere she looked it seemed that the spirit of peace had arisen. It was hard to realise that she had just seen an army, and harder yet to believe that beyond those blue Alsatian hills Ludwig marched beneath the black-cross banner of the enemy.

No, she could not think of war on such an afternoon of rest, for the road stretched out

towards Lembach and the woods echoed rustling music; so she breathed the pungent odour
of pasture and meadow, and thought of the day
long ago, when she sped her piebald pony
between that very double line of poplars, with
Ludwig beside her, and fat old Hans, so ruddy
and sleek, upon the box of her father's
barouche, puffing and pounding behind.
Every glade, every thicket, every white house
that slept by the roadside, brought back
memories of those days long gone

They struck the road to the village of Lembach and followed it upward through the
Hochwald, and when they reached the summit
of the wooded ridge, Marcelle could see the
pointed turrets of the grey château rising above
the trees of the park, and the winding, white
road down which they must travel. To the
right a wood path led off through the Mundat
Wald, and she remembered it was a short cut
to Grete's farm; Grete, her old Alsatian
"bonne," who had been a second mother to
her in those childhood days of which she had
been dreaming.

"Father," she said suddenly, "I haven't
been to Grete's farm since we got back. Let
me take this path and ride home that way.
It's only a little farther, and, oh, how glad
Grete will be to see me!"

General de Lembach looked dubious. "I don't think you ought to be riding about alone in war time—"

"War time!" she laughed; "as though there were danger here—on our own estate, within a few kilomètres of Lembach, where every farmer and every peasant are retainers! Danger, father—nonsense."

The General remembered the rides she had taken in Algeria, the fearless, careless way she looked upon danger—so like her mother, he thought.

"Well, well," he mused. "But you see those clouds—what if you should get caught out in a storm?"

"Then I'll stay all night with Grete," she laughed. "Good-bye," and wheeling her horse she was off through the woods at a gallop.

II

THE HOUSE IN THE FOREST

"If you pass the lines, Mademoiselle, you cannot return after sunset."

The captain in command of the outpost folded his arms and waited for Marcelle to reply. Beyond a line of picketed horses, swishing their banged tails, a group of booted troopers in pale blue tunics were stubbornly trying to incite a blaze with some sticks of green wood, and other soldiers lay stretched upon the grass. A boyish sentinel tarried on his beat, to turn a pair of admiring eyes at the pretty girl on the horse.

"Is this the last outpost?" asked Marcelle.

"The last of the First Division; the Second is at Wissembourg, or should be."

Marcelle tapped the grey skirt of her riding habit impatiently with her ivory-handled whip.

"And there is no way I can return to Lembach after sunset?" she asked.

"None, Mademoiselle,—our orders are positive.

"Then I must find a way," she answered, gathering up her reins.

"Our orders are to fire."

Marcelle looked at the officer and laughed; her whip stung the horse's flank.

"*Adieu, mon Capitaine*," she cried, and the boyish sentinel had scant time to leap aside.

The gallop soon brought her from the clearing where the chasseurs had bivouacked into the Mundat Wald again. Down in the valley the huddled village of Climbach glowed purple in the afternoon mist; the clouds to the south were banking high, and she heard the low grumble of thunder; but it was only three kilomètres to Grete's farm, and she had an hour at least before sunset; so she urged on her horse.

It was dark in the thickets of the forest, and she rode impetuously, now galloping, now letting the horse go as he would. He was winded and steaming hot when she reached the clearing and drew rein at the entrance to the court-yard of the little farm-house. She had laughed at the idea of fear when she had left her father's carriage at the cross-roads, but the sight of that bivouac of Ducrot's chasseurs, almost at the gate of the château park, made her ride as though a regiment of Uhlans was in pursuit. Every shadow looked like a Prussian sentry, yet she knew the Prussians were miles away across the Lauter. Alone in a forest in war time,—enough to try the heart of a man—and she was only a girl; so when the goal was reached she drew a deep breath of thankfulness.

The courtyard had but a single entrance. The low, rambling house with thatched gables and peaked roof, outbuildings and a stable, were all enclosed by a high stone wall, and as Marcelle trotted her horse through the gateway, she almost ran into a huge peasant's cart with a cover of white canvas which stood by the door of the house.

"Grete!" she called; "oh, Grete!" as she rode towards the open stable door.

A head was thrust through the kitchen window, and under the huge bows of an Alsatian peasant's cap she saw the rubicund face of her old nurse.

"Ma—Ma'm'selle Marcelle!" cried the peasant with delight.

"Yes, Grete," shouted the girl; "but where's Gottfried?"

"In the stable, Ma'm'selle."

"All right, I'll leave my horse with him and come to the house." The clatter of the hoofs on the flagstones of the courtyard had aroused Grete's husband, and he stood red and grinning in the stable door,—an honest face under the big round cap, bandy legs in the tight white breeches, a little fat body bulging out of a double-breasted waistcoat, and trim, tight jacket with two rows of buttons—it did Marcelle's eyes good to see the hale, hearty farmer beaming a welcome, and with a word of greeting she jumped from the saddle and threw him the reins.

"I've been with the wife three times to the château, Ma'm'selle," he said, "but always the same answer—Gone to Hagenau to see the soldiers."

"Yes, Gottfried, it makes my dear father young again to hear the drums beat."

"Ah, Ma'm'selle, aren't you thankful he is not going to the war?"

"I only wish I were going myself," cried the girl, with a rosy flush upon her cheeks, as the ivory-handled whip swung by its lash in her hand.

"*Gott in Himmel*, Ma'm'selle !" he exclaimed, in Alsatian German. "You go to the war!"

"If I were a man I'd ask nothing better."

"Heaven be praised, you're not," said the peasant, leading her horse to a stall. "Shall I take off the saddle?" he asked, looking over his shoulder inquiringly.

"No, I can only stop a moment. I have to be back before sundown You can give him some water though, when he is cooled off."

Then the girl noticed two rows of empty stalls.

"Why, Gottfried," she asked in astonishment, "what has become of your horses and cattle?"

"Up in the mountains, Ma'm'selle—horses, cows, sheep, everything—out of the way of the Prussians."

Marcelle's laughter rang through the empty stable.

"Afraid of the Prussians," she cried. "Why, Gottfried, they're leagues away across the Lauter."

"Leagues away," grunted the farmer, who, the horse fastened, now came waddling towards her. "Only last week a dozen Prussians galloped about here in broad daylight, swinging their swords and swearing like devils."

"Yes, I know," Marcelle answered, with a shrug; "those crazy dragoons that were all killed or captured at Scheuerlenhof—well, they got what they deserved—and there's no danger now, for General Douay marched to Wissembourg to-day."

"*Donnerwetter!*" said Gottfried dubiously; "if a dozen Prussians can do that, thinks I, how long will it be before the whole lot is on

top of us? So off I goes to the mountains
with the cattle and leaves my man Jacob to
watch them.''

Marcelle, still laughing at the fright that
wild exploit of Count Zeppelin and his Baden
dragoons had given the worthy farmer, walked
towards a door which stood open at the back
of the stable.   It led to the barnyard, she saw,
and was three or four feet above the ground—
a good jump for a horse, she thought.   As she
stood looking at the pasture and the flax field
beyond, raindrops fell upon her face and a
loud clap of thunder rumbled through the forest.

''Why, Gottfried,'' she cried, ''it's raining !
I may have to stay all night.''

''*Gott sei dank ?*'' exclaimed the farmer; but
a drenching downpour fairly drowned his
words, and Marcelle scampered away from the
door.

''How are we to get to the house without
getting wet ?'' she asked.

The farmer grinned, and without replying
walked to a small door at the side of the stable
and threw it open.   Marcelle caught a glimpse
of rows upon rows of milk cans and a tall
wooden churn.

''Ah, the dairy,'' she said.

''With a door to the house,'' he grunted.

''What a lot of wet feet it saves in winter at milking time!''

They passed through the cool dairy with its odours of milk and cheese, and entered the kitchen; then, with a cry of joy, the girl's arms flew about Grete's waist and her face was pressed against a plump, red cheek.

"And I thought my little Marcelle had forgotten her old Grete," cried the peasant—brushing away the tears of joy with one hand and leading the girl to the living-room with the other.

"No, no, Grete, you didn't think that," said the girl, catching the peasant's hands and swaying her back and forth, while Gottfried looked on beaming, his fat arms akimbo.

"A week at the château and never a thought of Grete," said the woman, shaking her head with its huge black bows.

"I came the first minute I could," exclaimed Marcelle.

The rain beat upon the window panes and the thunder shook the casements. It was growing dark, too, and the thought of the chasseur captain's warning came to Marcelle, but she did not care—it seemed to take ten years off her life to be there with dear old Grete.

Gottfried drew down the cast-iron lamp which hung by swivelled chains from the low

ceiling, and as he lighted it a glow of cheer
was shed upon the smiling faces of the peasants.
How far away were those marching regiments
and war, thought Marcelle, as her glance roved
about the cosey white room.

A Madonna and Child hung upon the wall,
an American sewing machine stood by the
window—the one she had given Grete—and a
row of flower pots were lined upon the ledge
before the white chintz curtains. There were
quaint carved chairs, too, a smooth oak table,
and a four-post bed in an alcove with feathered
coverlet and pretty flowered curtains—and
Marcelle romped like a child about the room,
examining every nook, looking into everything—even the huge clothes-press which stood
against the wall.

"Just the place for Gottfried to hide when
the Prussians come," she laughed, as she shut
the door upon shelves of linen, and hooks
bulging with Grete's best gowns.

The farmer grunted resentfully but said nothing, and meanwhile Grete scurried back and
forth across the room, until a cold goose, a
loaf of bread, and a cheese had been trans-
ported from the cupboard to the table.

"You can't go home in this storm, Ma'm-
'selle," she panted, in her efforts to draw a
cork from a bottle of *Tokaier.*

"I know it, you dear old Grete," exclaimed Marcelle, throwing her arms about the peasant's fat waist. "You'll have to undress me and put me to bed to-night, just as you used to do, and when you have tucked me in you must tell me fairy stories until I fall asleep.

"I know," smiled Grete, "'the Princess and the Elves.'"

"Yes, and the witch who lived in the Hochwald and stole all the naughty children," laughed Marcelle; and then she thought that if she were hungry herself, her poor horse must be so as well.

"Go to the stable and feed and water Moulaï, there's a good man," she said to Gottfried.

The farmer stumped off through the kitchen to the stable, and Marcelle sat down at the table beside Grete and rested her head upon the woman's broad shoulder. A hand stroked her forehead caressingly, and she closed her eyes and dreamed of a valley near far-off Ems where the water purled and the sunlight filtered through the leaves and there were glades and woodland lanes.

"Ah, how glad I am to be here!" Marcelle sighed. "It makes me forget such horrible things as war and duty."

"Does Ma'm'selle remember, ten years ago it must be, when she stole into Grete's bed at night and told her about the handsome young cousin from beyond the Rhine?"

"Oh, Grete," she cried, hiding her face on the woman's shoulder, "what made you think of him."

"Because Ma'm'selle told me she could never love any one else," Grete whispered softly, "and now it must be a fine young chasseur or a cuirassier—and that's why she talks of war and duty."

Marcelle made a brave show of indifference, and leaving the seat beside Grete she went to the window. It had grown quite dark, but the storm was lessening. The wind still came in furious gusts, but only a few intermittent drops of rain beat against the panes.

"Grete," she said, turning towards the peasant suddenly, "he is a Prussian Hussar, and every word I told you then was true."

"A Prussian!" exclaimed the woman, trying to understand.

The girl looked at her with a long, unmoving gaze.

"I had to tell some one, Grete," she said, in effort to keep back the tears. "Now, not another word." Then she walked quietly back to the table and began to help the Alsatian lay the knives and forks beside the earthenware plates.

Gottfried came from the stable, and Marcelle glanced up and smiled.

"Did you look after my horse?" she asked cheerfully.

"Yes, Ma'm'selle, I watered him, and now he is munching a full measure of barley."

"I hope you took off the saddle," she said.

"The saddle!" answered the farmer. "Why, no, Ma'm'selle, you told me not to."

Marcelle laughed. "Why, Gottfried, how silly you are. I said that when I thought I was going to stop only a minute, but it's dark now and storming, and they can't send for me from the château because Ducrot's chasseurs would not let them pass the lines."

Gottfried turned to go back to the stable.

"No, no, Gottfried," she called; "don't bother to do it now. Moulaï can't overeat with the saddle on, and supper is waiting."

While the peasants looked on laughing, she wielded a huge carving knife in futile efforts to carve the goose, but it put her in a merry mood once more and brought a pretty flush upon her cheeks. When, panting, she gave up her task and drew her chair beside the table the joy of the moment robbed her of any memories of marching columns or the black-crossed banner of the foe.

Her hale young appetite which coarse food could not spoil, the glow of light upon the ruddy, smiling faces of Gottfried and Grete, the cool, amber *Tokaier*—how far away war seemed!

"And to think that Gottfried was afraid of Prussians," she laughed.

Gottfried moved uncomfortably in his seat.

"The Prussians were here last week," he said; "they may be here again."

"You've seen the last Prussian this side the Lauter," scoffed Marcelle, "for General Douay has marched to the front," and raising her glass, she cried:

" 'Here's to our brave Gottfried, who kept cows in a pen
    Until he marched them up a hill and marched them
        down again' "

Grete nudged her man in the ribs and laughed uproariously, but he looked very sulky and glum—his pride was ruffled. Marcelle not wishing to hurt the old farmer's feelings, desisted from further bantering and began to eat, and as hers was not the only appetite at the table, the dimensions of the goose became rapidly less. Suddenly the girl put down her knife and fork.

"Listen!" she exclaimed,—for she thought

she had heard the sound of hoofs, and she wondered if it could be Ducrot's chasseurs.

Gottfried put his hand to his ear.

"The storm, Ma'm'selle," he said, after a moment.

But Marcelle left the table and stepped quietly to the window. Nearer, nearer came the noise. Yes, it was the pulsing of hoofs, not of one horse but of several.

She drew back out of the light, and going towards the door she opened it slightly and peered out into the darkness. The sound of the hoofs grew nearer, then two horsemen swung round the corner of the wall by the farmer's cart and halted. Others stopped in the night beyond.

By the light which streamed through the window she saw pale blue uniforms. Gottfried had crept beside her.

"Chasseurs!" he said.

But the girl heard a gruff command in German—and she stood for a moment cowed by her own heartbeats.

"Prussians!" she whispered finally; then closed the door quickly and turned the latch.

"Grete," she called in a low voice, "put out the lamp."

"Prussians!" cried the woman. "Oh, Ma'm'selle——"

"Hush, Grete !" said the girl.

The terrified peasant blew out the lamp, leaving the room in darkness.

Prussians in Alsace! Marcelle could not believe her senses. But those Baden dragoons at Scheuerlenhof last week, she thought, that gruff command in German,—what else could they be? Trembling, she crept to the window, her frightened brain a-whirl. She thought of her saddled horse and the way to the stable by the dairy, and her heart throbbed joyfully, but as quickly sank, for she heard the Prussian troopers dismounting at the stable door. Then an idea came to her—the chasseurs at the cross-roads scarce three kilomètres away.

"Gottfried," she whispered suddenly.

"Yes, Ma'm'selle," came through the darkness in a quivering voice.

"Gottfried," Marcelle went on, "at the cross-roads near Climbach there is a troop of chasseurs. Have you the courage to go and tell them that the Prussians are here?"

"But how can I pass the Prussians?" was the farmer's trembling answer.

"Listen, Gottfried," said the girl, feeling her way along the wall towards the clothes press—"and you, too, Grete."

"Yes, Ma'm'selle."

"Those Prussians are putting their horses in the stable; they will be at the door in a moment; they will help themselves to every-thing, and if they see me——"

"No, no," cried Grete, with a peasant woman's terror of soldiers. "They must never find you, Ma'm'selle, never! Ah, it would be too horrible!"

"Then there is but one way out of it," whis-pered Marcelle. "Gottfried must go for the chasseurs. Now, this is my plan. I will hide here in the clothes-press under the dresses, where, if they search, they may not find me. So much for me. Now, Gottfried, when they knock at the door, Grete will open it, making all the noise she can. It is dark, and while they are striking a light you are to creep through the door and hide under that big cart, —then watch your chance, steal through the gate and run as you never ran in your life to the cross-roads. Do you understand?"

"Yes, Ma'm'selle," he said meekly, but his heart went thumping against his ribs. He firmly expected to be pierced by a dozen bul-lets, drawn, quartered, and buried alive, but he had not the courage to refuse.

"And, Grete, remember—plenty of noise."

"Yes, Ma'm'selle."

"Hush!" whispered Marcelle, "there they

are now," and she drew open the door of the clothes-press.

A hand fumbled at the latch—then a loud knocking. Grete tiptoed towards the door, and Gottfried's shaking knees followed.

"Wait," called Marcelle, "wait till I tell you."

"Open that door!" growled a voice outside. The girl felt her way into the clothes-press, and fumbling found the fretwork of little holes which had been bored in the door for ventilation. They were just at the height of her eyes —fortunately, she thought.

"Open the door!" and the pounding grew louder. "Open, damn you, we know you're there—we saw the light."

"Open!" called Marcelle, shutting the clothes-press door. Then she glued her eyes against the ventilation holes and watched breathlessly.

The door creaked on its hinges. She heard the step of spurred boots and the rattle of steel.

"Light that candle you blew out," snarled a voice in German.

"'Tis a lamp, *Mein Herr*," shouted Grete.

"Well, light it, fool."

"Yes, *Mein Herr*." And Grete shuffled and stamped as though she were dancing the carmagnole.

"She's crazy—or it's a trick. Strike a match, quick."

Marcelle heard the grating of a match—then saw its flare. In the light two soldiers stood at the open doorway, and behind them Gottfried crouched. One held the match above his head and groped his way into the room; the other followed. Gottfried moved stealthily behind, and his dull peasant mind had an inspiration, for rising on tip-toe, he blew out the light.

"Confound that draught!" growled the trooper.

Grete's sabots clacked on the floor. Marcelle held her breath. Again the grating of a match—a glare of light.

"To stop the draught, *mein Herr*," said the peasant, quickly closing the door. The girl almost dreaded to look. Yes—Gottfried had gone.

Grete drew down the lamp which hung above the table and held it for the soldier to light, and Marcelle peering through her peep-holes saw two troopers in pale blue *attilas*, bulky Teutons, both; the one with a bushy beard and the chevrons of a sergeant upon his sleeve —the other boyish and without insignia.

Would Gottfried escape through the gate? She stood there, trembling, cowed, dragged out of herself by fear—for now that she had time to think, she realised her situation.

"Are you alone?" growled the burly sergeant to Grete, after a hurried glance about the room.

"Quite, *mein Herr*," answered the peasant, with a mock curtsey.

"That's strange," he muttered, glaring at her sabots. "I could have sworn I heard a soft step."

Possibly the sergeant might have given further vent to his suspicions had not the door swung open suddenly and two officers stalked into the room. The heels of the troopers sprang together, and their hands moved quick and rigid to "Salute." A Bavarian *chevau-léger* stepped into the light, and behind him in the shadow stood a Blue Hussar.

The Bavarian was somewhat of a dandy, with a curling red moustache, an eyeglass, and the swagger of the British Guards.

"Devilish hungry, sergeant," he drawled, flecking some mud blotches from the sleeve of his green tunic. "Found any forage?"

Captain Egerton! thought Marcelle, and her heart gave a throb of joy.

"Not yet, *Herr Rittmeister*," mumbled the subordinate.

"Where are your eyes?" laughed the Blue

Hussar, moving into the light. "Look!" and he pointed to the food upon the table.

Had he listened he might have heard the thudding of Marcelle's heart.

"Ludwig!" she almost cried aloud.

Meanwhile, a trembling figure crouched under the peasant's cart in the yard outside, while soldiers came and went with buckets of water and arms full of hay. The chance came at last, and he stole through the gate. A soldier heard the crackle of a twig and listened —then all was silent.

III

A TRAITOR TO FRANCE

Prussian scouts in the rear of Douay's Division! It seemed incomprehensible; but when Marcelle thought of Gottfried hurrying to the chasseur bivouac she longed to throw open the door and warn Ludwig while there was yet time.

But she remembered her father's words: "My daughter knows her duty." Ludwig was an enemy, and she had served her country. To her frightened reasoning it seemed that this handful of Prussians could never be so foolhardy as to fight. They would surrender, and when Ludwig was made a prisoner he would be in no more danger; so while she waited and listened joy and fear trembled together.

She saw Ludwig examine the remains of the supper with ravenous eyes.

"Barely enough for us, Egerton," he said in English. "I hope we won't have to divide with the men."

"Rather! I am a bit peckish, come to think," drawled the *chevau-léger*.

"My good woman," spoke Ludwig to Grete,

"fifteen hungry men,—have you food enough?
We will pay in good money."

Grete's eyes flashed, and she drew herself up
proudly.

"I have no food for Prussians—I do not wish
their gold."

"As you will.   Remember, we only pay for
what you offer willingly."

"I have no food for Prussians."

"Brave Grete!" Marcelle almost cried out.

"Sergeant, search the house," was the blunt
command.

The man took a step towards the clothes-
press.   "Ma'm'selle Marcelle!" thought Grete,
with terror.

"Pig!" she cried, "the food is there," and
she pointed towards the kitchen.

A muttered oath, and the sergeant's big
boots clacked across the floor, the private following; but when they entered the kitchen they
found the cupboard was locked.

"The key, confound you!" shouted the sergeant.

"Donkey!" sneered Grete; "do you expect
me to help you rob!"

At sight of an axe in a corner they made
scant ado about locks.   A few blows, till the
panels went crashing in.   There was provender
—as Grete knew—for the entire herd;   and

through the window to their comrades the fare was passed.

"Only three bottles of *Tokaier*, *Herr Rittmeister*," wailed the sergeant, when the larder had been stripped; and Grete trembled at thought of her casks in the cellar.

"Plenty," grunted Ludwig. "No fuddled brains to-night. An hour's rest for the horses, then 'March!'"

The man's hand fell from visor to thigh, and he stalked through the door.

Meanwhile, the dandy Egerton was bolting food without ceremony. Popular with his commanders, he had been billeted as Bavarian attaché on the staff of the Crown Prince Frederick, and despite his love for soldiering—for his preference would have been the fighting line—he had taken the post because he would be on the same staff with Ludwig.

A reconnaissance to get in touch with the enemy; to invade Alsace with twelve troopers and a sergeant—a reckless exploit for a daredevil, and he had volunteered with alacrity.

Ludwig had perhaps thought less of the danger or the glory to be won than that Lembach and the grey château among the beeches and firs were but a dozen kilomètres beyond the frontier. Count Zeppelin and his Baden dragoons had spent a whole night in Alsace, and perhaps—yes, it was the thought of Marcelle which had made him volunteer, and being Egerton's senior on the staff he was in command. So the two friends had ridden together into Alsace with their squad of Hussars picked from Ludwig's own regiment, and the result was that they had been outflanked by Abel Douay's Division moving on Wissembourg, and forced to make a long détour on the forlorn chance of reaching the frontier before dawn. In the rear of the French advance— the odds were against them, and in the storm they had lost their way. Ludwig knew that they were not far from the château, but the horses were fagged, and seeing the light of the farmhouse they had halted.

The tired, hungry officers dropped wearily into chairs beside the table. They did not notice the three soiled plates and that the peasant woman was now alone. Six hours in the saddle—dodging French outposts and then drenched by the storm—bodily fatigue and hunger had dulled their wits, so their only thought was food. They ate the remains of Grete's goose like ravenous beasts, and they drank the *Tokaier*, and then Ludwig began to think of their position.

"Guy," he said wearily, "I'd even pay my tailor to be well out of this."

"Bully grub," grunted the Englishman, and he went on eating.

Ludwig laughed.

"I believe you'd eat with a mine under you and the fuse lighted."

"Rather! Damned long journey to eternity —never travel on an empty stomach, my boy."

The young German helped himself to another generous ration. Grete stood behind him and scowled.

"Swine!" she muttered under her breath.

Egerton glanced up fretfully. The woman's frown annoyed him.

"Fat woman, remove thy face!" he drawled.

Grete only scowled the more.

"Melt, thou mountain of molten mush!" and a plate went sailing past the peasant's head.

Grete screamed and beat a hasty retreat to the kitchen. Marcelle meanwhile struggled to restrain her laughter. Ludwig and Egerton! —certainly there was no danger for her; and again she was on the point of making her presence known. But she saw her cousin unfolding a map, and again duty, or perhaps a woman's curiosity, prompted her to wait.

Ludwig laid the map beside him and studied it carefully between mouthfuls.

"Eight or nine kilomètres to the frontier,"

he said finally, "and the enemy in force at Wissembourg."

"Rot!" said the Englishman. "One division twenty miles from supports. By Jove! Think of it! Bothmer and our advance at Bergzabern, only five miles from the frontier. If we can get through with the news before those Frenchies are reinforced, the Crown Prince ought to bag the whole lot."

"Abel Douay at Wissembourg and unsupported—a prey for the first corps of Germans with the energy to pick him up."

The girl remembered her father's words. Ah, how thankful she was that she understood English! It was duty now—absolute and well defined.

"Guy," cried Ludwig, striking the table resolutely, "one of us must get through!"

"Even if they pot the rest, as they did Zeppelin's crew."

And Egerton drained his glass, as though six killed, captured or wounded, out of a party of seven, were a rare day's sport.

"Zeppelin had a few cavalry outposts to dodge; we have a whole army corps at our heels," said Ludwig, quietly folding his map.

"All the more glory in breasting the tape ahead. Besides, they haven't bagged us yet."

Ludwig raised his glass. "Here's to the luck of the devil—the thing we need most!"

The two sword-brothers touched beakers and drank; then Ludwig put down his glass with a start, for he had seen the ivory handle of a whip under the rim of the platter; the plain gold band, with the monogram "M. de L." He sat there askance, his heart drumming a wild tune.

"Should a woman's whip make a man stare like a madman?" thought Egerton.

Marcelle, breathing short and trembling, watched him spring from his seat and stride quickly to the kitchen door, watched him drag shaking Grete into the room.

"Where is the owner of that whip!" he cried.

"How—how should I know, *Herr—Herr Rittmeister?*" sputtered the woman.

"By God! you shall know!" and he shook her till she screamed for mercy.

Egerton caught a furtive glance towards the clothes-press.

"My dear chap," he drawled in English, "I'll lay a 'pony' the lady is in the wardrobe."

Dropping the woman in a heap, Ludwig wheeled towards the clothes-press, when, with a cry of fright—or was it joy?—the girl sprang through the doors.

"Marcelle!" he muttered, dazed.

She stood with her cheeks aflame, looking at him from under her brows; and Ludwig watched her like one stunned.

Seeing Marcelle, the Englishman had the tact to mumble something about looking to the cattle.

"Come with me," he grunted, dragging the stupefied Grete from the room.

Marcelle and Ludwig waited speechless for a short, throbbing interval—then he rushed to her with a hand outstretched.

"Marcelle!" he cried.

Inwardly the torrent swept her on; but duty showed a bold front above the whirling eddies, and she drew back quickly.

"Remember, Ludwig," she said in a low, frightened voice, "we are enemies!"

His hand fell to his side, and he stood there in a sort of dull consciousness, like one alone on a desert island who has seen the sails of a ship fade in the offing.

"Enemies!" he repeated, after a long silence, "and won't you even speak to me, Marcelle?"

"There is nothing I could say," she answered, turning her eyes away.

He took two or three swift turns across the floor.

"Do you think this is right, Marcelle?" he said, stopping finally near her, "or—or just?"

She stood very still, with a hand upon her bosom, and tried her utmost to quell a feeling far stronger than her love for France.

"I am a French girl," she said. "Ah, can't you understand?"

"No, Marcelle, I cannot," he answered, and his lips tightened.

"Don't make it harder for me," she begged.

He picked up her whip from the table and lashed the air with it in swift, impatient movements. Finally he laughed, but it was a queer sort of mirth.

"Am I to say that I care more for Prussia than I do for you?" he asked.

"Don't," she cried out, "please, don't torture me."

"Very well," he said, "I shall go through this war without a word or a sign, but all the patriotic sentiments you can string together won't make me stop loving you."

For the trembling space of a moment France and duty were forgotten.

"Ludwig," she murmured, "forgive me!" and she bent her head to him and stretched out her hands.

He drew himself up to his full height and folded his arms.

"Come, my little enemy," he answered laughing, for he had seemed to touch paradise,—"I am a Prussian officer and I found you hiding in a clothes-press, spying upon our movements—I shall have to order your arrest."

"Can't you see," she said, looking up at him with her clear, trembling eyes—"can't you see I have surrendered?"

"Then, Mademoiselle, I accept your sword," he answered, throwing his heels together, and swishing her riding whip to the height of his chin in military salute.

But she did not hear him.

"Listen!" she cried with a look of terror.

A shot—then another; hoarse shouts in the night outside; the rushing of many feet, and the clatter of steel.

He sprang towards the door, but she caught his arm and tried to hold him; and when he could not shake her off he dragged her with him.

"Don't," she cried, "don't go. They are Ducrot's   chasseurs.   The   house   is   sur-rounded.   It is useless to fight."

"Let me go!" he shouted gruffly, wrenching his arm from her grasp.

She staggered towards him, and as he threw open the door, she caught it with her trembling hands.

"Surrender," she cried.   "Surrender, before it is too late."

But he sprang past her at a bound, and
through the darkness she heard hasty orders
flying from his lips.

Marcelle stared into the night and while she
waited the thought that she had betrayed him
ran quivering through her. She saw the flash
of the guns, she heard the gruff shouts, the
hurried tramp of the Prussian troopers; but
what chance had a handful against a squadron?
Grete crept beside her, and taking her hand
tried to drag her away—but she motioned her
back.

"You are in danger, Ma'm'selle," pleaded the
peasant.

"Grete," cried the girl, "my cousin is fighting there—and I betrayed him. If I could
only do something to save him. Oh, Grete,
my heart is breaking."

"Poor Ma'm'selle!" whispered the peasant,
but her words were drowned by a volley
crashing through the night.

A covey of Prussians ready for snaring—
enticing bait for a squadron of chasseurs. A
sentry stalked while dozing on his post—easy
enough in wind and rain; the surprise were
complete had not the troopers, holding horses
down the road, heard the rustle of bushes.
They challenged, fired, missed—but gave
the alarm. It was Gottfried stealing into

the night. He had no stomach to face his prey.

Scant chance had this handful of Prussians, trapped in a courtyard, with bare time to snatch up arms before the onset. They rallied to Ludwig's call, and fought, snarling and frantic, like foxes run to earth. And Egerton, too, pumping a carbine snatched from a fallen trooper—a fierce British oath with every shot —magnificent, but unavailing.

In the doorway stood Marcelle, trembling for the man she loved, and Grete crouching with scared eyes. Out of the hot, gripping fight came shots, curses, groans, and the hack of sword on sword, then, sharp through the darkness, Ludwig's cries to his men. 'Twas valueless mettle thrown into the breach. Outcounted six to one—too niggardly odds for sport, or even a fighting chance.

A cheer—and the French seethed through che gateway, wild as a torrent in spring.

"To the house!" shouted Ludwig.

Too late! The outnumbered Germans were downed like schoolboys at football before a guard's back rush by men—some to die, others to surrender.

Out of the mêlée the burly sergeant dragged Egerton—a gun wound in his thigh, a sword gash on his cheek—while desperate Ludwig fought, step by step, to the beat of chasseur blades. Back—back against the house—all that was left of the handful.

"Surrender!"

The word rang gruff. The frightened women saw the levelled carbines. Time for a girl with wits to think.

Wide swung the door. Into the room tumbled the sergeant and the wounded man; Ludwig, too, dragged from under the hounding guns, and the door slammed, locked and bolted in the faces of the foe. The work of a girl and of panting Grete.

Ludwig had foresight to blow out the lamp.

"The window!" he cried. "Quick! Out of range!"

A volley from the carbines—a crash of glass. His words had near been drowned.

The table dragged against the door—then the sergeant at the window, stooping low, with orders to hold fire till a sure chance came— and, crouching, Ludwig, frenzied as a jungle beast, with gripped revolver and sword at guard. Only a wounded man and two women in reserve—they made a sorry garrison to hold against a squadron. They waited. The evil silence! What new manœuvre? they wondered. Then suddenly Marcelle remembered her horse, still saddled and waiting.

"Grete!" she whispered through the darkness.

"Yes, Ma'm'selle," came the trembling answer.

"The way through the dairy—my horse is saddled and there is a door into the barnyard."

"Yes, Ma'm'selle, I'll show you," whispered Grete, and groping on hands and knees, she found the kitchen door and drew it open.

"Come, Ma'm'selle," whispered the peasant.

"No, no, Grete—wait—you don't understand;" and she crept back through the darkness, and neared a writhing man.

"Bagged at last!" she heard the Englishman groan. Then she found Ludwig and he felt the touch of her hand.

"There's a door through the kitchen to the stable," she whispered; "my horse is saddled. It's about one chance in ten, Ludwig—will you take it?"

"I can't desert," he muttered between set teeth.

Egerton, limp at her feet, overheard.

"One—one chance in ten," he groaned. "It's your duty, Ludwig. I'll—I'll hold the fort!"

"And desert a comrade? Never!"

"Come!" cried Marcelle, trying to drag him away.

Meanwhile, the chasseurs were doing beaver work. The cart-tongue and some hop poles were lashed together as a makeshift ram with plenty of lusty arms to batter. Thud—it came against the door—thud!

The sergeant peered above the window ledge —levelled his piece — fired — loaded — fired again. A volley thundered through the night, and the window sash was chiselled deep with bullets. A head fell heavily against the floor —a brave man died.

"Ludwig, for God's sake, come!" urged a voice through the darkness.

The flare of a match in Grete's hand showed the way. He saw the sergeant dead, and seizing Egerton, he dragged him towards the kitchen door.

"The women first!" he cried, pushing Marcelle and Grete before him, and as they closed the door and dragged a dairy bench against it, they heard again the weight against the outside door—crash!—it came; the oak was splintered and, with a cheer, the French surged through. They found the corpse of the sergeant by the window, but the room was empty.

The thundering of war was lost in the damp stillness of the dairy, and with an arm about his wounded comrade and a hand in Marcelle's Ludwig clanged through the cellar, while Grete

guided with a flaming match, like a will-o'-the-
wisp. The stable, at last—and, after a stint of
groping, Marcelle found her horse, bridled and
ready—also the Prussian mounts; but she
backed her own animal from the stall.

"Take my horse, Ludwig—he's been fed and
rested."

"A fine Amazon I'll make," he laughed.
He was kneeling over Egerton, and with a
calico kerchief snatched from Grete's dress
he was binding the Englishman's thigh tight
with a tourniquet. In the yard outside
Marcelle heard the tramp and rattle of spurred
boots.

"Quick!" she cried, leading up the horse.
"The chasseurs!"

Ludwig sprang to his feet.

"Good-bye, Marcelle," he said; "God bless
you for this." A kiss might have thrilled the
blood in her, but she drew back frightened.
"No," she cried; "go, you haven't a moment
to lose."

So with a look that told more than she dared
believe, he vaulted to the saddle. She helped
his foot into the stirrup, and showed him the
way to climb to the pommel; then reaching
down, he grasped his wounded comrade's collar and with Grete's lusty arms to lift and
push, he dragged him up. At last they got

poor Egerton astride upon the horse's rump, with his arms around Ludwig's waist.

The door behind swung open, but the sound of the tramping feet was stifled in the trembling of the floor beneath the hoofs.

"Oh, Ludwig!" screamed Marcelle, "there's a jump—hold well!"

Paltry danger to that of armed chasseurs! Click, click—the carbines flew to the shoulder.

"Halt!" rang a voice.

Ludwig waved his hand.

"Good-bye," he called with a glance shoulder-wards.

Marcelle—trembling, praying, beaten out of her senses by fear, saw the plunge, the running start, and then, through the dark, she heard a man growling:

"Fire!"

The walls quivered at the yelp of the carbines. Through the smoke of a dozen guns, brisk words of command and hurrying feet hot in pursuit. They brought a lantern, finally, to search the place, and they found Grete bending weeping over the girl lying motionless upon the stable floor.

"*Canaille!* You've killed her!" the peasant cried, shaking her podgy fists in the soldiers' faces

A scented sprig of a subaltern held a light to the girl's face.

Marcelle partially opened her eyes, then closed them and sighed.

"Bah!" said the boy, "she's only fainted."

The dim light showed him her face.

"Beautiful!" he murmured, "very beautiful!"

Perhaps she heard—for her eyes opened once more in dazed bewilderment.

Chasseurs—ah, yes—she remembered now!

"Ludwig!" she called in fright. "Ludwig!"

The boy put his hand to his heart and bent at the waist with Gallic grace.

"*Mademoiselle, votre serviteur!*"

She heard the ring of spurs.

"No trace of them, my Lieutenant," mumbled a *maréchal de logis;* "The barnyard gate is open—they must have got away."

Marcelle's heart gave a throb of joy—then, as quickly, the smile left her lips.

Abel Douay at Wissembourg and unsupported! and Ludwig speeding with the news!

Like a goaded creature she sprang to her feet.

"A traitor to France!" she cried with shame, and the hot cheeks seemed to burn the hands that hid her face.

IV

THE DAY OF WISSEMBOURG

At the cross-roads, where a highway spreads
an arm over the mountains to Bitche and another southward across the vine-decked Geissberg, soggy tents of two line regiments—short
a battalion each—and the 1st Arab Tirailleurs,
loomed cheerless through the dim mist of
morning. Slim cannon, also, to the extent of
eighteen *bouches à feu,*—six of them dainty
mitrailleuses—lay dripping under their canvas
shrouds, while a mile or more away the 2nd
battalion of the 74th had been dumped between
the moat-skirted walls of mediæval Wissembourg, without guns and without supports,
useful as a pile of sand to stop an avalanche.

These eight battalions and the artillery, Abel
Douay's division less two regiments, detached
for Heaven alone knew what, a scant five thousand men in all, lay pointed towards Germany
like a shaftless arrow-head; for Ducrot, the
nearest, stood a day's march away.

As if that were not blunder enough, a squadron of horse chasseurs had just trotted into
camp after a morning's jaunt across the Lauter.
Too myopic, it seems, to see beyond the pol-

ished visors of their headgear; for the monster army of the Crown Prince was creeping through the shadows of the Bee-Forest, down in the valley to the east Prussians, Hessians and Silesians, men of Westphalia and Nassau, in all three army corps, and more at their heels, with Count Bothmer's Bavarian flank in advance, picking its way among the hills behind the red-tiled town.

Meanwhile, Abel Douay's men loitered in their slimy camp.   Long, yellow streams of muddy water gushed through the ditches, and dirty canvas fluttered in the morning air; coatless fantassins rubbed hard the breeches of their chassepots or coaxed the dilatory soup to steam, and in the Turco camp beyond, bedraggled Arabs crouched on their haunches in the mud to grin with shiny rows of teeth, while limp, rain-logged officers huddled together in groups to chat, and try to laugh blue devils away.

Down in the valley a mist was oozing from the pasture land, and like a box of tumbled toys the spires and peaked roofs of Wissembourg stood heaped behind the moss-tipped walls.   Beyond and around dull mountains rose in tiers of terraced vines to wooded peaks, with here and there a highway threading white amidst the green; and faint among the poplars and the willows of the valley the silver Lauter wormed its way past mills and villages and abbey towers, into the Bee-Forest depths.

Like a dormant lion the Geissberg hill lay couched at length between two valleys, and from their camp upon its crest the French might gaze across the Lauter into Germany and dream of Berlin. Up from the bottom-land the Geissberg rose, a jumble of hop-yards and gardens, vineyards and terraces, doomed for a shambles. A squat-towered castle with outer walls and inner court yards stood perched upon its ridge, and, crowning all, three meagre poplars—for the builder of the keep had been too humble in encroaching heaven-ward, and so the three slim trees looked down upon his work.

While the bells in the town below clanged eight, Douay and his staff rode out from camp to inspect the lines. With moustachios waxed and an imperial tuft upon his bulging chin, the General, glittering with epaulettes and orders, sat erect, as became a hero of Malakoff. The soggy earth splashed beneath the hoofs, while his spaniel yelped and frolicked about the charger's legs and sniffed the air with his tiny nose. Meanwhile, the General's eyes looked dreamy-wise from under his gold-leaved képi, but failed to penetrate the forest land beyond the towers of Wissembourg.

He halted finally to greet and question leading burghers of the town who had driven up from the valley to welcome their defenders. Little did he learn, however, and less would he believe, for rumours of the enemy were as vague as they were contradictory.

Finally the General gathered rein to ride on, when behind, at the picket line, a woman's voice rang trembling.

"I must see General Douay! I tell you, I must!"

He turned, but the guard tent hid her from his view. An aide-de-camp sidled his horse away and came back grinning.

"*Sapristi!* What a pretty girl, my General."

Abel Douay smiled, and the divining officer wheeled towards the guard tent. The charger pawed the ground and champed, and the spaniel capered. Meanwhile, the General's lustreless eyes roved along the hill crest, and did not see the pale, bare-headed girl rushing towards him like a hunted thing.

"The Prussians, my General! Then I'm not too late?"

He looked down startled.

"Marcelle de Lembach!" he cried in wonderment. She had grasped the bridle reins, and stood questioning with sunken eye.

"The Prussians!" she repeated. "They are coming through the Bee-Forest—unless——"

"Unless?" he asked in amazement.

"Unless you captured him."

"Him!" he exclaimed. "Whom?"

"A—a Prussian captain," and she turned her eyes away.

The General laughed.

"We haven't laid eyes on a Prussian since those crazy dragoons were caught at Scheuerlanhof."

"Then he got through the lines!" and her face lighted up.

"Through the lines!" he repeated.

"Prussian scouts were in the Mundat-Wald last night. I was there and I overheard them say, 'One division twenty miles from supports, and our advance only five miles off. One of us must get through with the news.'"

She glanced from side to side anxiously.

"And—and," she faltered, "one of them did get through."

"Prussians in the Mundat-Wald," he laughed. "My child, you are dreaming."

"A dream!" she said, in a low, quivering voice. "A dozen Prussians trapped by Ducrot's chasseurs, and all killed or captured but the Captain and a wounded comrade; was that a dream?'' She drew a hand across her forehead wearily.

"Go on," he said, with a show of interest.

"Ah, my General, I helped him to escape—because I—because he was my cousin."

She looked up into his face, her eyes filmy with tears.

"I was a traitor to France," she said.

"No, no, my dear,—not that," he answered reassuringly.

"They would not warn you, because they were Ducrot's men. 'The fellow would be captured,' they said, 'and it was no affair of theirs.' So they rode off with the prisoners and the Prussian horses, and—and—when I thought of you at Wissembourg, and realised what I had done——''

Faint with fatigue, she staggered forward and clutched the horse's mane. Her head fell heavily against a pistol holster.

"My poor child," he cried, bending to help her.

"It is nothing," she said between her teeth. "Nothing. I—I did all that I could. I walked alone through the storm. It was so black and terrible, and—when I could go no farther, I sank down by the roadside and must have slept, for it was daylight when I awoke. I should have been here sooner.''

"My brave girl!" and he stroked her hair tenderly. "Why, a patrol has just reported from across the Lauter, and there isn't a Prussian within miles."

She looked up startled.

"I heard what they said. Fall back on Ducrot, won't you, before it is too late?"

The veteran's eyes flashed.

"You," he cried, "a soldier's daughter, dare say 'Retreat!'"

"Forgive me," she said, glancing wearily across the valley towards the heights beyond the town; and as she looked, she saw a puff of something white against the hillside near the village spires of Schweigen—then another and still another little clot of vapour, quivering for a moment, soft as swan's down, then floating away in slender curls and wreaths.

"Look!" and she grasped the soldier's arm.

As she spoke, the gloomy mutter of cannon trembled across the valley on the morning air.

"Too late!" she moaned.

"Prussians!" the cry, and consternation on the faces of the gold-laced staff. Surprise complete, with no time for women, and scarce a chance for Marcelle to jump from under the hoofs, before the General and his cavalcade pounded along the hilltop, with guidon flat in the wind and sabres clattering.

Between the squatting rows of tents, surprised fantassins hopped hither and thither to the bugles and the mumbling drums like hens at feeding time; till, out of orderless, un-equipped dismay, slender oblongs of throb-bing blue and red were moulded together, each with its three-coloured fold of silk drooping beneath a wreath-decked eagle; and all the while in the valley below, the curve of shells over the frightened town, and explosions shot with fire !

Spellbound and trembling, the girl watched the battle. Near her the three slim trees upon the hill crest, and nearer still stood the quaking men from Wissembourg, praying for their souls.

Down in a hollow wavered a green banner with an open hand of red upon its field, and there a cohort of Turcos stood chafing in ranks. Untamed ochre-men from Africa with sky-blue jackets slashed with yellow arabesques, their tasselled caps askew, and the canvas bags about their legs caught into glove-like gaiters. Restless and eager they stood, as hounds in the leash, till the bugles called shrill the ad-vance, then, a wild shout of the desert, and a thousand red chechias hurled skyward in de-fiance, while nimble as antelopes, they herded down the valley side and deployed upon the plain below.

Those Arab tirailleurs had been her father's
"children" once, and Marcelle's heart
throbbed with pride as the regiment crawled
across the green in long, thin streaks of blue
and white, and faded out of sight among the
railway sheds and mills, the poplars and the
willows, down by the Hagenau gate. Then
the crack of volley firing mingled with Bavarian thunder from the heights of Schweigen.
A battery, too, rumbled superbly towards the
town with guns and caissons distanced as upon
parade; the drivers lashing the frenzied horses,
the cannoneers bolt upright on the chests,
and detachment chiefs riding hot on the flank.

Magnificent but bootless panoply, for there
to the north, beyond the walls of Wissembourg, Bothmer's men were making but a
parade of fighting among the hops and vineyards, while Kirchback's corps, and von Bose
as well, hurried the crushing odds of ten to
one towards the booming of the guns. Meanwhile, as brave a battalion as ever wore red
trousers was offered in sacrifice to fatuity behind the moats and ancient ramparts of the
town. St. Remy, too, with its abbey towers,
and the flanking lines of Wissembourg built
for defense in days gone by, might have held
the regiment now plodding aimlessly across the
Scherol pass. But what might better have been

was a shaft to the arrow-head, or eyes to penetrate the Bee-Forest,—or a voice to call retreat.

The terrified burghers fled to the Red Cross
flag fluttering at the Schafbusch farm, down in
a hollow to the rear.   So Marcelle was left
alone upon the hill-crest.   Charmed by the
mumbling incantation of the guns, she lay at
length upon the grass, a trembling worshipper
of the fetich war.

Above the exploding shells and lapping fire-
tongues, the spires of Wissembourg rose skyward from among the red-capped houses.
Down in the drowsy town, and at the railway
station, too, where the Turco chassepots sputtered and snapped, brave men were dying.

The tardy seconds grew to minutes, the minutes to an hour, while the Turcos in the valley
and the glorious battalion in the town held the
Bavarians in check among the vineyards, with
remorseless rifle fire.   Purposeless slaughter, it
seemed to the Crown Prince, just arriving on
the heights of Schweigen.   Two corps of
Prussians were hurrying along the Lauter's
banks over mud-soaked roads, and already a
column was debouching from the woods, so,
by his orders, the battle lagged.

The desultory firing; the Turcos holding
their position; the town unconquered!   Could

it be victory? The girl's heart beat fast with
hope.

Glory for the unknown soldiers dying for
France, pity for the General blindly obeying
the commands of folly; but not victory, for
Prussian cannon among the vines of Windhof
bellowed a welcome to Bavarian brothers on
the Schweigen heights, and other batteries
unlimbered behind the railway cutting near
the Nieder-Wald, while dark against the green
forest black masses crept from among the
trees.

The right flank was threatened. Marcelle was
soldier enough to understand, and with lips
parched and hands trembling and cold, she
lay among the waving tufts of grass watching
the movements in the valley. , Near her, on
the Geissberg, crouched the 50th of the line,
fretting in harness like high-strung horses
waiting for the coachman's chirp. Down the
hillside, by a cross-road, six fragile mitrailleuses, pert as a pack of goaded terriers,
yelped and spat defiance at the Prussian guns.
On the slope beside the battery, pale Abel
Douay loomed superb and motionless above
the wreathing smoke, while over the blood-red
képis of his gazing staff the headquarters' guidon
trembled in the mist, dim as the colours of a
phantom host.

The General turned and glanced for a moment towards the Geissberg castle. The girl read despair in his colourless face.

"One division twenty miles from supports. One of us must get through!"

The words went as keen as a knife-thrust deep into her heart.

"A traitor to France!" she cried again, in shame; but the voice was drowned by the battle's roar.

Still the sluggish moments dragged on. The blue-white Turco lines among the railway yards and willows wavered and fell back; the ground beyond the station and the tracks grew speckled with crawling things in black, and up from the valley rose the crackle of the needle-guns. The Prussian batteries, too, were seeking the range of Douay's mitrailleuses; their shells curved far above, then fell too short, exploding harmlessly in the air or sinking deep in the soft mud,—but nearer, gradually nearer.

The girl watched with eyes aflame. Splendid spectacle, those spitting things upon the near-by hillside, their limbers fifteen paces to the rear, the drivers erect and stiff in the saddle with eyes to the front, and spry cannoneers darting from caisson to gun. Among the stubble, too, white-faced infantry lay, hugging the ground, and there alone, in advance of his staff, Abel Douay, sitting his big horse, impassive and motionless, with dull, beamless eyes in melancholy gaze upon the retreating lines in the valley below—and all the while the roar and crash of a hurricane above the rasping, grating snarl of the mitrailleuses.

Splendid spectacle—till a poor devil was struck by a fragment of a bursting shell. A spurt of blood and brain—the girl hid the sight from her eyes. She felt a band about her temples—a sinking of the heart. When she had the courage to look, two stretcher-men were hurrying to the rear.

Then a shell burst only a few yards away and spattered her with earth. Her eyelids fluttered tremulously, her head was empty and light. She felt a strange nausea. Her impulse was to run; but through the smoke she saw a vision: Abel Douay, still sitting erect in the saddle, with eyes upon the foe, his trembling horse sniffing the air heavy with powder and the toy spaniel crouching in terror at the animal's feet. She dared not go. For the sake of love she had betrayed her country. She should not add the taint of cowardice.

So she waited, while the missiles screeched against the Geissberg, crouching as close to

the ground as the terrified fantassins upon the
hill-side. The shells, no longer curving harmlessly overhead or sputtering into the mud,
burst with rhythmical precision; more limp
things were carried to the rear; more bundles
of blue and red lay motionless upon the grass
—and then, two horses of a caisson, disem-
bowelled and writhing. But the girl's sight
grew accustomed to the awfulness, and, like
the patient drivers and the despairing General, she kept her eyes straight to the front—a
prayer to the God of Battles always in her
throbbing heart.

Suddenly, a roar rent the skies, and the
ground beneath her trembled as in an earth-
quake shock. Her eyes were blinded by the
flash; her ears were deafened. For a moment
she lay stunned. Then, when she dared look,
—a sight to make her sick at heart.

Beneath a cloud of smoke curling heavenward was scattered the wreckage of a caisson
exploded by a Prussian shell, and amid dis-
torted clots that had been men, wounded animals and gunners lay quivering. She saw the
nimble stretcher-men in grey spring alert from
the hillside, and the unharmed cannoneers
stagger back to their mitrailleuses, while artillery horses plunged and reared, or huddled
together in terror.

Faint and trembling she turned her eyes away. Beyond, on the slope where the commander had stood, excited staff officers were leaping from the saddle, or bending low over a form at length upon the ground. Hospital men hurried crouching through the grass—a riderless horse, with gold-embroidered holsters and saddle-cloth floundered in the mud, an aide-de-camp galloped like mad down the hillside—but General Douay, grand through the battle mist?

She looked with frightened eyes, and a cry of horror came from her lips.

Cold and inert as a thing of stone, she watched them bear the dying General up the hillside—watched the surgeon and the stretcher bearers until they passed—then, as the procession wended slowly towards the Schafbusch farm, where the Red Cross fluttered, she rose and followed.

V

FOR THE HONOUR OF FRANCE

A rifle at arms port closed the way, and a shock-headed sentry, with the jaw of a mastiff, muttered the word, "Halt!" Marcelle had come to ask the dying General's pardon, and the way to him was barred. She gazed at the closed door. Despair sat rigid in her face. She turned away.

The Schafbusch farm had been requisitioned for a hospital, and the house, the out-houses, and now the garden, were converted into wards. Marcelle stood watching the carts and ambulances come rumbling up, each with its bleeding load; and with pitiless regularity poor wretches in shell-torn uniforms were dumped among vegetables and flowers to await the scalpel. Some had received the hurried dressing of the battlefield; the wounds of others were gaping and raw. The shattered limbs, the open viscera, the oozing brains!—the girl gazed in horror at the scene. Meanwhile, faint rays of sunlight began to glimmer through the leaves, and the stench of anæsthetics mingled with the odour of roses.

A bulky surgeon, with fat arms bared to the elbow and apron gory as a butcher's, brushed past.

She seized his shirt sleeve.

"Major," she cried, "is there anything I can do?"

The man jerked his arm away.

"Get out of my way, confound you!" and he hastened on.

"Oh, let me help—do let me help," she pleaded, following by his side.

"Roll bandages," he grunted, "carry water."

She followed him, and in time won his confidence. Passing among the groaning men upon the ground, he picked out the urgent cases, and while he operated he let her help his staff of dressers and assistants. In a moment of grim good humour, he even ripped the Red Cross *brassard* from the sleeve of a stretcher-bearer who had died and fastened it upon her arm. She coloured with pride and gratitude, and the old surgeon smiled.

For a time the girl worked on in a delirium of pity and compassion—it might have been an hour at this labour of humanity—it might have been longer—but as she was staggering past the house under the weight of a bucket of water the door opened, and the shock-headed sentry's gun flew to present-arms. A staff

surgeon came out, bare-headed and anxious-
eyed and seeing Marcelle and the badge upon
her arm, called gruffly:

"Nurse, bring that water here."

She turned obediently and followed. The
way to the dying General was opened at last.

"Dead!"

A staff officer whispered the word. She
caught the look of dismay in the surgeon's
face, and the heart within her sank. The
door of a room stood open; and in the shadow
beyond was a Roman priest. She saw the
chalice and the consecrated oil, and at the
priest's feet an inert form at length upon the
floor. She touched her breast and forehead in
the token of the Cross, and fell upon her knees.
A prayer for a soul was mumbled on her trembling lips.

She arose at last, and stood in the open
doorway gazing at the face of the dead. The
soldier she had betrayed lay at length upon a
folded mattress, his head supported by an upturned chair, his eyes glassy and staring. A
rough blanket covered his stiffened limbs, and
upon it the faithful spaniel had curled himself
to guard the fallen master and snarl at the
.awed attendants.

Rough earthenware dishes and an untouched
peasant's meal stood on the bare deal table; a

flower bloomed upon the window ledge, while
from the clean white-washed wall a picture of
the Christ Child looked down upon the graven
face of the soldier. To Marcelle this hushed
room of death seemed almost restful after the
scenes of carnage.

She saw them close the General's eyes forever, saw them place the gold-leaved képi tenderly upon his head, and on his breast, above
the ghastly shell wound which they covered,
she saw the blood-red ribbon of Honour and the
unsullied Cross. Through an open casement
came the rumble of the battle.

"Nurse, there's work to be done."

The gruff voice startled her. The man was
the staff surgeon who had called her from the
garden to the house. She turned and followed.

For a time she worked among the wounded.
Unharmed fugitives began to come in from the
firing line, in twos and threes at first, then
more, and even more, till the road swarmed
with a pack of trembling cravens. The town
had fallen, they said, and the garrison had
been put to the sword. The Prussians were
upon the Geissberg, the army was in full
retreat.

"Fly!" they shouted; "fly!"—and on they
went to the westward.

"Cowards!" cried the girl.

More plodding fugitives shuffled along the road, and in a fierce ecstasy she watched them until the trudging of their feet seemed to cadence a requiem of shame.

"Cowards!" she cried again, "could you not die for France?"

She would not believe the battle had been lost. Hatred of the enemies of France thrilled in her. She heard the rattle of the musketry, the rumbling boom of cannon; her lips set hard together, her limbs grew icy cold. Unable to endure the suspense, she ran trembling to the Geissberg crest where the three poplars rustled in the wind, and stood gazing at the battle.

Near her a detachment of Turcos, cut off from the retreating regiment, lay flat upon their bellies, pumping their rifles. A sergeant had rallied them—a grim patriarch of the desert, with grizzled beard and eye of fire. The green banner with the blood-red hand was stuck in his gun barrel, and from time to time he waved it above his "children," and shouted defiance. Brave men of Africa, she thought, making the last stand for France! No, not the last, for, though fugitives choked the high-ways, men of the 50th, and 74th as well, still crouched along the hilltop with faces to the enemy. Down on the valley-side, too, a de-

tachment was charging headlong upon the captors of a gun, desperate lest an imperial trophy
remain to shame their France. And meanwhile, the squat-towered castle upon the Geissberg, five hundred paces to the right, belched
and crackled from cellar to roof.

"The fight is not lost," cried the girl.
"Only the cowards fly."

But the railway yards, where the brave
Turcos had stood off an army corps, and the
straggling streets of Wissembourg were swarming now with dull black Prussians and blue Bavarians with chenille-crested casques, and not a
single chassepot left to answer the bark of the
needle-guns. Down in the valley, too, they
were forming long sombre lines, like crawling
worms, and up the valley-side they came,
nearer, always nearer, while Prussian batteries
by the railway forks hurled shrapnel at the
wavering blue-red ranks upon the Geissberg.

The danger had a fiendish charm. Would
the French line hold? That was her only
thought. The crashing of a shell into the
Turco ranks gave answer. When the smoke
had cleared, she saw upon the ground beyond
the three slim trees the Turco sergeant dead,
with the banner of his faith grasped in stiffened
hands. She saw the brown Kabyles, too, waver
and fall back. A few shambled to the rear,

then, when a charge of shrapnel burst in their midst, the rest flew towards her in a panic-stricken horde.

Frenzied with despair, the girl sprang towards them.

"Halt!" she cried. "Halt!"

The terrified Africans stared with unseeing eyes, and stumbled on.

With lips half parted, and cheeks aglow, she ran crouching to the dead man on the ground and wrenched the green banner from his grasp.

Back towards the skulking Arabs she went, waving the Moslem flag.

"Children of the Faith," she cried in the Arab tongue, "you are cowards to flee before the Prussian swine. Charge! Charge for Mohammed the Prophet!"

The blood-red hand flattened above her streaming hair; the crescent cusps upon the flagstaff glistened like horns of fire; the sunlight kindled her uplifted face. Awed and trembling, the brown men bowed before this apparition of the battle-field, then fell upon their faces at her feet.

"Allah is great, and Mohammed is his Prophet!" they cried, with their lips upon the ground.

Above the roaring of the battle her voice rang clear: "Sons of the Prophet, I have come

to lead you.   I want no cowards.   Only brave
men shall follow me!"

With a wild shout of defiance they sprang to
their feet and hurled their red chechias heavenward.   Twenty frenzied Kabyles of the Algerian
mountains were ready to follow to a man wher-
ever she might lead.

Proud and erect, with eyes flashing and head
thrown back, she led them towards the firing-
line.   Her life for France!   She was in a fierce
delirium.   She breathed short, she panted; but
her brain was undimmed; she saw with the
clear instinct of a soldier.

That three-towered castle, with its low squatting roof, down among the gardens and the
hop vines, was the key of the French position.
Already the flanks, both right and left, were
turned—but while the castle stood, France
stood, so she led her Turcos there.

Crouching they went, dodging nimbly trom
tree to tree, and cover to cover, but following
always the girl with the green-red banner of the
Prophet.   A houri, she seemed, leading them
to Paradise.

They were fighting in the hop-yards and the
gardens, men of the 50th—fierce as beasts at
bay.   With a yell the Africans rushed crazed
and headlong into the battle, to die side by
side with their erstwhile conquerors.   No

need to lead them now, so the girl stood alone amid the uproar with the slender flagstaff tight in her grasp, while her hot blood surged and leapt—the blood of ancestors who had died for France.

Murky vapour curled in wreaths about the hedgerows; the chassepots spurted flame; the din was like a foundry in blast, with anvils shivering. Dim figures in blue ran, staggered, dropped and rose again. Trembling, she watched the struggle. Each step was contested; each terrace was a slaughter pen, till human courage could no more. She saw the red-legged infantry driven from the hop-yard, she saw the bluish forms of Turcos stumble past her; then, through the dull rampart of smoke hanging low in the hop vines came shadowy things in black, with beards and brass-tipped helmets. With a cry she reeled towards her comrades.

In an ecstasy of passion she had stood there spellbound, forgetful alike of danger and her sex—but those Prussians, looming through the smoke, with staring eyes and bayonets gleaming! A sight to make her a pale, trembling girl again, and quivering, throbbing all over like a hunted animal, she ran towards the fleeing soldiers. The green-red banner dropped from her weakened hands. She stumbled, picked herself up, stumbled again and fell, a terrified and helpless woman, by the castle gate.

She tried to rise, but had not the strength. The Prussians swam before her frightened eyes; she shrieked and fell back swooning; then a pair of strong arms seized her and a huge, sweating Turco bore her above the rush of men surging through the court-yard, as easily as though she were a child. Up the broad, outside staircase he carried her into the Geissberg castle. Seven comrades followed,— all that were left of her devoted band. In a chamber under the roof they laid her tenderly upon the floor.

VI

THE GEISSBERG SHAMBLES

Two hundred men against two army corps! Penned in a mediæval castle, they fought, without artillery, without supports, their comrades fleeing, their General dead. They barred the castle gates; they dragged the furniture against the doors; they stuffed the windows with mattresses and blankets; they hewed loopholes in the walls and in the shutters. From cellar to gable came the whirring, sputtering rattle of their rifles.

Meanwhile, Marcelle lay limp upon the floor in the chamber under the roof. She knew there were sounds and moving things about her, but the fury which had driven her was dead. The big Turco came and folded a knapsack under her head. "Thank you," she murmured, and she saw dimly two shining rows of teeth and a curled black beard upon a bronze face; her eyes closed listlessly.

She thought of the battle, but it seemed vague and far away. She wondered if it had not been a dream. It must be real, for here were her Turcos kneeling by the windows. Crack, went their rifles—crack, crack! The fumes of burnt powder filled her nostrils, and she shivered and covered her face with her hands. She was only a weak, frightened girl, throbbing at the sound of the rifles. The delirium of the battle-field was spent.

She thought of the farm house—of the fight in the court-yard, and Ludwig riding through the night. The surprise, the battle lost, the General's life, thrice wretched issue of her treachery—but she knew she would do it again under the same stress, for a woman is loyal first to her heart, and her heart was Ludwig's. An enemy to her people—yes; but was he fighting out there with the Prussians; had he reached their lines in safety? Oh, the misery of not knowing! She could bear it no longer; she must see; so, pale and quivering, she dragged herself across the floor.

The Turcos knelt behind the window ledges with pieces at aim; the breech-locks clicked, the rifles spoke; but none noticed her. She raised herself on hands and knees and gazed over the shoulders of her Kabyle friend. A mattress was stuffed in the window-sill; the shutters were partly closed, but through a crevice she could see the hillside beyond the high castle wall, the hop-yards and the gardens, the slope to the west rising towards the three slim poplars.

The walls trembled with volley upon volley
—every window in the castle jetted flame.
Smoke drifted into the room in hazy streaks;
it curled about the hedges and the garden; but
through the rifts she saw the tangled, surging
Prussians rolling up the Geissberg slopes in
helmet-crested waves.

To right, to left, and everywhere they came;
Silesians, Hessians, men of Nassau and of
Posen, Jägers and Prussian Grenadiers—United
Germany in two grim corps against two hundred men of France. On they came, slowly,
steadily, each unit in double billowing lines of
black, with officers to the front, and little flat
drums beating. Some wavered, stumbled, fell
—but the thinning ranks closed up. Would
nothing halt them? The girl stared with
frightened eyes. She saw a dim, white banner with a cross of black flutter above the nearest ranks. She saw it waver, fall and rise; she
saw it fall and rise again, and yet again—proud
flag of the King's Grenadiers passed from
dying hand to dying hand,—and then the
black line staggered.

Cheer upon cheer was shouted by the maddened French—cheer upon cheer of triumph.
The Prussians halted, though they gave not an
inch. They crouched behind the angles of the
walls; they burrowed into ditches; flash on

flash, their guns sputtered from the hillside,—
but the charge was stayed.

The panting Turcos staggered from the windows for a moment to breathe. They drew
hard biscuits from their haversacks, they
pressed canteens to their feverish lips, they
stared at the girl with their white, glassy eyes.
She thought of the green-red banner. Again
she was unworthy.

Her big protector came towards her smiling.
He held out a biscuit.

"*Taäm*," he grunted. The other Turcos
grinned.

Marcelle laughed. Army biscuit bore slight
resemblance to the native dish of Algeria, but
the humour was patriotic.

Marcelle was hungry, so she took the biscuit.
Meanwhile the tirailleur made a low salaam
with his forehead to the ground.

"O, noble white lady," he said, "never was
man so brave as thou."

"Say not so," answered Marcelle. "Unto
thee I owe my life."

"Nay, white lady, thou wouldst have fought
the cursed of Allah alone. Thy slave carried
thee hither because none had thy courage."

"Oh, son of the Prophet," she murmured,
"I am deeply grateful."

For a time she munched her biscuit in silence,

alone, with eight barbarians. She looked at her companions, sitting crouched upon their haunches, eating while the battle raged outside. They grinned and touched their fingers to their foreheads and lips, and she knew she had nothing to fear, so she turned to her champion.

"Thou art a Kabyle," she said, "yet thou speakest the Arab tongue."

"Thy slave is of the Aït-bou-Yoosuf," he answered, "in the snow land of the mountains of Djurdjura, beyond the Souk-el-Arba."

"I know thy country," said Marcelle eagerly.

"My father was Amin of his village," answered the Kabyle, proudly —"until the Holy War. His soul now rests in Paradise."

"And thy name?".

"Mohammed-Bin-Ali-Amin-Yoosuf."

"Tell me of thy father," she said, after a moment.

"He was a warrior of Kabylia. He died for the Faith. Dost know the village Ischerri-dhen?"

"I know it well," she answered.

"The men of the Djurdjura held it even against the great army of Si MacMahon. Si Bourbaki was wounded there. Dost remember, oh white lady?"

"Yes, yes, I remember."

The Turco stood up—a giant in height and sinew.

"My father," he said, with fiery eyes, "was Amin of the Aït-bou-Yoosuf, and his heart was like the lion of the desert. All the army of the Franks could not take Ischerridhen while my father lived. But when my father fell, and his soul went upward into Paradise, then——"

"Then," cried the girl, "my father, the Si de Lembach, with the Foreign Legion of his brigade, scaled the deep passes of the Djurdjura and stormed the village of Ischerridhen from the rear."

"Thy father!" he muttered.

Daughter of a Christian conqueror—son of the Moslem conquered—enemies by inheritance and faith—for a moment they stood staring at each other. His eyes had an untamed look. A high, bright flush was in her face.

"My father," she said, in a voice that trembled. "And to thee I owe my life, O Mohammed-Bin-Ali."

His breath came panting and quick. His eyes lost the look of the savage. His comrades were crouched listening, and he turned towards them.

"The father of the Lela Baida conquered our fathers—and to-day, when the Beni-Bou-Yoosuf fled before the accursed of Allah, she shamed us and led us back. None is so brave as she. The Beni-Bou-Yoosuf are her slaves. Is it not so, oh my brothers?"

"Aye, O Lela Baida," the Turcos cried in chorus; "thy slaves," and they touched their faces to the ground.

Then Mohammed stood up to his full height.

"Come, my brothers," he said, pointing towards the windows, and their eyes glowed with the fever sparks of battle.

"Death to the accursed of Allah!" they cried.

Back to the windows they went, and again their rifles spoke.

Trembling, Marcelle watched them. Brave fellows! Fighting for her France! Again the blood leapt up to tingle in her face, and she crawled to the window.

Bullets splintered into the shutters—Prussian sharpshooters firing at the windows—but, undismayed, the girl peered through the crevice above Mohammed's head.

Drums were beating in the distance—high-pitched snare-drums. Down in the garden hoarse trumpets blared, and always the rattle of the needle-guns, the crack of the chassepots. Through the battle mist she saw the hillside.

"Look!" she cried. "Cannon!"

Yes.   Guns and caissons, with plunging
horses, tugging and straining at their harness.
A battery of slim six-pounders, deep in the
mire, the cannoneers with shoulders to the
wheels, the drivers lashing, the officers riding
backward and forward, waving, gesticulating.

The Turcos grunted and aimed their rifles at
the Prussian cannoneers while the battery,
though exposed in column to the château fire,
slowly toiled upwards towards the poplars
upon the hill crest.

"Cannon," she moaned. "It means the
end."

She waited and prayed, and then she looked
again. The battery was unlimbering a scant
eight hundred paces from the castle walls—
three pieces only—for their fellows still floundered in the mire. Other batteries, too, with
horses tugging and drivers lashing with their
whips, came toiling up the Geissberg,—and
meanwhile Prussian Grenadiers hunted the last
brave remnant of the supporting French away
from the three slim trees.

The girl's heart sank. Two companies of
the 50th and her little Turco band now fighting
alone for the honour of France.

Bearded Prussians flitted about the gardens
and the outhouses, eager as buzzards at the

smell of carrion.   They tumbled blazing bales of straw against the embrasures, and tried to smoke out the hounded garrison, like foxes from the ground.   Then, with the pent-up fury of a mountain torrent, they beat down a gate with their rifle butts, and surged through the outer court-yard, only to break in raging impotence against the hell-charged masonry, and leave behind a trail of quivering wounded and motionless dead.   Cheer upon cheer, and the frenzied garrison fought on.

Boom! Again the thundering sound,—and yet again.   The castle walls trembled with the shock of solid shot.

The builder of the keep had been too humble in encroaching heavenward; the three slim poplars crowning the Geissberg crest looked down upon his work, and there stood the Prussian guns—the beginning of the end.

"Cowards!" cried Marcelle, shaking her little clenched fist towards the foe.   "You can't win in a fair fight, so you bring artillery. *Canaille——*"

A thundering explosion cut short her words and threw her stunned upon the floor.   The castle rocked and creaked, like a foundering ship; and amid a cloud of plaster and dust, the Turcos tumbled headlong from the windows.   The gable above their heads had been

struck by a shell, a yawning rent in the roof
and the shutter shattered in a thousand bits.

She opened her dazed eyes.   Two Turcos
were writhing, with hands to their middle; a
dead man lay pinned to the floor, a splinter
through his chest; and Mohammed, too, had
blood gushing from a rent across the temple.

She crawled towards her wounded friend.
He picked himself up and grunted.

"Nothing, Lela Baida, nothing."

She bathed the wound with water from his
canteen and bound it tight with her handkerchief.   Blood dripped along his cheek, and
when he grinned ran scarlet, but he seized his
chassepot and stumbled towards the window,
wild as a forest beast.

She went to the wounded on the floor—there
was little to be done.   One was dying without
a murmur; the other, with only a flesh wound,
bawled like a child with a cut finger.

Again the castle shook from cellar to roof.
In the hall outside and down the stairs feet
went hurrying.

"*Sauve qui peut!*" voices cried.

The fumes of burnt powder choked her, the
smoke dimmed her eyes, her ears seemed split-
ting with the din of rifle firing.   She crept
faint and staggering across the floor and seized
Mohammed's arm.

"Come!" she cried; "come!"

The frenzied Kabyle pushed her aside. The breech lock of his piece sprang open—a cartridge jammed home— Click! and the rifle flew to his shoulder.

Marcelle cowered close beside him, looking with eyes afright. She saw the court-yard empty, the gun flames spurting from the windows. Above the garden wall, where the smoke hung low, she saw the head and shoulders of a Prussian, and then a leg astride across the coping. He hovered for an instant on the wall; then she saw his light blue tunic frogged with white. Mohammed's piece was levelled. With a cry of terror she seized the barrel—the shot went wild. The Prussian dropped into the court-yard and ran crouching to the gate.

Mohammed reached for a cartridge.

"Stop!" she screamed, tugging at the rifle. "Stop!"

With a strength born of anguish, she wrenched the chassepot from his grasp and held it close to her breast. The Turco muttered and glared. She saw the levelled pieces of his comrades.

"Stop them," she cried. "Don't let them fire!"

The walls shivered at the screech of the chassepots. Her heart stood still. White and

trembling, she leaned far out of the window.
She saw the Prussian fumble at the fastenings
of the gate. From every crevice in the castle
the rifles snapped. At last the gate swung
open. He stood unharmed! She saw his
face.

"Ludwig!" she gasped. "God save him!"

Then the pale blue tunic was lost amid the
sombre flood of Prussian infantry which bil-
lowed through the narrow gate.

Across the walks and lawns they staggered—
a wild-eyed horde, with bayonets gleaming. On
they came in a surging sea of flat, spiked helmets, rushing, tumbling towards the castle.

The broad, low stairs winding outside the
castle front became the final shambles. Up
them the Prussians stumbled, battering at the
shutters with their rifle-butts, firing straight at
the windows in the face of rasping death. The
spitting French guns whirred like rattles; from
every casement frenzied soldiers leaned and
fired point-blank at the foe on the stairs. The
Prussians staggered, fell, recoiled, and then
came on to the throbbing of their little drums,
to the bellowing of officers. Pink-faced boys
fell whirling like pigeons at the traps, bearded
giants ran moaning with fingers to their
wounds; the twisted dead lay tumbled on the
gravel walks below, but always the crouching,

dodging living upon the terrace and the stairs; always the yelp of the needle-guns, till the goaded garrison despaired.

French bugles sounded clear above the battle, "Cease firing." They echoed from hall to hall, "Cease firing."

Hurried steps grated and creaked along the stairs.

"Surrender!" The shameful words rang hoarse, "Surrender!"

In the little chamber under the roof five Turcos knelt behind the window ledges; two lay motionless upon the floor, another moaned, while Marcelle's eyes still sought in the surging sea of black for a glimpse of the blue of heaven.

Again the bugles echoed through the shattered halls, and a Turco raised his piece to fire.

"Stop!" she cried. "We have surrendered."

Sullen as caged beasts, the Kabyles heaped their smoking pieces on the floor. They had fought for the honour of their conquerors. Their work was done.

VII

Marcelle stood gazing at the rifles heaped upon the floor. Her head fell heavily against her breast; sighs came from her breathing, but no words; her eyes were sunken and expressionless. Disheartened as the Kabyles squatting motionless upon their haunches, she awaited the coming of the victors. Through the shattered casement their cheers of triumph echoed: "*Hoch Preussen! Hoch Preussen!*"

At last the hallway creaked under the weight of booted men. Mohammed reached for a rifle.

She snatched the gun away and held it in her trembling hands.

"No," she cried; "No!"

The tramping feet came nearer. She saw the glimmer of gun-barrels, the flash of a sword. A squad of giants surged through the door; the word "Halt!" was grunted, and she saw the face of the officer, leering and red-hued, under a brass-spiked helmet—the face of a brute.

"A woman," he growled. "Damned if she isn't pretty. Caught red-handed, too, with a rifle."

195

She paled at the gaze of his tigerish eyes.

"Seize those Turcos!" he said, turning towards his men.

The Kabyles glowered with sullen hate, but offered no resistance. The Prussians dragged them to their feet and held them pinioned. She watched the brutish officer step towards the dead man lying with a splinter through his breast; she saw the white rims of his angry eyes, the flush of colour in his thick neck. He shook his huge fist at the helpless dead.

"You beast! You savage!" he shouted. "They bring you heathen swine to fight us Christians, and call themselves civilised! We ought to kill every mother's son of you. We ought to burn you alive,—yes, damn you, alive!"

Quivering with passion, he kicked the dead Turco again and again.

Marcelle sprang forward.

"Coward!" she cried, "you disgrace the uniform you wear!"

"Silence!" screamed the officer, wheeling towards her.

The girl's eyes flashed defiance

"You've conquered, but you shall not insult our dead."

He seized her little wrists with his big-boned hands.

"Yes, we've conquered," he chuckled; "conquered you, too, my beauty."

With maddened courage she fought him till his strength overcame her. His huge arms clutched her. His coarse lips pressed against her face.

Then a cry of rage—a scuffle. Mohammed had tumbled his unwieldy captors to the ground.

Lithe as a tiger he sprang at the Prussian's throat. The brute's hands unloosed her, and he fell, fighting for his life, while the stolid soldiers stared, wondering. Astride the officer's chest, with sinewy legs coiled around him, the angry Turco choked the man until his face was ashen; he beat his head against the floor; he snatched a hand from the Prussian's weakened grip and reached to his belt.

The bayonet flashed from its sheath—too late. Dull minds had begun to work; a dozen clumsy soldiers fell upon the Turco. Cursing, groaning, kicking, they all rolled fighting in a heap, till the weapon was wrenched from the frenzied African, and he was dragged from the throat of the officer.

Mohammed stood panting in the grasp of his captors.

Marcelle rushed towards him. A soldier dragged her back.

The Kabyle glared at his enemy. The brown veins stood knotted on his forehead.

"Lela Baida," he muttered, "I would die for thee."

They lifted the gasping Prussian to his feet. His throat was swollen in crimson welts, his tunic torn, a battered helmet lay upon the floor. He shook himself like an angry cur. His little eyes twitched with fiendish hate. For a moment he stood panting.

"Bind the prisoners," he growled.

They ripped off the Turcos' canteens, cut away the leather slings, and bound the prisoners' hands behind their backs—the wounded man's as well.

"To the wall with them!" shouted the officer.

Trembling, Marcelle stood searching with her eyes from side to side. She heard the guttural commands; she saw the Turcos dragged against the wall; she saw a file of men line up with rifles at "Ready."

"No, no,—in the name of Mercy, no!" she cried, falling on her knees before the officer.

He dragged her roughly to her feet.

"Out of my way!" he snarled.

"They are prisoners of war," she pleaded. "You have no right to shoot them."

"They are savages," he muttered; "they

attacked us after they had surrendered. They shall die like dogs."   ,

Behind her a voice rang clear.

"Let ' the Aït-bou-Yoosuf die — they are ready!"

She saw her brave Turcos — defiant and motionless against the wall. They were dying for her. With despair in her lifted eyes, she sprang before the rifles; her face was aflame; her breath came fluttering and quick.

"Don't!" she screamed. "Don't shoot helpless prisoners."

The rifles dropped. The soldiers stared hesitating at their officer.

Crimson with rage, he rushed toward the girl. He clutched both her arms and shook her.

She thought she heard the tramp of feet upon the stairs.

"Help!" she called. "Help!"

"Silence!" he hissed. "We have orders to shoot non-combatants found with arms in their hands. You were caught red-handed. By God, I'll shoot you, too!"

He dragged her trembling across the floor and flung her against the wall. She fell in a limp heap. The room swam before her eyes.

"Help!" she screamed again; "Help!"

"Ready!" growled the voice of the brute.

She heard the rifles click. Her blood ran cold. She closed her eyes. She prayed.

"Aim!"

The command was drowned by a rush of panting men.

"Stop!" thundered a voice.

Again the rifles fell.

Cold and motionless she waited, not daring to look.

"My God, lieutenant, what are you doing?"

The words rang trembling through the room. She half-opened her dazed eyes, and facing the brutal officer stood a blue Hussar with sabre drawn. Her heart throbbed faintly in her breast. She tried to rise, but had not the strength. Out of the quick struggle for breath came the word "Ludwig!"

With a cry he ran towards her. His arms closed about her—he lifted her tenderly. She sank drooping against his breast.

"Marcelle!" he called; "Marcelle!"

Her pale lips parted. She looked through trembling eyelids and saw his face, and she seemed to live, to glow, to drink of sparkling wine.

"Ludwig," she murmured. "Ah, if you had not come!"

"Sir," growled a voice, "that woman is my prisoner."

Ludwig wheeled towards the officer. A
quarrel meant Marcelle's name dragged
through the army.

"By whose orders are you shooting prisoners?" he asked.

"Prisoners," muttered the fellow. "The
savages attacked us after they had surrendered.
As for the woman, she was caught with a
rifle."

Marcelle clung fluttering to Ludwig's arm,
and the Red Cross *brassard* was hidden by his
sleeve.

"We had surrendered," she cried. "A
Turco seized a rifle—I snatched it away—and
then they came. Through all this terrible day
I have not fired a shot—God knows I wanted
to."

"A likely story," sneered the brute.

Ludwig could have struck him, but for Marcelle's sake he curbed his anger. Her conduct
was an enigma he dared not solve. Alone in a
house in the forest and then in the Geissberg
castle with a squad of Turcos. Was she a spy?
The thought made him shudder.

"Sir," he said, "do you doubt the lady's
word?"

The man laughed.

"You take a deep interest in the prisoner.
Perhaps you will honour me with your name!"

That leering red face, with the eyes of a beast? Yes, he remembered it now, and he knew the man's unsavoury record. It would be his final weapon.

"Captain the Count von Leun-Walram," he said, drawing himself up stiffly, "Aide-de-Camp to His Royal Highness the General Commanding."

"Oh," muttered the man, taken back, and his eyes wandered from the Turcos standing impassive against the wall to the handful of men who had followed Ludwig.

"A Captain of Hussars in command of infantry," he temporised, "I confess I was confused."

"Well, sir," said Ludwig, sharply, "will you apologise?"

The man was not a coward, but he knew his conduct would not bear investigation; least of all, by the Crown Prince.

"Sir, I apologise," he muttered, throwing his heels together and saluting.

"Sir, I accept your apology," and Ludwig turned his back.

Marcelle still clung to his arm, staring vaguely from under her brows.

She saw the officer wheel towards his men; she heard the quick words of command; she saw the Turcos dragged from the wall and the soldiers form about them with bayonets fixed. She saw Mohammed, too, proud and defiant above his captors.

"Ludwig," she called in a low, urgent voice, "he will shoot them."

"He will not dare."

"He insulted our dead," she whispered. "His insult to me was worse. A Turco broke from his captors to save me; he would have strangled the wretch, but they overpowered him. Then the brute ordered the prisoners shot. He would have killed me, too."

"Forward, march!"

She heard the gruff command, and then the tramp of feet across the floor.

"Save them!" she pleaded; "If you love me, save them!"

She threw her arms about his neck. He saw the Red Cross *brassard*. A nurse—not a spy! His heart leapt with joy!

"Halt!" he cried, springing before the marching men.

"I take orders from my colonel," thundered the officer. "Forward, march!"

"Lieutenant Bauer, surrender those prisoners to me."

The man drew back. His name on Ludwig's lips! It made him hesitate.

"The men are my prisoners," he growled. "I shall report to my commanding officer."

Ludwig looked him sternly in the eyes. "And I shall report to the General Commanding."

"Report," muttered Bauer.

Ludwig took his arm and drew him aside.

"Don't be a fool," he whispered. "You were court-martialed for conduct unbecoming an officer and a gentleman and sentenced to dismissal. You had a fighting record in '66. The Crown Prince remembered it, and you were pardoned. Think twice before you allow me to prefer charges. Shooting prisoners without orders is bad enough." He looked towards Marcelle. "But insulting and assaulting a nurse, protected by the Geneva Cross, and then ordering her shot!— What chance would you have with your record? Think!"

And Ludwig walked away.

A moment later he wheeled towards the man.

"Lieutenant Bauer," he commanded, "I am your superior officer. Surrender your prisoners to me!"

The officer's face flushed crimson. He took a step towards Ludwig—then his sword whisked angrily to "Salute," and, turning, he muttered quick orders to his command. The Turcos

were marched across the floor to Ludwig's
men, and Bauer's detachment wheeled into
line, awaiting the word of command.

"Forward, march," snarled Bauer. The
detachment moved on.

Marcelle listened to the tramping feet until
the echo died upon the stairs. Motionless she
stood, while the memory of the battle rose
before her in visions terrible. Somewhere a
Prussian band was playing, and she heard the
trombones groaning and the clang of cymbals;
the tears came then, and her wet eyes looked
at brave Mohammed, defiant behind the Prussian bayonets. At her feet lay the Turco dead.

"Come," said Ludwig, finally.

Her head fell wearily upon his shoulder.
"Ludwig," she murmured, "take me somewhere—somewhere away from here."

He led her towards the stairs. The little
escort followed with the prisoners.

The castle swarmed with Prussians, frantic
with victory. They surged through the halls
and cheered; they glared at the girl and muttered rude jests; and, trembling, she clung to
Ludwig. He dragged her finally into the open
air. The court-yard was alive with jägers and
grenadiers, and he hurried her beyond the
castle grounds and reached the hill crest. To
take her to a place of safety, to find the Crown

Prince, had been his only care. He saw the Red Cross flag at the Schafbusch farm, and hither he marched his little company.

Throughout the terrible day Marcelle had been swept on by a torrent of emotion—drummed out of her senses by the battle sounds; but now, when Prussian bands pealed victory, and her France lay bleeding, she dragged her weary feet along without energy and without hope. She had neither strength nor courage left.

There were questions Ludwig would have asked, but he had too much sympathy to press them. As they passed through a garden he gathered some flowers for her; she took them without a word.

A convoy of prisoners was forming in the farm-yard. Ludwig knew the officer in command, so he surrendered the Turcos to him.

"There is no more danger," he said to Marcelle. "They will be treated as prisoners of war."

She looked with dim, spiritless eyes into the face of her Kabyle champion.

"Thy life has been spared. I can help thee no more."

"O Lela Baida," he answered, "thy servant and all the Aït-bou-Yoosuf are thy slaves."

"Oh, brave Mohammed," she murmured,

and she watched the sad march of the vanquished till only the bayonets of the victors
flickered beyond the hill crest—then she turned
away.

The fleeing army had made a final stand at
the Schafbusch farm, and then had left the
brave defenders of the castle to vindicate
French honour. Trampled by victorious feet,
the evidences of strife lay strewn about her, and
again she was beset by leering Prussians
flushed with triumph. Feebly she clung to
Ludwig, while he hurried her half fainting
towards the house.

The door of the little room on the left of the
entrance where the vanquished General lay
stood partly open. The spaniel still crouched
snarling upon his master's body; the loyal
staff-surgeon stood bowed and sorrowful beside
his dead commander, and even the victors
hushed their voices and bared their heads as
they passed.

Marcelle and Ludwig entered softly. He
might leave her in safety there, he thought,
while he found his Chief. The surgeon stared
at them with glazed, expressionless eyes; the
spaniel growled, then seemed to recognize the
girl, for his tail began to wag. Again the
quiet chamber of death, with the Christ Child
hanging on the wall and the sunlight stream-

ing through the white muslin curtains, seemed restful after the carnage.

She laid her flowers upon the dead man's breast, as she gazed upon his peaceful face; she saw a vision of the battle-field,—Abel Douay, superb and motionless above the wreathing smoke; then a riderless horse with gold-embroidered holsters, and anxious faces bending over a form upon the ground. Her heart sickened, and she turned towards Ludwig. Remorse and shame swelled in her bosom.

"For your sake," she murmured, "I was a traitor."

He saw the beautiful curve of her face, the tumbled masses of her hair, and wondered at the meaning of her words, but dared not ask. Her head fell heavily against her breast, and she sank upon the bench by the window and sat gazing at the floor with dull, marred eyes.

Through the open casement she heard the clatter of hoofs, and cheer upon cheer.

"*Hoch! Unser Fritz! Hoch! Unser Fritz!*"

A band played "Die Wacht am Rhein." Then came the tramp of feet along the hall, and the door swung open wide. Ludwig sprang to attention, while the French surgeon leaned against the table sullen and downcast, and the spaniel growled.

Marcelle raised her weary eyes and saw the

Crown Prince of Prussia, majestic and tall, stride into the room. Behind came his booted staff, with sabres clanking. She arose in the presence of the royal victor, and stepped back into the shadow.

The Prince halted silent before the body of the fallen General; his head was bared, his hands were crossed upon his sword hilt. In the presence of death the heart of the soldier was softened, and he gazed in sorrow at the face of his enemy. Splendid as a bearded Rhine god he stood, with Prussian orders glittering on his breast. At his feet lay a hero of France. They had met—the living conqueror and the vanquished dead.

Through the open windows rang the cheers: "*Hoch Preussen! Hoch Preussen!*"

VIII

THE IRON CROSS

Beyond the royal soldier, stern officers with cap in hand, were leaning on their sabres, waiting. After a time, the Prince looked up and saw Marcelle standing there, with despair in her beautiful face.

"Mademoiselle," he said gently, "we both mourn a brave man's death."

In the torn grey habit, with loosened hair and face uplifted, she came towards him.

"He was my friend, Your Royal Highness."

"And you, Mademoiselle?" he asked.

Marcelle lowered her eyes.

"She is my cousin, Sir!" said Ludwig, stepping forward.

The Prince stared at the young aide-de-camp. He had supposed him dead or captured. Ludwig's heels clicked attention.

"Sir, I have the honour to report."

The Crown Prince turned his glance from Ludwig to the girl.

"The Count von Leun-Walram is—is your cousin," he said dryly, accenting the latter word.

"Yes, Your Royal Highness," Marcelle faltered.

"Oh," said the Prince, "I see."

He turned towards Ludwig.

"Sir, make your report."

The young officer looked straight at his Chief, and spoke modestly, in the manner of a soldier.

"Pursuant to orders, Your Royal Highness, Captain Egerton and I, with the men of our command, reconnoitred yesterday afternoon across the Lauter, entering the enemy's territory through the Mundat-Wald, near Roth. Towards dusk we got in touch with a division of the enemy going into camp near Wissembourg. His cavalry was surprisingly inactive, and we were able to skirt along the forest several kilomètres to his rear, keeping well under cover of the woods. If we were seen by the inhabitants in the twilight, as seems probable, we were no doubt taken for a patrol of the enemy. The command wore forage caps, and with our light blue *attilas*, braided in white, might pass, at a distance, for French Hussars, especially as, before crossing the Lauter, I had secured a bolt of red cambric which we wrapped around our legs when in the saddle."

"A clever expedient," interrupted the Crown Prince approvingly.

Ludwig's eyes glistened with pride.

"About dark," he continued, "we came upon a small patrol of the enemy, and were obliged to beat a hasty retreat into the Mundat-Wald—evidently undiscovered, as no pursuit was made. We were well in the rear of the force at Wissembourg, and thoroughly satisfied that one division of the enemy had been thrown forward hastily without supports. By making a long détour through the mountains we hoped to reach the frontier before daylight."

He hesitated.

"Continue," said the Prince impatiently.

"The horses were winded and the men were fagged. We came upon a farm-house in the forest. We found a peasant woman there alone."

"Alone," muttered the commander.

The color rose in Ludwig's tanned face.

"It afterwards appeared, Your Royal Highness, that my cousin, Mademoiselle de Lembach, was concealed in a clothes-press."

"A spy!" said the Prince, quickly.

"No, Your Royal Highness—not a spy," answered Marcelle, hastily. "The peasant woman was my old nurse. I had ridden into the Mundat-Wald to visit her—I was there when the Prussians came—I did not know my cousin was among them. It was very natural, Sir, that I should hide."

"Very natural that you should hide," said the Prince, looking at her quizzically; "very unnatural that a young girl of your evident position should be alone in a forest in war-time."

The Prince shrugged his shoulders coldly and Marcelle's eyes fell.

"Surely, Sir," said Ludwig, "Your Royal Highness does not suspect my cousin of being a spy!"

"The enemy is always guilty until proved innocent," he answered, but there was a twinkle in his gentle blue eyes which Ludwig did not see.

"Continue your report, Sir," he commanded.

Then Ludwig told modestly of the fight at the farm-house and his escape on Marcelle's horse with the wounded Egerton. He dilated with glowing colours upon his cousin's bravery, giving her full measure of credit for saving Egerton's life as well as his own.

She listened dumbly—staring with lustreless eyes.

"Where is Captain Egerton?" asked the Crown Prince, showing deep interest.

"In a peasant's cottage, Sir, near Riedseltz."

"A prisoner?"

"No, Your Royal Highness. The peasant is
from Baden. He and his wife live alone.
They can be trusted."

"Go on," said Prince Frederick, impatiently.

"When we left the house in the Mundat-
Wald we rode for our lives, thinking we should
be pursued. Under the double weight the
horse was winded. He floundered on at little
better than a walk. Egerton was growing
weaker with pain. I feared he would faint. I
lashed him to my belt. In the blinding rain I
lost my bearings. Finally we got through the
forest somehow into the open country. We
found a highway. I guessed it was the road
from Hagenau to Wissembourg. Trusting the
French patrols had no stomach for such a
night, we went on and saw at last the lights of
a town."

"Ingolsheim?" queried the Prince.

"No, Your Royal Highness; Riedseltz, as I
afterwards learned."

For a moment Prince Frederick paced the
floor.

"Ten or twelve kilomètres," he muttered;
"a good distance under such conditions."

Marcelle thought of the ignorance of the
French generals and she looked sorrowfully at
the dead commander. Alas for French valour
when pitted against such intelligence!

"We cut across country," Ludwig continued, "to avoid the town. We came upon a cottage—Captain Egerton was suffering terribly. He begged me to leave him. Trusting to mercy——"

"Come, sir, make haste," interrupted the Prince sharply; "you left Captain Egerton with the friendly Badener. Well?"

"I was forced to leave the winded horse of Mademoiselle, as well, and go on afoot. Dawn had begun to break. I met some peasants in a field—I hid in a hay-cock. The peasants were all about me—I dared not move."

The Crown Prince smiled.

Ludwig coloured and hesitated.

"From sheer exhaustion," he stammered, "I must have fallen asleep. When I awoke it was broad daylight. The peasants had gone— I could hear the sound of cannon."

Marcelle's heart beat wild with joy. The battle began before Ludwig reached the German lines. The surprise was not due to him. She seemed to touch heaven!

"I hastened to the sound of the guns," Ludwig went on, "and reached a forest. I met the 87th Nassau regiment debouching from the woods—my countrymen, Sir——"

"Well!" said the Prince suddenly.

"The battle had begun, Sir. The 11th corps

had already turned the French flank, and my information was valueless. The headquarters were upon the heights of Schweigen—five kilomètres across the battle-field. I was dismounted. It was impossible to report while the battle lasted. My countrymen were fighting."

He hesitated. The Crown Prince looked at him.

"You did what every Prussian officer would do—you fought."

"I reported to the colonel of the 87th, Sir," said Ludwig. "In the charge upon the Geissberg, a company lost its officers; I was forced to rally it and take command. In the Geissberg castle I found my cousin serving as a Red Cross nurse. I brought her here."

His hand swung stiffly to salute.

"Your Royal Highness, I have reported."

For a moment the tall, fair-bearded Prince studied the young soldier with his keen blue eyes. Meanwhile, a grey-haired officer of rank stepped forward from the door.

"Pardon me, Your Royal Highness," he interrupted. "Modesty has prevented Captain Count von Leun from making a full report."

"What have you failed to report, sir?" said the Prince sternly.

"Nothing of importance, Your Royal Highness," he stammered.

The grey-haired officer smiled. "He failed
to report, Sir, that during the final charge upon
the Geissberg position he scaled the high wall
which surrounds the castle. In the face of a
murderous fire from the windows, he dropped
into the court-yard and opened the gate for
our troops. I am a veteran of three wars, Sir,
but I have never seen a braver act."

A murmur of astonishment ran through the
room. Ludwig saw dimly the admiring faces
of his brother officers.

"Colonel von Grolman,' answered the
Prince, "I thank you for supplementing Captain Count von Leun's report."

Then, with dignity and kindness in his face,
he turned towards the young aide-de-camp.

"Captain Count von Leun," he said, "on be-
half of the army I have the honour to command,
I thank you for your services to-day. I shall
take personal pleasure in recommending you
for the Iron Cross."

Ludwig tried to quell the emotion rising in
his heart. Through glimmering eyes he saw
his young commander, broad-shouldered and
magnificent—a second Ariovistus leading his
warriors into Gaul. He could have kissed the
ground on which he stood.

"Ah, Sir!" he stammered at last, "I am
unworthy such an honour."

"I am the better judge," answered the royal soldier.

Then he turned away and gave some hurried orders to his chief-of-staff.

Beyond the crowding officers Ludwig saw Marcelle—very pale, very lithe and tall—Marcelle, fair, like a lily. Her hair was loose, her head thrown back; her eyes were afire with pride at the honour he had won—even against her France. The mere beauty of her, he thought—the loveliness!

Then orders passed and sabres clanged upon the floor, as muddy-booted aides sped to the bidding of the Chief.

The 4th Dragoons hurried in pursuit towards Soultz; the 88th Infantry deployed towards Riedseltz; the weary regiments were ordered into bivouac upon the battle-field. At last the commander had a momentary respite from the cares of war.

Ludwig, alert once more, placed a chair beside the table.

"Another for Mademoiselle," the Crown Prince whispered; then turning to Marcelle he said: "You look tired. Please do not stand."

The girl stammered her gratitude.

The peasant's meal was still upon the table, untouched through the battle, and he poured out some wine of the country.

"Drink this, Mademoiselle," he said; "it will refresh you."

She took the seat beside him.

This handsome blonde soldier, whose voice was so kind, whose glance was so gentle! It was hard to believe he was the heir-apparent to a throne; harder still, to realise he was a foe.

"Ah, sir," she murmured, "if all the Prussians were like you, we French would have to love our enemies as ourselves."

His blue eyes glowed like sapphires.

"It is treason enough, my dear," he laughed, "to love one enemy."

She tried to appear unconcerned, and failed utterly. But she looked very charming, he thought, with the conscious flush in her pretty face.

"Mademoiselle," he said, after a moment, "I would not venture to command you to report as I do my officers—but I am as curious as a woman. How came you in the Geissberg castle, when only last night you were in the Mundat-Wald aiding Prussian captains to escape."

Her eyes filled with tears.

"Ah, Your Royal Highness," she said, "I thought I had betrayed my country. I came to warn our General. I came too late."

She covered her face with her hands, and let
her head fall forward on the table. He took
her hand in his.

"Won't you tell me the story, my dear
child," he said. "Perhaps I might help you '

Not daring to look up; frightened by the
beating of her own heart, she told him, in
quick panting words, of her adventures. She
told him all except the affair with Bauer,
which she withheld for Ludwig's sake. It was
a delight to unburden her heart to some one.

Ludwig listened breathlessly. Her strange
talk of treason—the mystery of the Geissberg
castle! He understood at last.

As the story progressed the Prince smiled
from time to time—smiled kindly. He was
amused at the thought of this modern Maid of
Orleans tramping through the storm to save an
army, nursing wounded soldiers, rallying
Turcos on the battle-field, merely to atone for
having been so thoroughly feminine. He
thought her very romantic, very French, very
much to be loved.

"My dear child," he said, when she had
finished her story, "you heard your cousin say
he did not reach headquarters. Let me tell
you that yesterday, at four o'clock, the order to
cross the Lauter was issued—the army to march
at daybreak, traversing the Bee-Forest by four

routes and moving to the attack of Wissembourg. Your cousin's plucky reconnaissance in
no way changed the order of events. Your
treachery to France consisted merely in saving
his life."

The girl looked up—a glow of happiness was
in her face.

"Ah, Your Royal Highness," she murmured,
"how can I thank you?"

An amused smile stole across his handsome
face.

"You are my prisoner, Mademoiselle," he
laughed. "I shall release you on parole.
That is, if you give me your word never to bear
arms again. You are too valuable a general
for our enemies," he added, rising from his
seat. "Should you lead any more French
armies, we might be driven back across the
Rhine."

She seized his hand and touched it to her lips.

"I promise, Your Royal Highness, I promise."

He looked at her benignly, with gentle
eyes, then turned to the aide-de-camp:

"Captain Count von Leun," he said, "you will
prepare a room in the farm-house where Mademoiselle may rest. Then you will take an
ambulance to the cottage where you left Captain Egerton. I hope he can be moved."

"His wound is not serious, Sir,—a ball through the fleshy part of the thigh."

"When you return," continued the Prince, "you will, with an escort of cavalry, conduct Mademoiselle to the French lines, under a flag of truce."

"Yes, Your Royal Highness," muttered the young officer. He stood erect and stiff, with hand at "Salute," but his heart beat a wild tattoo of joy.

The Crown Prince turned away. For a moment he stood gazing at the fallen General. The faithful spaniel growled, but was awed to silence.

"I detest this butchery," the soldier murmured sorrowfully. "Yet it is my fate to be led from war to war, from battle-field to battle-field. It is hard for one who cares only for the welfare of his people."

Thus they parted—the living Prince, whose strength was to be ever dimmed by a father's glory, and the inefficient dead.

"Come," whispered Ludwig, and he and Marcelle followed.

Before the cottage a regimental band was playing the Lutheran hymn "*Lobe den Herrn, den mächtigen König der Ehren.*" To the glory of God the Victor the chords of praise resounded, while fair-haired soldiers bowed their heads in reverence. Splendid in the "blood-red sunset of a dying chivalry," the royal conqueror stood listening.

Later, Marcelle stood in the window of her room gazing at the battle-field. Near the mournful poplars bivouac fires glowed through the night, and she could see the shadowy sentinels pacing their dreary beats. About the camp fires muffled officers sat smoking quaint German pipes, and beside the rifles stacked in double rows along the hill crest lay the bundled forms of sleeping soldiers. Furled in its glazed black case, a regimental standard rose like a monument of grief amid the silent drums and trombones of the band.

IX

BETWEEN THE LINES

Rifles glimmered in the early light when Marcelle rode forth from camp, and Prussian trumpets bellowed hoarse from hill to hill. The unpitying rain which had fallen again during the night had ceased, and for a little while the sun shone warm and bright upon the valley-side; though while the drums rolled and the bugles blared, she dreamed not of arms but the man, for Ludwig rode beside her, stiff in the seat of the *Reit-Schule*.

They walked their horses slowly up the mountain side towards Lembach, and the gullies and brooks beside the road droned to the music of swollen waters. In the valley below, the spires of Wissembourg loomed grey through the river mist, and the low-towered shambles on the Geissberg crest stood white and quiet as a convent of nuns. It was a day when all nature seemed awakened and robed anew; when the air arose fresh and pungent to fill their lungs with the fullness of youth and life. An escort of Uhlans clattered slowly up the road ahead, with slim, pennoned lances

athwart their red-braided coats of blue, and the
plumes of their brass-tipped *czapkas* fluttering
in the morning breeze.

Though Marcelle listened to the rattle of the
sabres against the booted legs, though the ban-
nerets upon the lance heads were the sable and
white of the enemy, though behind her stood
the Geissberg carnage pen and the slender
poplars of the battle-field, the memory of all
that horrible butchery seemed afar off; for she
thought of a valley at Ems, and as she breathed
the morning air she seemed adrift on roses.

She was refreshed by sleep, she rode her own
horse, she was with Ludwig—and "the roaring
of war had ceased upon the air."

He seemed to read her thoughts, for he
drew from next his heart a bow of scarlet ribbon.

"Always!" he said, pressing it to his lips.

"The colours of an enemy," she murmured.

He leaned towards her from the saddle.

"Ah, Marcelle," he whispered, "there is a
love which is deeper than love of country."

She smiled and patted the neck of her horse
—then her face grew thoughtful.

"Have you forgotten what I said that day
when you came to bid me good-bye?" and as
she spoke she kept her eyes fixed full upon the
ground.

"No, Marcelle," he cried, "you said *'noblesse oblige,'*— and it told me other women are to you as withered field flowers to a splendid rose, and when my eyes had seen your daring I knew that it was true."

A pure, throbbing fire thrilled in her heart and crept up to burn within her face, but she made a bold effort to quell it.

"Ludwig," she faltered, "I fear you have forgotten what I said to my father that day. I told him that should we meet again, we would not forget our duty."

"Does duty forbid me to think only of you, to breathe only for you, to live only for the day when this hateful war shall be ended, and I may come to you and say; Marcelle, I have loved you always?"

He must have seen—for he gazed long enough—the quickened play of her breath. But while he waited for her to answer, she looked above his ruddy, soldier face to his brown fur busby, and from the silver scroll above his brow she read aloud the words emblazoned there:

"With God, for King and Fatherland!"

The wind caught the waving hair which curled about her neck; her lips had the curve of the love god's bow—and he thought that her eyes put the sunlight to shame.

"Then, Marcelle," he said in a low, thrilled voice, "I am a traitor to my King—for I would die for you sooner than I would for him."

She grew blush-red and divinely happy.

"And I am a traitor to France," she murmured trembling, "for Ludwig, I love you——"

"Oh, blessed Marcelle!" he cried; but the words he wished to speak seemed all inadequate.

So, for a brief time they rode on in silence, while fear and joy trembled together in Marcelle's heart as on that night in the Mundat-Wald. Only the fear was vague and undefined, like a shadow in the night afar off,—and the joy was like the glad sunshine about her. But when she saw the clouds above the mountains banking high she trembled, for she feared her happiness would be as short-lived as the warmth of that August day.

Ludwig riding beside her heard the bells tinkle on the necks of grazing cattle, and remote brakes and woodland places seemed to welcome him to loiter. The way lay through sweet-smelling pines, past hamlets white and red-roofed in the forests of the Vosges, and the rustling language the leaves whispered seemed to speak of a joyful eternity, till faintly, faintly up the valley-side rose the blare of Prussian trumpets.

"We are born to think, Marcelle," he said suddenly; "we are never a moment without thinking; but all our thoughts are merely of two things—love and ambition."

Marcelle smiled. "When I was at the convent," she said, "I obtained unknown to the sisters Pascal's '*Discours sur les passions de l'amour.*' I read and re-read it, and I almost know it by heart, and he says just that."

"Don't think I crammed up Pascal for the occasion," Ludwig interrupted, laughing.

"Pascal says," Marcelle went on, "that however grand the human heart may be, it is capable of but one great passion, and that when love and ambition meet, each falls short of what it otherwise would be."

"The very thought I was trying to express," he answered eagerly. "I believe, Marcelle, that love is the only thing in life worth attaining; and to have heard the words you spoke to me just now I would gladly give up all the honours and crosses and rewards my King could bestow."

Tremblingly she lifted her eyes to his.

"Let me say them again, Ludwig," she whispered, "I love you—I love you."

And as the sunlight kindled her crimsoned face and glistened on her smiling lips, the Uhlan troopers of the little escort's rear guard

looked at each other and smiled. They did
not understand French, but they understood
glances. Yet for Ludwig at that moment there
were no troopers.

"You are splendid, Marcelle!" he cried, "I
will never cease to love you!"

"No matter what comes in this hateful war?"

"Though all the world should go to war."

"Oh Ludwig, I fear—but—but never mind; I
love to hear it."

"But I seem to keep wandering from the
point," he laughed. "And yet the point is
you. What I wish to say is this. No ambition since the world began was ever gratified.
Alexander, Cæsar, Napoleon—anybody you
may select—always had a new world to conquer; but it is not so with love."

"Some people make it so," she said. "They
are never satisfied with the love they have, but
always sigh for the new——"

"That is because, like the Napoleons, they
do not realise it is greater to conquer one's
own spirit than it is to take a city."

"Oh," she said, arching her brows and looking up at him, "so you think you must conquer
yourself in order to love me."

"Marcelle," he answered thoughtfully, "I
think it is far harder to keep love than to win
it."

"I don't understand," she said.

"I mean this. If we build a hearth fire, or if we start a conflagration in a whirlwind, it will go on burning just so long as there is fuel for the flames. Now the conflagration cannot last, because there would never be fuel enough, but the hearth fire can burn forever if it is replenished day by day. It takes thought, it takes care, I believe, but it must be so worth the while."

She sat quietly for a moment in the saddle, wondering.

"I think I understand," she said. "Yes, I do understand—and—and I know you are right."

"Marcelle," he said in a low, earnest voice, "you and I have been in the whirlwind, such a whirlwind of strife and battle as I cannot realise,—but if we both live it is only the beginning. Dearest, I have waited all my life for you, and now I have found you, I can't let you go, I can't lose you; and I mean to try to do something each day I live to make you realise I value the only thing in life worth having, —perhaps if I try to do that I may keep your love always."

He was near, and she could see the keen light in his eyes, and she rode beside him for a moment breathless.

"Pascal," she murmured finally, "said that

'great souls require an inundation of passion
to disturb and fill them; but when they begin
to love, they love supremely.' "

"Haven't you any thoughts left but Pascal's?"
he asked, laughing.

"No, Ludwig, for you have them all."

"Even those about duty?"

"Don't be cruel," she protested, "I sent for
the chasseurs and when they came—I forgot
duty and France and everything when you were
in danger."

A mischievous smile swept across his face.

"And yet you read the device on my busby
and lecture me because I preach the very thing
you practice so superbly."

She turned and watched him with a long,
steady, unmoving gaze of admiration.   She
was thinking of the moment when the Crown
Prince had commended him before his brother
officers, and of the pride she had felt.

"Could you have done more for your King
and your country," she asked, "than I saw
you do?"

A blush crept up which he could not hold
back—a blush of honest pride.

"If you mean the battle, Marcelle," he said,
"I only did what I thought some one ought
to do, and as I was there, and no one seemed
anxious, and I was terribly excited, I was fool·

hardy enough to scale that wall and open the gate. If I had been shot, I should have been called a fool; as I got through all right I shall wear a cross and a ribbon."

"Ah, but you know you did well," she exclaimed, "and you're proud of that cross and ribbon."

"Of course, I'm proud of it, Marcelle—just as I'm proud of you—because it's something I had to fight for; and I mean to keep on fighting in this hateful war, and doing what I'm told to do, and what I think I ought to do, because fate has made me a soldier. But all the time I shall be thinking of you and your people, and my heart would be breaking if I did not know that if I live until it is over, you will be waiting for me. The motto on my head is not the motto in my heart, for that reads: 'With God, for Marcelle.' I shall fight for King and country, because it is my duty; but if you were a spy and I captured you, I should let you go—even if they shot me for it. And that's what I meant when I said I was a traitor, because I love you more than I do my King, or my country, or anything else in the world. And that's exactly how you proved you loved me, when you helped me to escape that night in the Mundat-Wald; so now, will the dearest girl in the world stop talking about pride and duty and ambition, and confess that love is the only thing worth living for?"

As she looked up into his face smiling her brown eyes trembled over him.

"Yes, Ludwig, I will acknowledge it," she murmured, "but isn't all you have said only a long, roundabout, beautiful way of saying '*noblesse oblige*'?"

"I hope Pascal did not write that," he laughed.

"No, Ludwig, but it is written in every word you say, and in everything you do."

"Once more you are wrong," he protested, "for in my case it should read '*l'amour oblige*.'" And again he took her bow of scarlet ribbon from his breast and pressed it to his lips.

And so they rode into the heart of the day; the sunlight thrilled, the keen air tingled; beyond, on the edge of the forest, French sabres gleamed.

While Ludwig rode slowly towards the enemy's lines escorted by an Uhlan trooper with a flag of truce, Marcelle sat alone in the saddle waiting. In the road ahead was a picket of French dragoons, and beyond among the beeches and the firs were the pointed turrets of a grey château. With brimming eyes, she saw an officer ride forward from the French outpost, saw the exchange of salutes, and when the brief parley was ended, the Blue Hussar swing his hand to his brow and wheel his horse towards the group of Uhlans on the green knoll beside her.

How splendid he looked, she thought, as he trotted up the highroad, erect in the saddle with sword a-clanking and sabretasche of silver, blue and red flapping against his charger's shining flanks, his handsome, sunburned face aglow beneath the red-bagged busby with its unsullied plume of white. How proud she was of this tall, blonde enemy she loved; but she knew the parting must be until peace came—or forever—and the heart within her sank.

They said but little as they rode together towards the French outpost, for words seemed miserably unequal to their thoughts, but after a time he glanced up suddenly with a hopeful look in his blue eyes:

"Headquarters will be at Soultz to-night," he said eagerly, "and the 2nd Bavarian Corps should be at Lembach. It would be safe for me to ride across."

"No, Ludwig, not until peace comes. Remember, my father is a General of France."

"Yes, Marcelle," he answered, "I understand."

Cold, merciless rain began to fall then, and

Marcelle shuddered, and as they rode on in silence, the red-legged dragoons astride their chargers gazed at them from under their shining helmets and wondered at all this panoply of a Hussar officer and an Uhlan escort to bring one pretty French girl through the lines. But, like the blue lancers of Thuringia, they understood the language of glances, so when salutes had been exchanged and the coldly civil greeting of enemy to enemy, and they saw the Prussian officer spring from the saddle and take the hand of the girl on the horse, they looked at each other and smiled.

He would have kissed her, then, before the dragoons and the Uhlans—or all the armies of France and Germany, had they been there—but in his burning glance she read his thought.

"No, Ludwig," she said, and as they watched the rain drops dot the ground, a strange, sad beauty was upon her face. Her deep brown eyes were soft with vague desire, but tears filled them as he touched her hand to his lips and through her heart swept an undetermined fear.

"*L'amour oblige*," he whispered.

X

THE DAY OF WÖRTH

On the morrow cannon thundered through the forests of the Vosges. All day the black guns belched and the château trembled. Down in the valley of the Sauer, where the village of Wörth nestled white and the green heights rose up to Fröschweiler, little clouds of vapour formed and broke, as the French guns echoed faintly through the hills. While the battle raged Marcelle watched beside her father in a turret window of the grey château.

All day they gazed toward the south, and everywhere upon the miles of valley road were blue-black tunics and low, spiked helmets, and columns of little midgets—as they seemed—marching through the valleys, deploying in the shelter of the hills and mounds, or dashing forward to the charge. The veteran's practiced eye scoured the forest edge with his glasses and he waited breathlessly, hoping those helmeted minims would recoil, and a streak of blue and red flicker along the hill side beneath the wreathing smoke. Marcelle watched with wide tearless eyes, praying for victory—and for Ludwig.

But as the day lengthened, the veteran's face grew sadder, and the words he spoke were of rage and despair—for he saw the blue Bavarians to the right encircling the heights of Fröschweiler, while the fight raged hottest, now down by the village of Wörth, then across the willowed banks of the Sauer, where the little hamlet of Elsasshausen glimmered beside the green "Nether-Forest."

When the numbers were even the French lines more than held, and fickle victory hovered above the imperial tricolour and all but perched, but the odds became as eighty-seven to fifty-four multiplied by thousands. Then the lancers and cuirassiers of France charged and charged again, always in vain, upon the dull black centre of the enemy, while the Turcos and Zouaves were mowed down in heaps by the shrapnel shells of the Krupps and the bullets of the needle-guns. Off to the right the blue Bavarians and to the left the Württembergers drew closer the circle of death about the last stronghold of France upon the heights of Fröschweiler. The veteran's eye roved anxiously then across the mountains to the west, for he knew that at Bitche, scarce a day's march away, a corps of Frenchmen chafed within sound of the guns,—but like brave MacMahon, down in the valley there beneath a walnut tree, he looked in vain for the corps of de Failly, and as the crimson sun disc sank behind the forests of the Vosges, he heard the cry of victory rise panting on the evening air—victory for the black-cross banner of the foe.

Night fell at last upon the blood-red field of Wörth, upon the upturned faces of the dead, and while MacMahon's beaten army fled panic-stricken towards the passes of the Vosges, the bivouac fires, the burning villages, and the lanterns of mercy and of human ghouls shone out in the darkness. The veteran turned, then, from the turret window, and with Marcelle's fluttering hand in his, tramped wearily down the spiral stairway to the floor below.

Since morning the château had been alive with Bavarian reserves, their rifles stacked in rows upon the terraces, the flower beds trampled by the booted feet of those stocky little Germans of the South, with blankets slung across their pale blue tunics and queer mediæval helmets tufted with chenille, above their russet faces. Now, as the girl walked slowly down the stairs she saw as she passed the windows camp fires glowing in the night, and heard the guttural chanting of war songs and hymns of praise; and her heart filled with sad-

ness for the silent dead and pity for the
wounded living.

The château had been requisitioned as headquarters by a brigade commander, and as they
left the tower they heard the clanging steps of
hurrying aides-de-camp, so General de Lembach stiffened himself and met the stare of the
bearded orderlies and dandy staff officers with
a proud, defiant gaze. But Marcelle's slanting
eyes saw glistening upon their helmets, beneath
a royal crown, the letter "L" and a quick
tremor went through her, for the name of their
King was Ludwig.

Marcelle and her father dined in the library.
The Bavarian commander sent an aide-de-camp
with his compliments and an invitation to join
his mess in the dining-room, but it seemed
both insult and injury and was curtly declined.

During the meal General de Lembach sat
staring at the table-cloth with dim, unwinking
eyes, and the food before him remained almost
untasted. From time to time he put a few
mouthfuls to his lips, but his head would fall
forward on his breast and he would sit motionless as before, staring at nothing.

He was thinking of the army of the Crown
Prince—horses, cannon and victorious men
shaking the earth of France—of MacMahon's
beaten troops fleeing through the passes of the

Vosges; and he pictured to himself the morrow with the sun blazing on the fields and the wind sighing through the poplars, while the stricken horde fled on. He seemed to hear the cry of "Prussians!" moaned from town to town, the rumbling carts, the bleeding cattle; seemed to see pale women cling hysterically to sobbing children and gaunt despairing men trudge through the dust.

Then he thought of the time when Abel Douay had ridden away, laughing as he went and talking of Berlin. Douay was dead, Mac-Mahon was beaten, and now the chanting of Prussian war songs beneath his window—only four days since that afternoon when he waved good-bye to the General riding so proudly to the north at the head of his fantassins and Turcos—but it seemed an eternity of shame.

Marcelle, too, thought of General Douay—but white and staring on the floor of the Schaf-busch farm-house. Then the memory of the time when he had ridden laughing to the north, with epaulettes and orders glistening in the sun light, came to her as well, but it filled her heart with trepidation, for she remembered the question he had asked and her father's answer: "My daughter knows her duty!"

When the servants had cleared the table and they were alone, Marcelle went and knelt be-

side her father's chair and took his lean,
wrinkled hand in hers. As she looked up into
his motionless eyes, a regimental band beneath
the window crashed out a love song and the
refrain was taken up by a thousand soldier
throats:

> "Steh ich im finst'rer Mitternach
> So einsam auf der stillen Wacht,
> So denk ich an mein fernes Lieb
> Ob sie auch treu und hold mir blieb."

The girl listened trembling to the chorus
with its mingling of love and war, and she
thought of Ludwig; and as she waited she saw
out of the shadowy background of books and
armour and carved oak chairs, beyond the sputtering candles in their silver holders, the face
of her mother gazing at her from a gilded
frame upon the wall. How she longed for her
at that moment!

Perhaps it was the summons of her soul to
his which made the sere old veteran turn his
lustreless eyes to the portrait of his wife. But
he seemed to forget as he gazed at her beautiful face, the rumbling of the slim black guns,
the fluttering Uhlan pennons. He thought
then of the time long gone, when unknown to
her, he had gone to a modiste's shop in the
Rue de la Paix, to select the wrap which hung

about the shoulders of the old-fashioned
square-cut bodice.

"Benvenuto Cellini" velvet and "Rachel"
crêpe—that was the way the pretty girl in the
shop had described the garment, and he smiled
to think that he should remember those names
once fashionable.

What a thrill of pride he had felt when he
first saw the picture with the garment he had
chosen painted without his knowledge, as proof
of his taste—or was it of her love he wondered.

That tall, slight figure with the well-poised
head, that face so calm and spiritual in repose,
with the clear white skin, and the keen brown
eyes set wide apart,—were it not for the parting of the chestnut hair upon the forehead, and
the quaint poke bonnet with the ostrich feath-
ers, it might be the face of Marcelle, he
thought; and to see the living image of his
wife, he turned and looked at the girl who
knelt beside him.   As the tenderness of the
past stole into his face, she felt that now if
ever he should know.

"Father," she said, gazing up at him with
the brown eyes of the portrait, "if you had
been a young French officer—say about seventy
years ago—and my mother had been a Prussian
girl, and you had fallen in love with her just

before Napoleon crossed the Rhine, should you
feel that you had done wrong?''

General de Lembach smiled, then gazed
once more at the portrait of his wife and
thought of that moment by the woodside when
the shadows deepened on the turf and the sun
faded behind the purple hills, that moment
when the sweet country vapours scented the air
and she had whispered her answer.

Then he met the eyes of Marcelle and their
tenderness must have thrilled him, for his arm
crept softly around her, and when, after a long
silence he spoke, his breath caught in his
throat and the room seemed throbbing like his
heart.

"My dear," he said, "it could not have been
wrong to love your mother at any time; but if
it were wrong—I believe that I should have
done it all the same."

She crept nearer to his side and then drew
his arm about her tightly as she whispered:

"And suppose my mother had been—shall
we say Marshal von Blücher's daughter?—and
that after Jena and Auerstädt mother had gone
to him and told him that in spite of her loyalty
to him, in spite of her duty to Prussia, she
loved a young French officer with Napoleon's
conquering army—do you think he would have
forgiven her?''

General de Lembach understood her meaning too well not to frown, but the humour of the girl's strategy overcame him, and though he laughed a curt, distant laugh and tried not to meet her eyes, he could no more have refrained from lifting her to his arms and kissing her at that moment, than he could have halted in the charge upon the redoubt of the Malakoff.

"If Blücher had had such a rogue for a daughter as you," he smiled, "I'm afraid he'd have forgiven her anything."

For a long time she sat on the arm of his chair with her head upon his shoulder and as the Bavarian soldiers sang beneath the windows she told him of the day at Wissembourg.

"Well, well,'' he said at last, as he thought of the Turcos following her green-red banner and the fight in the Geissberg castle, "even if you have your mother's Yankee independence —you've some of your old father's blood——"

"And you will forgive me?"

"I hope for Blücher's sake that he never had a daughter," he smiled, as he kissed her again.

The Bavarian soldiers were sleeping beside the stacks of rifles and the sentries pacing their beats while Marcelle sat by her window gazing out into darkness. She could see the glow of bivouac fires and lanterns flitting among the hills like will-o'-the-wisps. She pondered over the shadowy battle-field, watched the lights of the searchers for the wounded glimmer faintly through the night and she could not help feeling that Ludwig might be out there on the hillside. The thought drove sleep away.

When the first ray of morning gleamed beyond the forest, when hills and sky were blending in a bank of purple mist, and light, fleecy clouds floated spirit-like among the stars, she heard the Prussian trumpets blaring from camp to camp, saw the sleeping dots upon the hillside spring to life. Birds twittered beneath her window then, and as the sky glowed vivid crimson and a flood of golden light streamed across the mountain tops she turned away. Day had dawned—but the dead still slept upon the hillside. Ah! the misery of not knowing.

Soon her heart beat out a wild tune of joy, for while the soldiers in the château park were forming for the march, an orderly rode up the long avenue between the beeches and firs and halted by the fountain with the stone-hewn nymphs. She saw him coming and hurried trembling to the terrace, for she had seen the pale-blue *attila* of the 13th Hussars.

The soldier gave her a bunch of lilies tied

with a bow of scarlet ribbon. On the card
with the flowers Ludwig had written:

"A rosebud set with little wilful thorns,
And sweet as English air could make her, she."

The dreary weeks of war rolled on. Though
the armies of Germany tramped past the
château park and wound like huge snakes down
the valley side, though her heart filled with
pity and shame for her country she waited at
the grey château, hoping for the hour when he
would come.

And while the days went by, Ludwig rode
with the Crown Prince through the heart of
France to Sedan, thinking of her and repeating
again and again to himself: "There is a love
which is deeper than love of country."

Four weeks of war and France lay humbled.
Saarbrücken the overture, Wissembourg the
prologue, then an act of seething tragedy—
brilliant in conception, ceaseless in action,
pitiless in motive. Like a company of well-
drilled actors the generals of Germany played
their relentless parts; like a troop of faltering
amateurs the marshals of France stumbled,
awkward and confused, before the pitying eyes
of Europe.

Frossard, dreaming of a marshal's baton,
while Steinmetz drove him from the heights of

Spicheren and comrades marched and counter-
marched within hearing of his guns; Mac-
Mahon's veterans crushed to a pulp at Wörth
by Crown Prince Frederick, while de Failly
slumbered fitfully at Bitche to the distant
lullaby of cannon; brave Canrobert aban-
doned at St. Privat, and the French army of
the Rhine hurled by the Red Prince of Prussia
back against the walls of Metz, while sluggish,
scheming Bazaine coddled the Imperial Guard
and dreamed of victory won, if not of empire
grasped.

Thus the first act ended, and bewildered
France gazed aghast at the scene of Gravelotte
blazing red as the curtain fell.   Meanwhile a
disheartened, beaten army grumbled at Chalons
while the stage was being set for Sedan and a
pitiful dummy in imperial robes was trundled
into place for the tableau of the downfall.
The Crown Prince coursed unchecked beyond
the Meuse;   unruly Steinmetz and Prince
Frederick Charles growled before the gates of
Metz, while grim and wrinkled Moltke infused
three monster hosts with life.   Three armies
overrunning France, three heads thrust forward from a single heart, a Prussian Cerberus,
had been unleashed upon a bleeding land.

III

I

EN CABINET PARTICULIER

"Love is like climbing a steeple," said Clotilde Berthon. "You think you're near heaven, but you're only far enough from earth to fall."

The others at the dinner table laughed.

"Yes," said Paul D'Arblay, glancing at Marguerite Clairon, "in one case you break your neck, in the other your heart."

"Therefore love is preferable to steeple climbing," said Yvonne le Tellier of the Châtelet, from across the table.

Marguerite gazed at the blue-white cloth.

"It all depends," she said, after a minute; "love is the nearer heaven of the two—therefore, the fall is farther."

"Well," said the banker with the piggy eyes, "I'd rather break my heart than my neck. Wouldn't you, Marguerite?"

"It all depends," she answered.

"Marguerite must be in love," laughed Clotilde Berthon.

"O la-la," said the banker, and he pressed Clotilde's hand judiciously beneath the table and whispered——

"She's jealous—let's give her cause."

Meanwhile the arm of the Russian sitting next Yvonne le Tellier stole round her waist as he murmured near her cheek: "Let us climb the steeple and jump off together."

A candle, burning to its socket, spluttered. Marguerite quietly blew it out, snuffed the wick with her fingers and sank back into her chair.

Paul D'Arblay watched her intently. "Why is she so obdurate?" he wondered; "so impregnable—I'd almost give my life to hold her in my arms."

She knew that he was looking at her and she played with the stem of her glass watching the sparkling bubbles.

Rumpled napkins, half-burned candles, salad-stained plates, the carcass of a bird — that phantom of a feast seemed to stifle her. Yes, her life was as cramped as that low-ceilinged *cabinet particulier* with its red damask curtains, its mouldings of gilt. A mirror hung on the wall before her and she thought of the women with scented skin and wasp-like waists who had gazed flushed and smiling into the mocking glass while they etched their names with the diamonds of their frailty. She could almost see the soft, alluring eyes, the little earthy mouths, almost see the men, too, who had knelt beside them on that broad red divan:

some, boys with young, wilful faces; others, cruel and hard with thinnish hair and turgid eyelids or sleek bald spots and fat red jowls.

What a story that room could tell! To-night it belonged to the banker with the piggy eyes. And to think that she— oh! the misery of it!

"Life," she thought; "immunity to man—to a woman, immolation."

A waiter came, noiseless and imperturbable, to clear the table. To him it was a thral-dom of crumbs and silver pieces. But it was respectable.

Through an open casement came the murmur of the boulevards, the unceasing plaint of the city—now low and mumbling, now shrilled by the cries of vagabond humanity. She longed to break down the walls that cramped her and soar upward into the night—then float at peace among the stars.

She touched her glass to her lips and put it down with the wine untasted. Looking up she saw the ashen face of Paul D'Arblay.

"Marguerite," he said, "you are like sweet champagne. You take me out of myself; but you always leave me with a heartburn."

Her glance was openly contemptuous.

"And you are like the cork," she answered, "you merely serve to restrain my spirits."

His face darkened.

"Really!" he said, "but a fine French *cuvée* might grow flat and stale in a Prussian blue bottle were it not for the despised cork. You see it has one commendable quality."

"Yes," she said, crumbling a piece of bread and quietly brushing the crumbs away, "the quality of lightness—like your fingers, Monsieur D'Arblay."

His eyes had the hard glitter she had seen that night when he said: "I am content to wait."

"*Vraiment!*" he exclaimed, "but if the cork keep firmly in its place, some day the bottle may break—and that will be the end of the champagne, but not of the cork, *ma chère*."

She looked at him from beneath her arched eyebrows.

"A fool often tries to hide behind a threat," she said, "but it never covers his cap."

"*Le roi s'amuse;* but sometimes the fool has his revenge."

"*Tiens,*" she answered and turned away.

She saw the banker with his arm around Clotilde Berthon, and the smile on her pink and white face. But she did not heed the petty triumph of her friend, because she was thinking of a balcony at Ems.

"Wake up, Marguerite," said the banker,

"you are solemn enough for a *croque - mort.*
The Prussians haven't reached Paris yet."

"That's why she's so solemn," taunted
Clotilde.

"Please, Mademoiselle Clairon," said the
Russian; "one little smile,— the party is so
dull."

"Well, I like that," cried Yvonne le Tellier,
turning her back upon him.

The Russian edged towards Marguerite and
tried to take her hand.

"Your bear has escaped, Yvonne," she
laughed, drawing away, "and I am no tamer.'

"He will dance when he hears music,"
answered Yvonne.

"Please, Mademoiselle Clairon," said the
Russian with a hand upon his heart, "one little
song."

"Yes, Marguerite, sing," pleaded Yvonne,
"and my bear will dance attendance forever."

"What! Sing in presence of the Bouffes
Parisiens," Marguerite laughed with a chal-
lenging glance at Clotilde; "you forget we are
not musical at the Palais Royal."

"*Eh bien,*" answered Clotilde. "A song for
Marguerite," and she went to the piano.

She ran her fingers over the keys and the
notes she played had a rhythm of merriment,
until the banker came and stood beside her,

when they grew sombre and tremulous, like the moaning of a dirge.

"Why a funeral march?" he asked.

"For the *croque-mort*," she answered, so that Marguerite could hear. "Shall it be a song to suit her thoughts?"

"If you know my thoughts," said Marguerite, in an effort to smile.

Clotilde played a few light chords; then, with an improvised accompaniment, she chanted in a taunting, sentimental way two stanzas of de Musset's Chanson de Fortunio:

> "Si vous croyez que je vais dire
>   Qui j'ose aimer,
> Je ne saurais, pour un empire
>   Vous la nommer.
>
> Mais j'aime trop pour que je die
>   Qui j'ose aimer,
> Et je veux mourir pour ma mie
>   Sans la nommer."

"Brava!" cried the banker and the Russian, "Brava!"

"The song of the Prussian Blue Hussars—" said Clotilde.

"Treason! Clotilde," laughed the banker, "Treason!"

"Yes," she said with a shrug; "When a French girl loves a Prussian. Do you like

this better?'' And, running her fingers over
the keys, she sang:

"L'amour s'enfuit, le temps s'envole,
    Le temps emporte nos plaisirs
    Comme les flots une gondole !"

"Yes," thought Marguerite, "what I said to
him that night is true. A woman who really
loves cannot dissemble. Let them laugh if
they wish. Such a man exists, it is enough for
me to know it."

Clotilde finished her song, and for a brief
moment revelry seemed awed by a strange
stillness, coming as a ghost to the feast.
Marguerite gazed at the faces about her:
Yvonne, with her big celestial eyes and little
terrestrial mouth; Clotilde with her yellow
hair—fair as a poisoned opal in a setting of
gold. Beside the fat banker she might have
been Circe still charming swine. How vapid
and unreal and bloodshot these people seemed!

"My life is like one of these candles in the
crystal chandelier," she thought; "I shine for
a few moments among the mirrors and the
gilded frames, but I shall sputter and go out.
Yes, and in the unattainable heavens glows a
star."

The piping cries of newsboys, clamouring in
the street, broke upon the stillness of the
moment.

"*Voila le Temps!* Special Edition; Bazaine Defeated. *Voila le Temps!*" Up the streets piercingly came the voices:

"Bazaine Defeated; *voila le Temps!*"

Alas, poor France, she thought. Wissembourg, Forbach, Wörth, and again that panting cry—defeat. Like the shrieking of Nemesis it seemed, and even the revellers about her paled and gazed at one another askance.

The banker hurriedly opened the door.

"Quick, Émile, a paper!" he called to the waiter in the hall. "*Mon Dieu,*" he muttered as he closed the door, "there'll be another panic on the Bourse and I gambled on victory —after we had held our own at Mars la Tour."

"Well," said Clotilde, "after us the deluge," —and she played a waltz.

"*Sacré!*" cried the banker when the waiter had brought the paper and he read of Gravelotte with feverish eyes. "The army of the Rhine is defeated. Two hundred thousand troops cooped up in Metz. Only MacMahon and his beaten troops between the Prussians and Paris."

With a trembling hand he drained his glass.

"An army of lions led by an ass," said D'Arblay, lighting a cigarette. "Monsieur Bazaine had better put his famous bâton back in his knapsack—and shoulder a chasse-pot."

"I am long on Suez canals," muttered the banker, staring at the cloth before him with a dull gaze. "Stocks will go to the devil."

"*Mon vieux bébé*," murmured Clotilde, glancing over her shoulder with suggestive eyes— "If the stocks are going to the devil we'll all go, too. So *en avant!*" and she played a quickstep.

"Nero fiddled," said D'Arblay, "and Clotilde plays. *Vogue la galère!*"

"*Fichtre*, but you are all cold-blooded," cried impressionable Yvonne with a shudder; but she let the Russian take her hand.

"Think of the poor soldiers," said Marguerite; "think of the wounded." She left her seat, walked to the window and stood gazing into the lighted street.

"Self, nothing but self," she thought. "Pleasure the beginning and the end. Dear God, must I live with them always!"

She heard the turmoil of the street, the murmurous underflow of voices, saw the gnome-like crowds moving beneath the gas jets. Each breathing creature there, an entity to himself and an atom for eternity; and the street —a double row of glistening lights converging into nothingness; and Paris—a perversion of

souls. No, no, her heart cried out within her
—even if belief in the life immortal is but
misery at finding this life mortal, it is better
than disbelief—for reason without belief is
only a rudderless bark on the sea of despair.

Through the night she heard the shrieking
of clarions, the mumbling of drums—near,
gradually nearer came the throbbing sounds
until the windows shook and the street was
filled from curb to curb with marching fantassins. The glistening pavement rang to the
weary footfalls as, bent to knapsack and kit,
the regiment tramped on, band, staff and line
in close formation, and red legs opening and
shutting like a thousand pair of shears.

She saw the gaunt boy faces of the lagging
soldiers.

"Poor fellows," she said; "yet they fight for
France;" and as she watched the tangled
rifles glinting, she thought of the field of
Gravelotte—the staring faces of the dead, the
parched, unsuccoured wounded, grey as the
ashes of dead fire.

"If there were only something that I could
do," her heart cried out, "anything to help my
country."

"Another regiment for Vinoy," muttered the
banker behind her, "he goes to reinforce Mac-

Mahon—one more sacrifice to imbecility."
With a laugh he turned away.

"Another meal for the **cannon**," scoffed
D'Arblay beside her.

"Have you no patriotism?" she cried.

"Patriotism," he laughed, "the cant of
demagogues and the shibboleth of fools!"

"Paul D'Arbay," she whispered, pale to her
lips with anger, "I have kept the secret of that
night at Ems. Don't tempt me. I might cry
'Trickster' to all Paris."

"On the word of a **Prussian**," he laughed;
"take my advice: Don't."

"Have you no honour?" she cried, "is there
nothing you believe in?"

"You, Marguerite, you." He spoke eagerly
and she saw his eyes a-search for advantage.
She threw her head back——

"You may leave me out of the question,"
she answered coldly.

"Never, Marguerite."

"When Greek meets Greek," she answered.

A flush of anger crossed his face and his brow
knitted—in the argot of the time "Greek"
meant "sharper."

He showed his teeth for an instant.

"I am content to wait," he replied, "until
the shadows lengthen and the prey goes forth
to water."

"Tiger," she answered in a deep breath, "why do you pursue me?"

"Because I enjoy a puzzle."

She looked up strangely towards him.

"Would you like the key?"

"If it opens the way to you."

"The prey of a tiger dies in his claws," she answered, her eyes half closed, her lips pressed together; "but not for love of him."

"Should you like me better in the plumage of a dove? I doubt it."

She gazed at him long and curiously—"You saw the marching regiment—you might try the rôle of man."

"Not a bad idea," he laughed. "You remember the Ardennes—or have you forgotten you were the innocent belle of a village, until a poet, who writes great plays and therefore must study young emotions, came to spend an idle hour at Wasigny? I loved you then. The tiger is constant, you see. Have you forgotten?"

His words were like the cold breath of the forest after the sunlight has gone.

"I have not forgotten the *mauvais sujet* of the village," she answered with a nervous little laugh. "Ambition makes events."

"Possibly," he shrugged. "But the *mauvais sujet* knows the Ardennes. They are forming corps of francs-tireurs, they say—and the Prussians may pass that way on their road to Paris. A Blue Hussar might pass."

Marguerite shuddered, for his smile seemed as frozen on his face as it had been that night at Ems.

"Are a fool and his threats never parted?" she laughed as she turned away—but a feeling of dread stole through her.

The banker was holding Clotilde's *sortie de bal.*

"We are going to Clotilde's," he called.

"What a joy not to have to go to the theatre," said Yvonne, suppressing a yawn with her little hand. "I wish life were all a *relâche.*"

"Come," whispered D'Arblay, holding Marguerite's wrap.

"Into the tiger's claws?" she smiled. "Not yet."

Her victoria stood before the door, first in the line of waiting carriages. What a relief to escape, even for a moment, she thought, as she breathed the cool night air; then sinking back against the cushions, she saw the banker with his foot on the step.

"Clotilde has a vacant seat," she said.

He flattered himself that she was jealous.

"Where to, Madame?" asked the smart little carriage groom who tucked in the robe.

"Anywhere."

II

THE MADELEINE

Marguerite's carriage turned a corner and she saw the glaring boulevard—two rows of lighted shops, two parallels of gas jets. For a time she watched the restless crowd. "Roaring, surging Paris," she thought; "to glimmer on the wave crest or to be swept down by the moiling undertow—Chance; nothing else. That girl beneath the street lamp, decked in her flimsy finery. She is submerged—but her life and mine?"

She shuddered and drew her wrap tightly about her shoulders, for she thought of a far-off balcony. "He pointed the way and I did not follow."

The carriage turned into a narrow street and behind her the tides of people surged on beneath the lights. The way beyond was long and shadowy and above was the night, a dome of porphyry encrusted with stars. For a time she drove on, trying not to think. "Oh, the despair of groping in the darkness, and where are these vague thoughts leading? Not to misery, for it is here; not to hope, for it is

passed; not to belief, for it is too far off—
except my belief in him."

She passed a library. "Behind these frowning walls," she thought, "thousands upon
thousands of books stand in their dusty alcoves
and each is the record of a life."

Lean paupers shambled by her and in their
pale, sunken eyes she saw a plea for money,
money, bread. "And I," she thought, "I
have the money and the bread, but what else?"

A statue loomed white beside the carriage
and by the fountain beneath it she saw the
muses of comedy, and she thought as she
passed of the question a king once put to a
man of letters. "Who is the greatest genius in
France?" he asked, and Boileau answered,
"Molière, Sire."

"The greatest genius in France," she smiled,
"yet while he lived the courtiers did not think
him good enough to smooth the king's sheets.
Yes, and he blackened his face daily to produce the moustache of Sganarelle, and when he
died the church refused him absolution. 'The
greatest genius in France' and he loved a faith-
less woman to the end. Another soul starving
for the unattainable. Greatness, love, peace
—always the unattainable while we live—and
then? An unmarked grave, or at best a
statue."

"Drive faster, Guillaume," she called to the coachman.

The lights of the Palais Royal shone out ahead—bulwark of despotism and debauchery, birthplace of liberty; to her it meant vaude-villes and farces; the petty triumphs of her life.

She thought of the pretty theatre and the eager faces beyond the flaring footlights, the bravas and the hand-claps.

"To think that once it gratified my self-con-ceit. But once I was content to be a country girl and once a poet—well, he made the amend, for he wrote me a clever piece and trained me for my début—and when I won my little triumph I forgot that I had a soul. Ah, Ludwig, until you came I was contented." She heard the rattle of a soldier's spurs be-neath the arcade beside her— "The battle-field," she thought—"the dead."

"Faster, faster, Guillaume," she called, and the carriage rolled from the narrow streets into a blazing square.

It made her less lonely to be among the lights, but it was only momentarily, for once more she entered a shadowy street. A market cart with a peasant dozing on his cabbages blocked the way and the carriage followed at a walk. Under a low awning she saw flushed faces huddled about a sidewalk table and as she passed she caught the muttered words, "*À bas Bazaine; à bas l' empire.*" Then suddenly she turned a corner and saw a palace, black and frowning in the night, and a sentry in his box staring and motionless as a mummy long entombed.

"The Empress," she thought; "is she sleeping peacefully behind those walls or is her mind torn by unrest like mine? She cannot hear those words; '*À bas l'empire,*' but she can dream of a queen who slept until the drums rolled and the pikes gleamed in the night. Swiss sentries stood motionless in their little boxes then—perhaps!"

The thought made her shudder and she turned her eyes away from the darkly silent palace. A row of lights twinkled beneath the arches of a dim arcade and through the iron palings of a fence, she saw the murky forms of trees. "Rivoli," she thought, "but there will never be a *Rue de Gravelotte*, never in France at least. And the Empress in the palace I have passed loves the hand-claps and the bravas and because it is her war— Forbach, Wörth, Gravelotte! Does she think of the hisses, I wonder?"

She remembered then the gaunt boy faces of the regiment she had seen passing and D'Arblay's sneering words, "Another meal for the cannon."

"If there were only something that I could do," she sighed. "Perhaps they would accept me as a Red Cross nurse"—she smiled at the idea—"'La belle Clairon goes to the front with Vinoy's corps'—an item for every paragrapher in Paris—*quelle réclame?*"

But that thought of the applause made her feel mean and petty. "Am I as vain and selfish as the Empress?" she asked herself— "La belle Clairon of the Palais Royal. Yes, I am rightly named, for I belong among the vaudevilles and farces!"

The carriage rolled on and beside her flamed a broad square ablaze with a myriad lights. She saw pale statues and misty fountains and, pointing to the stars, an obelisk. "'Place of Concord,'" she thought. What an irony of words, for through the night she seemed to see the gleam of the guillotine and hear the rumble of the tumbrils. And again she trembled and drew her cloak tightly around her. Near her loomed the figure of Strassburg, white and ghostlike in the shadow, and she thought of a wretched city besieged by the conquerors.

An orderly galloped past the carriage and she saw the gleam of a cuirass—the glint of a horse-hair plume. "Perhaps a Blue Hussar is

riding through the night," she thought, "with
the enemy's despatches," and she remembered
D'Arblay's threat, "They are forming corps of
francs-tireurs—a Blue Hussar may pass."

"Ah! why do I love him?" her heart cried
out. "Why does the memory of that one
night come back to me again and again? Is it
to make me realise that the greatest gift God
could send me would be he—or is it to make
me feel that I am not worthy?"

Then the carriage turned into a broad,
lighted street and between the converging rows
of lamps she saw a church.

She sank back against the cushions, thinking
of nothing definitely, trying not to think. Her
eyes closed and like one at a revel her life
passed before her—the hand-claps, the bravas,
the laughter, and the wine; and the men she
had known arose in a flame-hued imagery about
her; all except one who stood beside her upon
a balcony at night and whispered, "I am waiting for the best the world can offer."

"Why didn't I wait?" she thought. "*Mon
Dieu*, why didn't I wait?"

For a time she sat quite still and it seemed
to her in those moments that her childhood
was beside her—the forests of the Ardennes,
the valleys and the white villages, the church
where she made her first communion. She

paused to listen, for voices seemed to be singing afar off, voices singing as they walked in
procession:

"Venez, venez, Toi que j'adore!
Venez, venez, venez encore!"

She saw candles burn upon an altar; she
was dressed all in white with a chaplet of
flowers upon her reddish curls; she carried
a lighted taper; as she knelt before the
Host a strange exaltation of the soul overcame
her and she seemed to be taken out of herself
and borne afar off with the voices still singing.
She was not sure whence they came—her own
heart, perhaps, or echoes brought by the wind.

Looking up suddenly she saw the stone pil-
lars of a church and through the bronze doors
came a faint glow of light.

"Guillaume," she called in a strange impulse, "stop at the Madeleine."

Candles flamed upon the altar as she entered,
and black-gowned women knelt praying for
the dead upon the battle-fields of France. A
few looked up at the rustling of her dress.
Her laces and her jewels seemed to them
strangely out of harmony with the house of
God and the perfume in her hair like the
tainted breath of a defiling spirit. "Why had
she come?" they wondered.

Her step resounding through the shadowy stillness seemed to fill her heart with awe; she would have turned and fled, but the altar blazed before her and pale in the gloom beyond she saw Saint Mary Magdalene borne heavenward by two angels; so, trembling, she knelt and prayed.

Next her was a wrinkled woman with a face pinched and hard. She cast a look of envy at the girl, for once she had been as she, a beautiful creature with silks and jewels. The woman saw the flare of the candles on the face beside her, the reddish hair ablaze where it clustered on the forehead, the soft white lace against the delicate skin, the dark, mysterious eyes, the lips like blood rubies. "A lover dead upon the battle-field," she thought, "and some day she may be like me—a *concierge*."

She did not see the look of envy in the woman's face. As she prayed her eyes were fixed upon Saint Mary Magdalene white in the shadow beyond the tapers, and she seemed to hear again the voices singing:

"Venez, venez, Toi que j'adore!
Venez, venez, venez encore!"

Mingling with the droning of the hymn came the far-off throbbing of drums, the shriek of clarions and she seemed to see the upturned faces of the dead, the pale, unsuccoured wounded—and then upon her sleeve a cross of red. "It might make atonement," she thought.

In that moment a feeling of rest stole over her, and for a long time she knelt alone in the silent church—after the black-gowned women had gone.

III

EAGLES OF EMPIRE

The rays of the sun were slanting in the west. Upon the hill crest stood the grey-haired King of Prussia, with glasses levelled at the battle-field; near him lounged the Great Headquarters Staff, princes, generals and court officials glittering in the light of a September day. In the valley below, the river Meuse coiled past the moated walls of Sedan, and beyond stretched the brown plateau of Floing, where an Empire crumbled.

Ludwig reached the group and halted his winded horse; leaping from the saddle he threw the reins to an orderly and strode towards the King.

The battle had raged since dawn. He had been with the Crown Prince on the hill at Piaux while the blue Bavarians of von der Tann stormed the blazing houses of Bazeilles until the gallant French marines had burned the last cartridge. He had ridden then to the northward with orders for von Gersdorff, and had found a dying General. A moment on the firing line at Floing, where his countrymen of the 87th were making a noble fight, a greeting shouted to brother officers of two squadrons of the 13th Hussars chafing in a field near St. Menges, then back to headquarters. His memories of the battle were mostly of tramping, sweating regiments on sun-scorched roads, of rumbling caissons, and the boom of cannon on the hills beyond Sedan. It had been a day of galloping, galloping, or picking his way along troop-choked highways. How different it had been at Wissembourg, where the blood tingled through him. But the thought of Wissembourg and Marcelle——

Mechanically he touched the brim of his busby.

"Your Majesty, His Royal Highness the Crown Prince commands me to report——"

The tall, thin officer standing by the King looked up at the sound of his voice—grey, wrinkled Moltke, with the pale, drawn face of a cloistered monk and the eyes of a hawk. He listened while the young Hussar told in a few blunt words of the successful flanking movement of von Kirchbach's corps; a smile trembled on his thin lips; Givonne had fallen; the Guards were debouching from the forest of the Ardennes; the army of Chalons was caught between the flanges of his iron vise.

"*Es stimmt,*" he muttered to himself, then

he turned to Ludwig. "You may wait for
orders, Captain," he said, and stepped away,
but Ludwig's face flushed with pride, for
the great man's eye had rested on his Iron
Cross.

He saw von Moltke unfold a map and ex-
plain the movements of the troops to a short,
thickset little man, in the dark blue uniform
of some foreign service. The stranger had a
ruddy, weather-beaten face with keen, snap-
ping eyes, a bulging neck, and a tuft of beard
on the chin under his curled moustache. He
looked a soldier every inch. Who could he
be? Ludwig wondered. His dark blue cap
with the three silver stars had the cut of the
French chasseurs; his blouse was severely
plain, without galloons or orders—yet he must
be a soldier of distinction. He heard von
Moltke speaking English and he remembered
then that Sheridan, the famous American cavalry commander, was at headquarters.

Standing with Moltke and Sheridan was the
Chancellor of the Confederation in cuirassier
tunic and boots, towering like a giant of flesh
and muscle above the little American. Sheridan's hands were resting on his sabre hilt, his
white forage cap was tilted backward towards
his beefy neck. Those bull-dog eyes, shaded
by bushy brows, with the puffed and swollen

underlids! That jaw of iron! What a face of will and strength.

He edged nearer and listened, while the Chief of the General Staff explained the movements of the troops: The Prince Royal of Saxony on the right bank of the Meuse, the Crown Prince on the left, advancing like the arms of a horseshoe, with MacMahon's hapless army between them.

"Napoleon will likely be one of the prizes," he heard the little American say.

Bismarck shook his head incredulously. "Oh, no; the old fox is too cunning to be caught in such a trap; he has doubtless slipped off to Paris."

Ludwig caught the piercing eye of Moltke. He had approached too near, and, covered with confusion, he stepped back among the crowd of Hereditary Grand Dukes and Serene Highnesses, aides-de-camp and court functionaries, who encumbered the Great Headquarters with their swaggering, glittering presence. But he despised this flotsam and jetsam of royalty, so he drew away and sat down on the ground to rest. He was tired and hot and sick at heart as well. Marcelle, Marcelle! Always the thought of her. Would this war ever end?

With his glasses he scanned the valley of the

Meuse, which lay so green and peaceful under the cloudless sky! Peaceful! What an irony of thought—for there, on the edge of a wood scarce half a mile away Uhlan pennons fluttered in the autumn breeze, and Bavarian batteries thundered at Sedan. Above the red-tiled town floated a yellow-tinged cloud of dark grey smoke, while mingling with the deep-voiced detonations of the cannon, a rasping sound arose from the forest of Garenne, like the crackling of a million twigs. Off to the right the charred and ruined houses of Bazeilles still smouldered, and beyond Sedan, upon the hillside where a hundred German guns were massed, little white puff-balls formed, broke and floated away in streaks of filmy grey.

This panorama of battle, viewed in safety from the royal box—sublime, absorbing spectacle! New to his eyes as well, for at Wissembourg he had fought in the van of the firing line, and when the Crown Prince arrived upon the field of Wörth he had been sent galloping in hot haste towards Spachbach, to hasten the march of the Württembergers.

With his powerful lenses he could see distinctly dark masses of Prussian infantry toiling up the hillsides before the hamlet of Floing, and, on the broad plateau beyond, shrapnel

shells were bursting in the ranks of the panic-
stricken regiments surging towards Sedan.
Men were dying there, a bleeding testament of
the power of kings to slay, "while numbers
sanctified the crime." War, horrible war; it
was kill, kill, with all the passion of brutes
unleashed. He could feel only pity for those
shattered regiments, he could not think of
them as enemies. Marcelle was right: deep
down in his heart he was not a soldier.

Suddenly a cry of admiration started from
his lips. There to the north, in a hollow of
the brown plateau, French cavalry were forming for a charge—five regiments of mites—mere
splatters of blue on white where the chasseurs
rode, or a glint of steel in the western sun in
the line of the cuirassiers. Right front into
line the squadrons wheeled; before them a
streak of Prussian skirmishers on the hill ahead
of the battle line, and, enfilading the plain
they must pass, a hundred Prussian guns.

They were off! Entranced he watched those
brave men ride straight at the line of the foe.
Into the volley fire, into the pelting death they
rode—on through the skirmishers, up to the
solid battle line, till courage could no more.
Against the stone-walled infantry they broke,
like the waves of a maddened sea, then back to
their lines they stumbled in shattered, scat-

tered fragments, and the dun plateau was speckled white where the chasseur horses lay. But, undismayed, they formed again in the hollow of the road, then up to the black massed infantry they charged, up to the belching guns; to front, to right, to left of them; again and yet again.

Breathless the young soldier watched, with glasses glued to his eyes—then he uttered a shout of joy. There in a hollow by the Gaulier road, two squadrons of Prussian horse in echelon were charging the flank of the cuirassiers. His regiment! The 13th Hussars; he knew by the position.

Steady! There come the foe, a gleam on their breasts of steel, their sabres pointed tierce—a shock—curses—groans—and horses rearing high. Down go the front men, as if from a lightning flash; the riderless mounts recoil upon the line, the rear rank men press on; they are falling in front in a heap—but on, on we go, with the bugles sounding charge. Victory! · Victory! The ground trembles to a thousand hoofs as, with a mighty rush, we sweep the plain.

It was Ludwig's frenzied dream, for those charging mites were full three miles away. For half an hour the battle raged, charge upon charge—and then only the white specks were left dotting the brown plateau, while the living remnants fled towards the forest of Garenne.   Brave, final gasp of a dying Empire—all for the honour of France.

The firing gradually grew less, until only the disheartened, spluttering shots of fleeing troops answered the victorious skirmishers who closed about Sedan; then, a white flag fluttered above a gate, and a Bavarian officer rode towards the town to summon a beaten army to surrender. Meanwhile, the declining sun spread over the valley its rays of burnished gold; a pillar of dense grey vapour floated above the shambles of Bazeilles, and from two burning houses in Sedan dense clouds of bluish smoke arose, like incense from an altar of despair.   Meanwhile, the princelings on the hillside were eating a luncheon of chops and peas and drinking bumpers of sherry and claret—the guests of an Emperor-to-be at the grave of an Empire dead.

In the valley below a wretched man sat writing in his heart's blood: "Not having been able to die at the head of my troops, there is nothing left to me but to place my sword in Your Majesty's hands," while in the street outside his windows the tumbrils of the wounded rumbled amid a seething, surging horde of fugitives.

Ludwig watched the Grand Dukes and the

Highnesses eating, drinking, laughing while the royal host did the honours of the *al fresco* board. His heart filled with sadness. Poor France! home of his childhood days—he loved her yet—and, alas, somewhere to the southward beyond those bluish hills was Marcelle.

He arose and walked alone along the hill crest, but he no longer heard the faint and intermittent rifle shots, the laughter and the clinking glasses. He was thinking of that grey day between the lines and the words she had spoken: "I am a traitor to France; for, Ludwig, I love you!"

The hoofs of a cavalcade clattered behind, but he did not look up.

"Ludwig!" shouted a voice and Egerton swerved his horse aside.

"Guy," he called, with a thrill of joy—Egerton at headquarters and recovered from his wound! He must have reported that morning. Beyond rode the Crown Prince. Ludwig's heels flew together and his hand to "Salute," as his Chief and the galloping staff drew their sweating mounts up standing.

The feast of the mighty was over, and the Crown Prince joined his royal father. Bismarck and Moltke were with the King, and the great War Minister, von Roon, as well—guile, strategy and method, an unmatched triumvirate,—and as they chatted the Bavarian officer who had gone to Sedan rode up the hillside and reported to the King. The staff crowded around, eager to hear the news—then a murmur of joy ran along the hill crest: The Emperor was in Sedan, a *parlementaire* was coming from the town, there would be no more fighting. The victorious monarch turned to his officers: "It is a great victory," he exclaimed; then to his soldier son he said: "I thank thee for thy share in it," and the Crown Prince kissed his father's hand.

Their triumph another's downfall: did they think of another father and another son, Ludwig wondered. Von Moltke touched his royal master's fingers to his lips, then the King grasped the Iron Chancellor's hand and together they stepped aside to converse in low, inaudible tones, while the pretentious Grand Dukes and Highnesses, who had been ignored, were left to nurse their nettled pride.

Egerton joined Ludwig and they strolled along the hillside away from the crowd.

"I can't tell you how glad I am to see you, old fellow," Ludwig exclaimed.

"I'm damned glad to be here," the Englishman grunted, "the hospital was a beastly hole."

There were a thousand things Ludwig wished

to say—but his thoughts crowded upon each other so rapidly that for a time he walked beside his friend in silence. During the long forced marches when the Crown Prince was outflanking MacMahon's doomed army and cutting off its retreat Egerton had been always on his mind—when Marcelle did not fill all his thoughts. But Egerton had been with her that night on the Cursaal terrace and again in the Mundat-Wald when Marcelle had saved their lives; so, in a way, the Englishman was linked with her in his recollection.

Now that the fighting was over, for a time at least, Egerton thought the moment opportune to ask a question, and he did it with characteristic bluntness.

"I dare say it's no affair of mine, old chap—but I'd like to know about your pretty cousin. I heard all about her playing the rôle of Joan of Arc. Did you see her again after Wissembourg?"

"Yes," Ludwig said, rather stiffly, "I was detailed to escort her back to the French lines."

"Not a bad detail, I fancy," smiled the Englishman.

Ludwig did not answer and the blunt soldier picked up a handful of pebbles and began to hurl them down the hillside towards the beleaguered town.   Finally he turned to his friend.

"Ludwig," he said; "that girl's a thorough-bred and if I know anything about women she loves you."

Ludwig could not restrain a smile.

"I shall not question your knowledge."

"Then it's true," said the Englishman eagerly.

For a moment Ludwig ploughed furrows in the loose earth with the toe of his big cavalry boot.

"Guy," he answered finally, "I'm the hap-piest man in two armies.   If it weren't for this hateful war——"

"You'd be the happiest man in the world," and the big - hearted *Chevau-léger* grasped his friend's hand: "By Jove, but I'm glad!" he cried.

"I oughtn't to have told you," said Ludwig, "but I had to tell someone."

Egerton stroked his moustache for a moment.

"What's the use of having a pal," he answered, "if you can't talk out to him what you think— By Jove, I thought at one time that little red - haired actress would end by making an ass of you——"

"That little red-haired actress," thought

Ludwig, and the memory of that night at Ems came back in vivid colours to his mind—her face in the mirror, the dreamy eyes, the curving lips half parted, the subtle perfume. Then she stood beside him on the balcony and whispered—in a low, trembling voice: "It is the way a woman feels—until—until it is too late."

"Guy," he said, "that little actress is a good sort. A man might go a long way and fare worse."

"Rot," said the Englishman, "I know them, and they're all alike."

Ludwig felt the warm blood tingle through him, but he had the good sense to keep his thoughts to himself.

"Guy," he said suddenly, "you remember that fellow D'Arblay?"

"Not a bad chap," mused Egerton.

"You may know a lot about women—but your judgment of men is not worth that," and Ludwig snapped his fingers.

"I say, that's rather frank."

"Then let me tell you," Ludwig went on. "You remember the bet we made. Benedetti interfered with the settlement, but I'd have won it because I'm an amateur card-sharper; and because I am, I caught that fellow cheating you."

"You're dreaming, Ludwig," laughed the Englishman, "I've played cards all my life."

"Nevertheless, we had a frank discussion on the subject and if it hadn't been for Marguerite Clairon I might not be here. She caught his arm just as he was hurling a carafe at my head."

"The devil you say," exclaimed Egerton.

"Yes, and he acknowledged that he was cheating, and it was he who sent you the five thousand thalers."

The Englishman stared at him in amazement. "Why didn't you tell me this before?" he asked.

"I shouldn't have told you now," said Ludwig quietly, "if you had not spoken as you did about Marguerite Clairon. She behaved like a trump that night. I tell you they're not all alike."

Egerton twirled his red moustache furiously for a moment, then he screwed his glass into his eye and scowled.

"I'd like to meet that beggar face to face."

"No, Guy, the quarrel is mine," said Ludwig, "and I have a feeling that some day we shall have it out. I saw a look on his face that night I shall not forget."

"I hope that I shall have the luck to meet him first," Egerton muttered.

"No, Guy, no," Ludwig said.

"Rot," said the Englishman. "Didn't you save my life?"

Men say little at such moments. It is enough to feel that mysterious grandeur of the soul which is friendship; so for a time they stood together in silence—and meanwhile Ludwig's thoughts wandered again to Marcelle. Marguerite was but an incident.

While the shadows lengthened in the valley and the crimson sun sank behind the western hills, a little group of horsemen rode slowly towards them, and a white flag trembled in the golden light of the dying day.

"There comes the *parlementaire*," said Ludwig at last. "Ah! if it only means peace!"

"By Jove, it ought to," cried Egerton, "if we've bagged the Emperor!"

"You don't know France," said the German thoughtfully. "This war has only begun."

Then together they wandered towards the group of officers upon the hilltop.

Some giant cuirassiers trotted up astride their ponderous chargers to serve as a guard of honour, and, as the white flag fluttered up the hillside, the medal-decked officials ranged themselves behind the King. A hundred yards or more away, the little group of horsemen halted while an officer rode forward to report that the *parlementaire* was with General Reille, Napoleon's adjutant, bearing an autograph letter from the Emperor to His Majesty the King of Prussia.

The aged King stepped to the front alone, and the Crown Prince followed, together with Bismarck, Moltke and Roon: Then Ludwig saw a General of France, with bared head bowed in shame, toil slowly up the hill, with his master's letter of submission held in his trembling hand.   Swordless he came, with blouse unbuttoned, like a faltering figure of despair, and, as his grey head bent before the King, Ludwig's heart throbbed a wild discord of triumph and pity.

IV

OMNIA VANITAS

From the inundated low lands along the Meuse a mist was rising, and the morning air had the first chill of autumn. Ludwig dropped the reins upon his horse's neck and let him walk along the tree-lined highway. He had galloped at dawn with orders to the Bavarian headquarters—he had seen the battle-field, and he wanted to forget the smoking ruins of Bazeilles, the horrible, discoloured faces of the dead. To think that men should call it noble to kill, kill for the honour of nations!

Ra - ta - ra! the bugles sounded from a near-by cantonment; *ra-ta-ra-ta!* they echoed from the plains beyond Sedan, then a battery rumbled into line upon the hill beside him, and long, slim guns, unlimbered, were pointed towards the town. He thought of grim, ascetic Moltke, with those hawk-like eyes. The flanges of the iron vise were being tightened; the crushed and bleeding army of Chalons must choose: capitulation or annihilation.

Finally he stopped his horse and let him

browse upon the bank beside the road. He was thinking now of a shadowy room in far-off Paris, where the light fell soft upon the draperies and manikins, the easels and the unfinished sketches—a room in the realm of sympathy, where the soul was monarch, and the courtiers were fancies and day-dreams. Why was he a soldier? he asked himself. The answer was, "*noblesse oblige.*"

Then he heard the sound of hoofs, and looking up he saw the American general, erect and soldierly, riding like a part of his horse, and beside him an officer in plain blue tunic and chasseur cap, with two gold leaves upon his shoulder straps.

The little General reined in his horse. Ludwig caught the look of those quick, shrewd eyes, and his hand flew to his forehead in "Salute."

"I wonder if it's safe to tackle this officer in French," he heard him say to his companion.

A smile trembled on Ludwig's lip.

"It's safe to tackle me in English, sir."

General Sheridan laughed.

"Since Gravelotte I take no chances. A squad of soldiers held me up there, and were going to shoot me on the spot. My forage cap and my goatee," he added, with an indicating gesture to the tuft upon his chin, "have a

French cut, I guess, and, as I couldn't speak German, and they couldn't speak English, and I daren't speak French, I thought surely my hour had come, till an officer of the General Staff came along and rescued me."

"The hero of Winchester deserves a better fate, sir."

Sheridan looked at Ludwig closely. "Are you an American?" he asked.

"My mother was, sir."

"Your name?"

"Captain, the Count von Leun-Walram, aide-de-camp to General H. R. H. the Crown Prince."

"General Forsyth, my aide-de-camp," said Sheridan, turning towards his companion.

Ludwig and the officer saluted.

"We've lost our carriage," continued the General. "I guess they've pressed it into the hospital service."

"Can I help you to find it, sir?" asked Ludwig.

"You can help us look; besides, I'm mighty glad to find someone who speaks English."

They rode on towards Sedan, while the General plied Ludwig with questions; and fell to telling stories of his own campaigning—Indian fights in the far West and incidents of the Civil War. Ludwig was charmed by his frank, straightforward manner and keen insight; he felt that the little soldier was a man among men.

They passed a corpse by the roadside—a Turco with his jaw shot away, staring to heaven with his filmy eyes. It made Ludwig think of Wissembourg. Perhaps that Turco had been one of Marcelle's defenders.

The General's quick eye caught the young man's look of pain.

"The older you grow, my young friend," he said, "the worse such sights will seem. You will never get used to the horror of a battle-field."

Ludwig was silent a moment.

"I was at Bazeilles this morning," he said finally. "The slaughter there was terrible, sir. I shall never forget those charred and ruined houses; the Bavarian and French dead, heaped together in the streets; the odour of burning flesh. The miserable inhabitants had fought side by side with the marines, and the maddened Bavarians, when they stormed the place, stood the poor inhabitants against the walls and shot them like dogs—men whose only crime had been to fight for the protection of their homes. Is such cruelty necessary, sir, even in war?"

Sheridan's face grew thoughtful, and his lips set together firmly.

"War is war," he answered, "and ununi-
formed inhabitants who take up arms must be
summarily dealt with, else war becomes a campaign against guerrillas, the mere hunting
down of hidden assassins. The proper strategy
consists first in inflicting as telling blows as
possible upon the enemy's army, and then in
causing the inhabitants so much suffering that
they must long for peace, and force their government to demand it. The people must be
left nothing but their eyes to weep with over
the war."

Ludwig looked at the great commander in
surprise. This view of war seemed, at first
sight, so heartless, so unnecessarily brutal; but
the more he thought, the more he realised that
the General was right. It was war from a soldier's point of view. His heart, however, went
out in pity towards those poor, misguided
people of Bazeilles.

Meanwhile, Sheridan was examining the
batteries being hurried into line about the
town, and he inquired the reason for this
activity.

"The Emperor had relinquished his command," answered Ludwig, "and only offered to
surrender his own sword. General Wimpffen
has not yet signed the capitulation."

"Oh, I see—those guns are being placed in

position in case he is foolish enough to try to break through.

"Yes, sir," said Ludwig. "Poor Wimpffen was at our headquarters most of the night. He pleaded for the honours of war, and he pleaded for himself; for he had only arrived the day before the battle, and when MacMahon was wounded he had been forced to take command when the battle was already lost, and now he was asked to put his signature to an unconditional surrender. In a frenzy of despair, he returned to Sedan threatening to continue the fight."

"And meanwhile, Moltke is not caught napping," mused Sheridan, with a significant glance along the German lines.

At the picket line near Sedan they drew rein, while Ludwig made inquiries about the lost vehicle. While they were there a carriage rumbled through the gate of the town and drove towards them along the highway.

Ludwig glanced up curiously. A strange sight in war-time, he thought—that imposing barouche, with the gold-laced liveries and three French officers galloping beside it. As the carriage passed he saw the letter "N" surmounted by an imperial crown upon the brass-tipped harness. Within sat four French Generals with white-gloved hands resting upon their sword hilts. One was smoking a cigarette. His head had dropped upon his breast, and his long grey hair fell from under his crimson képi upon the collar of a military cloak.

That heavy, silent face, with the puffed underlids to the dreamy, watery eyes and the drawn corners of the mouth under stiffly waxed moustachios—that face of ghastly pallor! Ludwig glanced at his companions.

"The Emperor!" whispered Sheridan.

Meanwhile the soldiers by the roadside stared in stolid wonder at their fallen foe; and the barouche rumbled on along the tree-lined road towards Donchery.

Eager to witness events, Ludwig and the two Americans turned and followed. A mile or more beyond, the imperial carriage stopped, and again they saw the wretched Emperor staring down at the white roadway with those sunken, lustreless eyes, a look of silent agony in his pale, drawn face. Then they heard the clatter of hoofs, and the giant form of Bismarck loomed through the dust. The Chancellor dismounted and strode towards the barouche. As the heels of his cavalry boots clicked together and his hand swung brusquely to the visor of his cap, the Emperor glanced up as though rudely awakened from a dream; and his face blanched with a look of fright, then he hurriedly removed his képi, while Bismarck snatched off his white forage cap as though reluctant to disregard the Prussian regulations about uncovering the uniform. After an exchange of words, which Ludwig could not hear, the Chancellor mounted his horse again and the carriage drove on.

By the roadside near Donchery, between a clump of green bushes and the white blossoms of a potato field, stood a little yellow cottage, and there the captive Emperor alighted to wait until the King of Prussia should deign to receive his sword. After he had been for a time with Bismarck within the house, he came into the garden and sat upon a humble weaver's cane-seat chair smoking interminable cigarettes, while his big arch-enemy tortured him with coldly civil diplomatic cruelty until his colleague of war should have given the final twist to the iron vise. Lean, shrivelled Moltke came at last, and it was safe to let the imperial captive meet the gentle-hearted King —safe because the hapless Wimpffen had agreed to the surrender, and mercy to the fallen could not avail.

After the Chief of the General Staff had ridden away, the Chancellor's big boots clanked down the path before the cottage, and Bismarck, seeing the little American soldier, stopped to greet him.

"Did you notice, General," he asked, "how the Emperor started when we met?"

"Yes, Your Excellency," answered Sheridan; "I noticed it."

"Well, it must have been due to my manner, not my words, for I said: 'I salute Your Majesty just as I would my King.' "

What irony! thought Ludwig, as he watched the Chancellor swing into the saddle.

"You had better go to the Château Bellevue, General," he heard him say. "The formal surrender takes place there." Then the bluff giant galloped off towards Donchery.

Staff officers came and went, filling the road with their dust, while the silent Emperor paced to and fro beside the white blossoms of the potato field, his gold-leafed cap aslant upon his bended head, his white-gloved hands twisting together behind his stooping back—and still a cigarette between his lips. What must his thoughts have been? Boulogne, Paris, Solferino, Mexico—and now Sedan. Exile, adventurer, President, Emperor—and now to be an exile again. To Ludwig, gazing in pity at that broken man, so pale, so gentle, it seemed beyond the ken of reason that in one life could be such adversity, such triumph, and at the last such misery.

The Chancellor rode up finally with an escort of bearded troopers in glittering corselets and tunics of white, and when the Emperor had entered his carriage, the cavalcade moved on towards Bellevue; while Bismarck, resplendent in the clean new uniform he had donned, with a steel-spiked helmet a-tilt upon his massive head, rode proud and triumphant beside the imperial barouche — hale, crafty Hercules of modern times, bringing the Gallic boar to his master's feet.

Ludwig followed in the dust of the escort and saw the meeting with the King at Bellevue, saw the pale Emperor's eyes fill with tears; then he carried a basket of decorations while the Crown Prince distributed rewards among his exultant officers. It was a day of eager faces and loud huzzas, as the King and his victorious Generals rode in triumph from camp to camp; but it was a day of sadness for the young Hussar, for Marcelle and her bleeding France were always in his thoughts.

At last he got his orders. All day long reports had been coming to headquarters of a French division falling back from Mezières in the hilly, wooded country to the westward. Rheims was the apparent objective of the retreating French—large bodies of the enemy were reported assembling there,—so towards evening orders were sent to the front that the 6th corps and the two cavalry divisions which had been hanging on the enemy's flank should march direct upon the city.

When later it was known at headquarters that the retreating division had turned to the northward at Saulces, Ludwig was, despatched with orders to General von Rheinbaben, whose cavalry had been last engaged, not to retire on Rheims, but to keep in touch with the French column and inform the commanders of the 6th corps and the 6th cavalry division of the enemy's movements.

Twenty miles or more through the night, in the face of a blinding rain—all in a soldier's life, and he made the best of it. Von Rhein-baben had been at Tourteron in the morning, but he thought he must have gone to the front when his troops were engaged, so he took the road along the railway, hoping to find the General somewhere in the neighborhood of Saulces. He came upon detachments of Uhlans and cuirassiers—men of the 6th cavalry division. They had kept up a running fight all day; the French were at Corny la Ville and Bois Notre Dame, they thought. General Rheinbaben's headquarters? The question was

beyond them, so Ludwig rode on into the
storm until he met a patrol of Hussars—an
outpost of the 5th division. The bivouac of
their squadron was near at hand, they said,
and he turned aside into the forest.

Huddled about the spluttering remnants of a
fire he found a group of bedraggled officers in
rain-soaked cloaks.   Gratefully accepting a
biscuit and a swig of brandy from these
brothers-in-arms, he munched his hard tack
and tried to gather information. The French
were at Novion Porcien, not a mile away;
Rheinbaben's headquarters were either at
Tourteron or Le Chênois; Ludwig's best
route was to cut into the highway and turn to
the left at the first *carrefour*, where there was
an outpost of Brunswick Hussars.

After his steaming horse had caught new
breath he swung into the saddle again. There
had been a lull in the storm, but the rain began
to fall again in torrents.   He could not see
beyond the horse's ears—he could only trust
to the animal's instinct.   Finally he entered a
highway. He thought it was the road he had
left to visit the bivouac, and that soon he
would reach the *carrefour;* but in the blinding
storm he had taken the wrong path in the
woods and so passed the last outpost of the
Prussian cavalry.

The cold rain beat upon his face; his clothes clung soaking to his shivering body; his tired knees pressed tremblingly against the slippery saddle—and meanwhile the weary beast slumped on through the mud. To give himself courage, he spoke a cheering word to the horse. The animal pricked up his ears, and it made him feel less miserable. Alone in the darkness and the storm, with those huge soughing trees and the pattering, pattering rain; it took all his courage to go on. No, it was not courage, he thought, but the knowledge that he must—must, because it was a soldier's duty. What a weak, insignificant atom of life he was, after all. Only a breathing particle; only one of a million of monads in the pitiless organism of an army. Suddenly, out of the night might come the knife-thrust of a franc-tireur—an order undelivered, a body to rot by the roadside; who would know, and who would care? Would Marcelle? The word "Yes" fluttered faintly in his breast; he seemed to see her brown eyes tremble over him.

"Marcelle!" he called aloud. "Marcelle!"

"*Qui va là?*" came gruff through the darkness.

His horse crouched trembling, and dazed he started from his reverie.

"Halt!" cried a voice. He saw a dark figure, and it became the thought of an instant to ride the man down and reach the Prussian lines he supposed were beyond. Into the horse's side he dug his spurs; his head bent low upon the animal's neck.

The sentry jumped from under the hoofs; a shot rang screeching through the storm, but unharmed he dashed ahead.

Shadowy forms sprang up from the roadside and tried to stop his horse; he heard cries and shots behind him. Were they francs-tireurs? Were the French advancing under cover of the storm? Had he passed the *carrefour?* A jumble of excited thoughts surged through his brain; his heart thumped wildly against his side; deeper into the horse's flanks went the spurs. Then the road bent suddenly and the lights of a village gleamed ahead. He heard a French bugle sound "To arms," but he could not stop the maddened horse; he was in a road between two walls, and he could not turn; so, into a winding street he dashed, where rain-drenched stones glistened between two rows of lights.

Men sprang towards him from the doorways; he heard shouts and cries of "Halt!" in the language of the foe, then, suddenly across the road ahead he saw the glint of bayonets.

He threw his weight upon the reins; the horse slid and stumbled over the slippery pavement; he tried to turn him, but a hand had seized the bridle. In the frenzy of the moment he drew his pistol and fired—then a gun flashed almost in his face.

He felt a quick, stinging pain; the earth sprang up; the lights danced before his eyes—he was falling—slipping. The night grew red, the earth grew red, and in an overpowering moment vague images crowded upon him—his mother, his aged father, and, floating in a crimson haze before his dim and quivering eyes, the face of Marcelle. Was this the end, he wondered—was this dying? Then a terrible weight fell upon his leg, and, without pain or regret, he became unconscious.

"Will he live; oh, Doctor, will he live?"

He heard the words as in a dream. Indistinct forms moved about the room; a woman's face bent over him; a cool, refreshing liquid touched his lips.

"Where am I?" he murmured.

"Hush!" came in a voice he seemed to remember vaguely. "You are too weak to speak."

The room faded before his eyes. He felt

them carry him away, felt the jolting, jolting of a cart, and a terrible aching pain—then black grew the night, black the unknown into which he sank.

V

THE BADGE OF NOBILITY

On the table beside the bed were phials and bandages and the room was strange, but it was clean and white, and through the open casement warm sunlight streamed. Ludwig tried to raise himself upon an elbow, but he felt a sharp agonising pain; the room swayed and grew indistinct, and he closed his eyes.

A woman's step fell softly beside him, but in his delirium he murmured the name of Marcelle.

His soul fought long within its shattered prison to escape, yet the thin walls held until the fluttering pulse beat stronger and the watcher by the bedside knew that a life had been spared.

Again he saw the clean, white room and a woman watching beside him. Yes, he remembered that moment in far-off Ems when he stood with her upon a balcony, and a single star shone bright above the mountains; but that dress of grey, with the Red Cross on the sleeve? His eyes grew dim, his throat was afire.

"Water," he called.

She placed a tumbler to his lips and he drank—drank; then he felt a cool hand on his burning forehead, and he looked up and smiled. That face with the dreamy, mysterious eyes!

"Why are you here?" he murmured.

"Don't ask. When you are stronger I shall tell you."

When he looked again a man stood beside his bedside—a stranger with a wise grey head, a kindly smile.

"Those army surgeons did their work well," he heard him say. "Poor chap, it's lucky the bullet didn't pass one centimètre higher. Apparently it just grazed the subclavian artery, which of course would have been hopeless from the start. It is apparent that the fellow who fired that shot was at close range, for one seldom sees a more lacerated and ugly wound than this. The hæmorrhage must have been profuse, and those men were clever to find that bulging in the back which indicated the proximity of the bullet. Even then, when his temperature rose and he refused to rally—I think we must thank your nursing, my dear."

"And my prayers," sighed the girl.

It seemed all vague and strange, like an unfinished dream, and when they were alone again he watched her moving quietly from place to place, putting the little white room aright, watering the crimson flowers upon the window ledge.

"Marguerite!" he murmured. "Marguerite Clairon!"

Her sad face lighted up. He had remem, bered her name.

The hours became a day, the day another, and then, when the shadows in the room were dimmed, he whispered softly.

"I am stronger; won't you tell me?"

She drew a chair beside the bed—the fading sunlight tinged her white face golden.

"It was terrible there in Paris—the excitement, the mobs, the despair; and then my life seemed so futile."

It was the rich, soft voice he remembered.

"*Quel succès!*" she laughed suddenly. "La belle Clairon an ambulance nurse with Vinoy's corps. The company gave me a supper; the papers were full of me—*quelle réclame!*"

"I was with Blanchard's division," she went quickly on, in an altered tone. "We were hurried on to Mezières, to reinforce Mac-Mahon. We arrived too late, and when we learned of the disaster of Sedan, General Vinoy, who was with us, ordered a retreat on Rethel."

"Go on," he said impatiently.

"All that day we kept up a running fight with Uhlans and cuirassiers, and then we learned towards nightfall that the enemy was at Rethel——"

"Hoffman's division!" exclaimed Ludwig eagerly.

"Our retreat to the west was cut off," she continued, "so we turned towards the north. At dusk we went into camp. The Prussians had shelled our rear guard, and we improvised a hospital at a village inn. Late that night, when I was at work among the wounded, I heard galloping and cries in the street outside and as I ran to the door I heard a shot. A horse was floundering in the mud and beside him lay a wounded Prussian—a courier, the soldiers said, and by the lantern they brought to search for despatches I recognised your face."

The sunlight had gone, and in the dusk he caught her long gaze fixed upon him.

"The surgeons said that you would die, but I told them you must live—must, because you breathed her name—the one for whom you had been waiting."

His eyes brimmed with tears, but the words he would have spoken died upon his lips— they were too inadequate.

"They said it was a waste of time, for Frenchmen needed them," she went on quickly, "but
I made them operate, and then, during the
night, we got orders to march. For fear they
should not take you I covered you with an army
overcoat and put a dead man's képi on your
head. At last, they tumbled you into a market
cart with a poor little recruit who was dying,
and I got upon the seat with the driver. The
roads were blocked with soldiers; it was raining torrents; the night was very black, but
when I saw we had turned to the north,
towards Wasigny, I formed a plan——"

"What! You knew the country?" he exclaimed in astonishment.

Her face was eager; her eyes shone and were
clear.

"When I was a child I lived here in the
Ardennes—this is my aunt's house."

He moved his lips to speak.

"Hush," she whispered, "let me tell my
story."

He smiled feebly and she went on.

"I had snatched a bottle of brandy from the
stores, and I gave it to the peasant beside me.
He drank and drank, and when his head fell
forward on his breast I took the reins. In the
rain and the darkness the soldiers did not
notice when I turned to the left near Wasigny,

or perhaps they did not care, for what was one
cart of wounded, more or less, on such a night
of agony. I stopped and listened, but I was
not followed. Ah, how my heart beat when I
saw the little white cottage of my aunt suddenly in a flash of lightning!"

He saw her stoop from above him.

"The little recruit was dead," she said in a
low, thrilled voice. "The drunken man was
still asleep, and when we carried you here I
started the horse towards home. No one
knows but my aunt and the dear old Doctor
who brought me into the world."

"You trump," he cried. "Ah, how can I
thank you?"

He caught her white hand. It was cold as
steel. He tried to kiss it.

"No, no," her lips framed, then suddenly
the great drops fell unchecked and she turned
and ran headlong from the room.

He lay for a long time in the twilight trying
to understand the devotion of this strange girl.
When she came back he had fallen asleep, and
she went to the bedside and kissed him, trembling lest he should awake. Would the other
give him her heart's blood, she wondered. He
owed his life to her—let the other look to herself. Ah, but if she conquered, he would be like
other men, he would be dragged down by her.

As she sat looking into his face, she thought
of a day at Ems when she had met him in the
colonnade beside the Cursaal. She could see
him coming towards her, erect and soldierly in
his smart blue uniform.

Smiling through the tears she could not keep
back, she unbuttoned her dress. A plain gold
locket hung by a little chain about her neck
and unfastening the clasp which held it, she
opened it and gazed long at a faded rose.

It was the Jacqueminot the little flower girl
had pinned upon his *attila* that day.

"How strange life is," she thought, "I met
him when we had not thought of meeting, and
in the impulse of the moment, he gave me this
flower. 'Until we meet again' he said—how
strange the meeting. Yet until he came I
was contented with that other life," and she
pressed the rose to her lips.

"Love," she thought; "it is only in its moments that we live at all. We forget the
physical as soon as it is gratified, but the
spiritual can never end; it must reach beyond
eternity." She paused as if standing before
a glorious revelation, yet she was mortally
afraid and sat in a sort of a dull consciousness looking into the glow of the candle which
burned beside the bed, not daring to move.

"God! Dear God," she said, "it was good

of Thee to send him to me, even if I must give him up."

She heard the door open softly, and a step upon the threshold startled her. Looking up she saw the kind face of the Doctor. She put down the locket quietly among the phials and bandages on the table beside the bed and stepped towards him with a finger on her lips.

"I did not think that you would come until morning," she whispered.

"I thought it safer to come at night," he answered, walking on tip-toe towards the bed; "francs-tireurs are in the forest of Avaux."

"Francs-tireurs," she repeated shuddering.

The Doctor gazed at the sleeping soldier.

"They shot a Prussian courier last night," he said; "they make no prisoners."

"*Mon Dieu!*" she cried out in terror. "Is there no place of safety?"

He shook his head. "To move him now would mean his death. We must wait."

"They are forming corps of francs-tireurs. A Blue Hussar may pass—" Those words ran like fire through her blood as she closed her eyes and tried not to think of an ashen face with a cold-set smile upon the lips; but her breast rose and fell like the unresting sea.

The wounded man moved uneasily upon the pillow.

"Come," whispered the Doctor, "sleep is the best medicine," and taking her hand he led her to the adjoining room.

She closed the door behind them softly.

"Doctor," she said, looking at him with large, unwavering eyes, "do the people in the village suspect?"

"My dear child," he answered. "Yesterday, when I was leaving you I thought as I turned into the high road that I saw behind a hedge a sheep-skin cap—the glimmer of a gun barrel."

"Then they are watching the house," she said, and the heart within her grew cold.

"Perhaps my old eyes did not see well," he answered in a cheerful tone. "At all events we must hope for the best."

"How long will it be before he can be moved?" she asked.

"Two weeks at least, and then it will be dangerous."

"Two weeks," she said in a voice low and trembling, "and if the house is watched already?"

"He is as safe here as anywhere else," muttered the doctor as he opened his satchel and searched for a chemist's phial he had brought, "we must wait until another Prussian column passes."

"If those francs-tireurs were not beasts," she said with a shudder; "if they fought like men."

"Every cut-throat and rascal for miles around disguised as a patriot," mused the Doctor; and having found the package he sought he closed the bag. "It'll do no good to worry," he went on," our task is to get our Prussian well enough to be moved."

"But not well enough to fight," she said, trying hard to smile. "That would be treason."

"No danger, my dear— It'll be months before he can be fit for duty. The war will not last that long."

"Months," she thought, "and then?"

"Come, don't look so doleful," he laughed. "When the war is over La belle Clairon goes back in triumph; her Prussian lover comes. Paris hears the romance and falls at her feet. Look at the bright side, my dear."

In the dim light he did not see that her eyes were like dead fire.

"Come, here's a tonic to build him up," he continued, handing her the phial.

She glared at the red label.

"Arsenic," he said. "The dose is two drops in a wine-glass full of water three times a day, increasing a drop each day until you are

administering four drops. Take care, ten drops
mean death."

"Arsenic?" she repeated with a questioning
look.

"The best tonic in the world," he laughed,
"for depleted blood or a misspent life, but be
careful not to take it for your complexion."

"My aunt might," she smiled, "so I'll keep
it locked up. Two grains you say?"

"Yes, three times a day, increasing one each
day, remember. And now I must be off," he
added, turning up the collar of his coat, for
the mountain air had the chill of autumn.

"Good-bye, my dear," he said, touching her
hand to his lips.

Impulsively she threw her arms about his
neck and kissed him.

"Doctor," she cried, "dear Doctor, how can
I ever repay you?"

The old physician blushed and beamed.

"If I've done my little Marguerite a good
turn I ask no thanks. We are very proud of
you here in the Ardennes. Those of us who
are not priests or old women," he added
laughing.

She placed her hand upon the door latch—
"All who are not priests or old women," she
thought, then suddenly she turned and put out
the lamp.

"The francs-tireurs," she whispered.

"Very wise, my dear,' he said, and he stooped and kissed her again.

She listened to his steps until she could no longer hear them, then, closing the door, she returned to the room where the wounded man still slept. Stepping to the bureau she placed the phial under lock and key. "My complexion," she thought. "Shall I ever care?"

At the closing of the drawer Ludwig awoke.

He saw her pale and beautiful in the dim candle light and he tried to think, but his head was feverish and for a moment he lay watching her with a dull, unmoving gaze.

"Marguerite," he called faintly.

She turned at the sound of his voice and came towards him.

"Water," he murmured.

She held a tumbler to his lips.

"You are tired, *chéri*," she said, "I'm afraid I talked too much to-day."

"Why are you so kind to me?" he asked.

He felt her hand upon his forehead, smoothing his hair softly for a moment.

"Because—because I can't help it," she said with a little nervous laugh.

"Because you are an angel," he whispered.

She felt the gaze of his eyes fixed upon her; but she was thinking of a scented room where the candles flickered before a mirror, and she seemed to see him bending towards her, flushed and trembling.

"You forget, Ludwig; you are waiting."

"Waiting," he repeated with a puzzled look.

"For the best the world can offer," she answered.

He understood but vaguely, for the fever burned in his temples.

"What is that?" he asked, his eyes upon the open locket beside the bandages and phials.

She grew red as the rose and stood with her eyelids drooping.

"I said I should keep it."

Then, trembling she snatched it away, afraid lest he had understood.

VI

ONE PLAY AND ONE ENDING

During the weeks while he lay convalescing
Marguerite seemed to Ludwig like the sunlight of those grey September days. She filled
the room with brightness when she came and
left it cold and cheerless when she went. Day
by day her face grew sweeter, and when she
sat beside the bed, happy in the consciousness
of being near him, the "crimson wing of conquest" seemed to flutter far away. What mat-
tered it to him that an empire had fallen and
guerre à l'outrance was the clamour of France,
when the radiance of her eyes filled the little
room?

More than once a cross of red upon a
woman's sleeve has seemed a badge of true
nobility, and more than once a wounded man
has come to think that love's ideal is near to
being love's recipient. Not that Ludwig had
failed in thoughts of Marcelle—she was his
faith, his promise—but he could not fail in
gratitude to her who had nursed him back to
life.

Poisonous darts in the quiver of the little

naked god are gratitude and propinquity, and
often the one when quickened by the other
will play a rôle not unakin to love. He would
not have confessed it, even to himself, but during those days when he lay recovering, Marcelle, though still his faith, remained within
the shadow of his heart, while, rejoicing for
the moment in its sunshine, was Marguerite
Clairon, devoted in a hundred other ways than
words.

Often he tried to make her tell him of herself, but she only laughed. She knew that she
was too much a creature of impulse to talk of
self without revealing her love for him. But
one day in the twilight when he had grown
strong enough to sit propped up by pillows in
a big arm-chair, he asked her suddenly why
she had deserted France to nurse a wounded
Prussian.

She shrugged her pretty shoulders. "I wish
to study new sensations," she said. "I wish
to know how it would feel to love an enemy.
When I return to Paris I shall abandon farces
and vaudevilles to play Camille in Corneille's
Horace. I expect to score a big success."

"Then I am but a subject on the operating
table of your heart?"

"Who knows?" she laughed. "Some day I
may write a play, and you shall be the hero.

In the play I shall love you, and gratitude will make you think you care for me, and we shall go away together. Then, for a brief moment, I shall be happy."

"Only in the play," he said.

He was close, and she could see the sudden light in his eyes.

"Ah, but you will leave me," she went on quickly, "and the other will forgive. Then you will forget, and I shall die, like *La Dame aux Caméllias*, only no Armand will come."

He sat very still with his eyes turned towards the window. He could see the brownish hills and the sere forest of Avaux. He was thinking of Marcelle and the day they had ridden together up the mountain-side towards Lembach, while the brooks and gullies droned to the music of swollen waters and the Uhlans with their pennoned lances clattered up the road ahead.

"All my life I have waited for you, Marcelle," he said to her then, "and I mean to try to do something each day I live to make you realise I value the only thing in life worth having."

He turned and looked at Marguerite, sitting beside him in the twilight.

"If to enjoy every moment she is with me," he thought; "if to begrudge every moment she is away is to be untrue to Marcelle—then I must have failed to keep my promise."

"Please tell me the truth," he asked suddenly. "What made you go with Vinoy's corps? I know it was not for new sensations or *réclame*."

She turned her eyes away and looked through the window towards the bleak hills, now shadowy in the dusk of evening.

"You guessed the truth the night we met," she said. "He was a poet and when he touched his lyre my soul was thrilled. He spent a summer here in the Ardennes, and when he left he took me to Paris. He wrote plays and he thought I had talent so he gave me an opening on the stage. But a poet must have new strings for his lyre and when the end came, I went on living somehow. I won my little triumph in the only arena open to a woman when she has picked herself up stunned and bruised, but my soul was lost somewhere."

She managed to hold back the tears and the words she dared not speak, and after a moment she said in a lower tone.

"Until one night in Paris when I had been dining with the friends you met at Ems a regiment passed beneath the window, and somehow the sight of those poor fellows marching to the front made my life seem so futile and vapid and the air with its odour of perfume and smoke seemed to stifle me. When I thought of the wounded I longed to do something to help my country and—and—when I left those hateful people I went to a church—'' Her eyes had a pleading, hunted look. "Oh, can't you understand without my telling you?"

He touched the softness of her hair. "Sympathy is a poor, abused word, dear," he said, "but now when I want to tell you all, I feel, it is the only one I know."

"It is a blessed word when you long to hear it," and a smile tried hard to tremble on her lips.

"God was very kind to me, Marguerite," he said, "when he sent you with Vinoy's corps."

She looked up trembling.

"It must have been for her sake, Ludwig. I saw you with her that morning in the park at Ems when the King and Benedetti met, and when I heard her name upon your lips, I prayed that you might live."

He could not speak.

"Tell me about her," she whispered after a moment.

He told her the story and she listened to the end.

"I shall never write the play," she said,

when he had finished, "because it is already written."

"But the end?" he asked

"The Doctor says you will not be able to fight again. You will pass through Alsace on your way to Prussia and stop at a grey château; a stern parent will relent and the curtain fall upon a beautiful drama!"

"But you, Marguerite?"

"I shall go back to the vaudevilles and the farces without the one brief moment."

At the thought that she had said too much her cheeks burned and her eyes dropped. "But I am not in the play," she continued quickly. "The nurse is broad comedy and the first old woman always plays the part. I shall have to search for a more congenial rôle."

"A miracle play, Marguerite," he said in a deep breath, "and you shall wear the white robes of a saint."

She gazed for a moment through the window. Night had fallen while they were talking and the moon hung large and silvery through an opening in the trees. The stars were thickly spread in the sapphire blue above.

"And if it should be true," she thought, "and we were to go away together—a moment of happiness for me—then, misery for both."

"No," her lips said at last. "There is but one play and one ending."

He looked up suddenly. Her face was white and beautiful beneath the coiled masses of her hair. and he remembered a moment when he had stood before a mirror—watching her eyes with their curling lashes and arching brows. How gentle her face had grown since then, he thought.

Yes, he had breathed the scented air that night, and with a courage born of despair beaten back a wild flood of passion. But now she stood before him purified—must he wage a new fight, and this time with love?

VII

THE FACE AT THE WINDOW

October came and the Doctor said that if a
Prussian column passed, Ludwig might leave
the little white room, though he could not go
back to the clamour of war. He will be in-
valided, Marguerite thought, and on his way
to Germany he will stop at a château in the
forests of the Vosges.

When the Doctor left she waited in the doorway listening to the rumbling of his gig upon
the highway. For a time she stood, afraid to
move, and slowly a temptation mastered her.
Closing her eyes, she saw a room with gilded
chairs and damask curtains, not in far-off Ems
but in Paris; when he stood behind her he
stooped and took her in his arms, and it seemed
as if their souls were laid bare. But the
image of purity she had worshipped from afar
was shattered in fragments of clay. In the
temple of a pagan goddess stood an idol of
flesh and blood. "Ah, no," she thought.
"I have been in the temple before and I know
the feverish rites. Better the image, though it
stand upon a pedestal beyond my reach."

"Marguerite," she heard him calling from the other room.

"Yes, *chéri*," she answered, and went to him.

"What did the doctor say?" he asked.

"That when a Prussian column passes—" but she could not finish.

He took her hand.

"Marguerite dear," he said, "if I could only find the words to tell you——"

"Don't try, Ludwig," she cried, "please don't try!" The sunlight caught her white face and glistened on her trembling lips.

Not since that night in the twilight had they spoken of themselves; but, if he did not speak, it was because he understood.

She stood for a moment by the window and her eyes wandered beyond to the forest of Avaux.

"If the Prussians would only come," she sighed.

"Am I such a burden that you cannot wait?"

"I was thinking of the francs-tireurs."

"The francs-tireurs?" he repeated with a questioning look.

"They are in the forest of Avaux."

"Well," he asked, "what is that to us?"

She turned to him an anxious face.

"One evening when the Doctor left he thought he saw some one watching the house

Since then he has always come at night through the garden. To-day he drove up by daylight in his gig."

"Not an unusual way for a doctor to make a visit," he smiled.

"But if they should know that you are here," and a feeling of dread crept through her.

"A French prison instead of Germany," he said.

"They make no prisoners," she answered.

"You can't frighten me," he laughed, "for even francs-tireurs would not harm a defenseless, wounded man."

She knew her fears were too vague for him to understand, and in time she began to believe they were unfounded.

A week went by. He grew stronger day by day and could walk at last across the room; but his arm hung helpless in a sling and it would be months before he could regain its use completely.

Though the Doctor came and went by daylight in his gig he assured Marguerite that this very boldness would disarm suspicion.

"But the village must know you have a patient," she said.

"My patient is Marguerite Clairon, and she lies ill of small-pox contracted in the hospital where she was nursing wounded soldiers."

"A second Vidocq for artifice," she laughed as she kissed him.

"I can drive up in comfort," he chuckled, "without scratching my hands on the thorns; meanwhile the priests and old women are praying for your soul. '

The Doctor never spoke to Ludwig except professionally.   To save a wounded man's life was a duty, to keep a charming woman's secret was a delight—but talk to a Prussian! —*nom de Dieu*, that was treason.

When he had gone Marguerite told Ludwig the story and together they laughed at the priests and old women.   Then one day at nightfall, they heard the blare of trumpets down the highway towards the South.

"Prussian cavalry!" he said.

"So soon! So soon!" she whispered.

He saw the look of her startled eyes, heard the quickened play of her breath, caught her hand and held it close.

"I shall never forget what you have been to me.   Never—never!"

She drew her hand away and brushed back the tears.   When he dared look she stood by the window beautiful in the dying light.   On the road beyond were Uhlan pennons waving.

"Don't, Marguerite," he cried.   "Don't

think that I do not care." He went and stood beside her.

"Ah, Ludwig, I knew the moment must come, but it has seemed vague and far off—like death."

The sun was fading behind the hills as he gazed at the passing squadron, the splendid chargers, the shining arms, the soldier faces ruddy in the crimson light.

"All that men care for but love," he said, "and that is an afterthought with most of them."

"There is nothing in the world but Love," she cried impulsively. "Fame, Glory, Money—they are nothing, nothing."

And in that moment her eyes burnt through him, and he saw a woman's imprisoned passion.

"Shall we write the play?" he whispered in the impulse of a feeling he had never thought would come.

A colour of deep rose glowed over her; she listened to a voice whispering, "Marguerite, he belongs to you."

He waited, for he was seized with a sudden terror of himself. His will was being taken from him; yet when the anguish of the struggle was nearly over he looked beyond the hills and saw in the night a single star.

"The play," he repeated, "with but a single ending."

For the space of a moment she stood trembling, throbbing all over in an ecstasy of mingled joy and thankfulness.

"Ludwig," she said, looking up at him with large, honest eyes where courage burned steadily. "I know now that happiness is but the habit of good impulses."

He took her white face between his hands and kissed her trembling lips.

"Tell her, dear," she whispered. "She will understand."

"Heaven grant that she may!" he said.

For a while they stood watching the dim stars wake. He saw the grace of her little head with its heart-breaking beauty, and a keen pain swept through him, for he thought of the time when he parted from Marcelle.

"*L'amour oblige*," he had whispered then. Through the night he heard the Uhlan bugles in the village.

"With God, for Marcelle," he thought. "It is the only way. But love has its obligations, too, and when I tell her of Marguerite Clairon I believe she will understand."

Faintly, faintly, came the bugle calls. *Halt! Dismount! Break Ranks!*

Marguerite raised her face to his and a

delicate fire stole up to burn there unreproved.

"Ludwig," she said, "until to-night I believe I have never lived."

She waited, awed by the luxury of the sacrifice she had made, until at the window she saw a face.

The man's cap was drawn low over his eyes, but she saw the ashen cheeks, the retreating chin with the pointed beard, the smile on the set lips, and fear thrilled every fibre of her body.

White and rigid as a thing of marble she watched the face at the window—then gathered courage and drew the curtain quickly.

"Why did you do that?" Ludwig asked, for he had not seen the franc-tireur.

"Ludwig," she said, "you are very weak remember and you must rest. I am going to send word to the Prussians you are here. Promise me you shall not leave this room until I return." Her eyes did not waver from his glance, but in the dim light he did not see the look of terror in her pale, quivering face.

"But Marguerite," he protested. "You must not go—to the village—alone and at night."

"I saw at the window a peasant whom I know," she said. "He will take my message."

He caught her hand as she left and touched it to his lips.

"God give me courage," she prayed as she went out into the night.

VIII

THE TIGER'S CLAWS

Marguerite passed into the garden and stood among the shadowy vines with her ears strained for the coming danger. The air was sweet with country vapours; fleecy clouds hung motionless above the trees, the winds were still and the pale fire of the moon kindled her face and her shining hair. It was a night in which to dream away the world, but it was a dirge her heart drummed out, as a footfall rustled the dead leaves and D'Arblay came towards her, glancing from side to side.

He wore a képi low upon his forehead and a sleeveless sheep-skin jacket over a peasant's blouse; a revolver was stuck in his belt and a sword hung at his side. One by one she saw his francs-tireurs step from behind the trees, their rifles glimmering in the misty light.

"The tiger's claws," he said, pointing towards his men, and he grinned fearfully.

Half defiant, half terrified, she watched him with a steady, narrowing gaze.

"The fool is still hiding behind his threats, I see," but she trembled at her daring.

"He need hide no longer, *ma chère*.   He
has waited patiently and his time has come."

In the shadowy light she saw the set smile
which neither grew nor faded, but seemed cast
upon his lips.

"Well, what is the fool's revenge?" she
answered with an attempt at courage, but a
deep tide of despair came sweeping over her.

"When the francs-tireurs of the Ardennes
find a Prussian in hiding they are apt to suspect him of being a spy and they don't quib-
ble much about courts-martial."

He spoke with sarcasm, but in his eyes she
saw a look of craft and venom. Like a
caught animal she stared about her. The
sense of her impotence overcame her. The
catastrophe that overhung Ludwig, the fate
so treacherously prepared for him, confused
her brain almost to delirium. In lightning
flashes of her mind she forecasted what would
happen: Ludwig in the hands of those cut-
throats—the horror filled her with helplessness.
She strove to think, to calculate the chances,
to invent some way to save him.

"The Prussians," she thought, "scarce a
kilomètre away." Her heart gave a great
jump, then seemed to stand still—for before
her quivering eyes were D'Arblay's ruffians,
with their rifles gleaming in the night.

Mercy! The man knew not the quality of it. Ah! but he had one vulnerable point—his passion for her. Time and again she had seen him tremble at her glance, but dared she hope?

"Strategy," she thought, "the rôle of *commédienne*—and if I fail—tragedy!"

He was very close, but she crept nearer until he touched the softness of her dress and her breath fanned his face.

"Really, Paul D'Arblay," she said, looking up at him with insinuating eyes, "you have missed your calling; you should have been a barytone."

"A barytone!" he repeated in amazement.

"Yes, *mon cher*, a barytone in opera bouffe," and her little low laugh trembled through the night.

His face flushed, his dark brows knitted.

"Take care, Marguerite," he muttered, "I'm in no mood for raillery—I'm here for a purpose."

"What an impressive barytone villain we are," she said with a feigned shudder, and for a moment she hummed a tune. "What a superb *coup de théâtre* we have planned," she went on after she had raised her eyes to his and lowered them gently, after her lips had smiled half parted.

"The chorus of loutish peasants steals on in

the moonlight disguised as fierce brigands. Their chief, the barytone villain, holds the centre of the stage while his cut-throats surround the bower where the gipsy maiden nurses her tenor lover back to life——"

"Stop," he growled, his blood afire with anger. "Stop, I tell you; this is no time for *badinage*. You are concealing a Prussian spy. I am here to do my duty."

"Bravo!" she cried, clapping her hands. "Bravo! You have rehearsed your part superbly—now I will listen while you sing a solo—about revenge."

"By God, Marguerite," he shouted, "you shall hold your tongue," and he clutched her arm and shook her.

She felt pain in her wrist, but she never took her eyes off him. "Ridicule," she thought; "the weapon a man parries worst."

He loosed her arm; she looked up and laughed.

"Now the gipsy pleads for her lover—ah, but wait. I'm not made up for the part."

Trembling, smiling and afire, she tore open her dress and folded it back to form a broad collar. He caught the gleam of her white breast and as her hair fell loose upon her shoulders in a wavy, glinting mass he saw her beautiful beside him in a night of wonderful brilliance—saw her curving lips—her fathomless eyes with a glance that set his pulses throbbing.

"Well, Monsieur *le scélérat*, shall we go on with the piece; shall it be a duet?" and she threw her arms around his neck.

"Dear villain, sweet villain, a maiden prays," she whispered close to his face. Her breath came fluttering and quick; in that moment as she held him in her arms, a fierce torrent swept through him, but, like a drowning man, he fought to breast it.

"Do you think I don't see through your tricks?" he muttered. "You must be a fool."

With a mocking laugh she sprang away.

"No, Paul D'Arblay, but you are."

"Take care," he growled.

"What! More opera bouffe?" and she rattled the sword by his side and sang in a taunting way:

"Voici le sabre, le sabre de mon père."

"I'll put an end to this nonsense," he cried, wheeling towards his men.

She saw them beyond in the night—wiry, savage-eyed rascals fingering their gun-locks. The horrors which had beset her seized her anew and filled her with a maddening sense of fear.

"Wait," she said in a dry, low voice—"Let me ask one question."

"Well," he answered with a shrug, half afraid to meet her eyes, for all the passion of his fiery nature trembled through him, the pent-up passion from years of scorn.

"You knew when I brought him here, why did you wait until to-night?"

As she spoke the Prussian bugles in the village sounded the beautiful notes of "Tattoo" softly on the night air.

"To let you hear those Prussian bugles," he answered with a laugh of triumph, "and think that your lover was—safe."

"So the revenge was for me?" she said quickly.

He took a step towards her and caught her arm.

"You have played the rôle of Torquemada —so can I!"

Tense as a swordsman before an adversary, she watched him, for she knew that the moment had come to conquer or fail.

"So the torture is for me!" she said. "I supposed you remembered a pack of cards."

He looked so threatening with his dark, harsh face that she feared she stood to lose all, or more than all she had won by her boldness.

"I could have settled my score with him

long ago, but for you, my beauty," and he laughed a low laugh of content.

A woman less brave would have given up the contest. But though her colourless face showed she knew what she had to fear, though her heart was sick with downright terror, she held her ground.

"As for me, Monsieur," she said, looking up at him with a taunting smile, "I acknowledge you are devoted beyond my fondest dreams."

"Devoted?" he answered between his teeth.

"Yes, and jealous, Paul D'Arblay, and a fool into the bargain because you fancy I am in love with this Prussian," she hesitated. "*Mon Dieu*, if you knew women better."

"*Sacré!* Not in love with him; another trick—" but his eyes devoured her.

"My dear Paul," she said, stealing very near him, with the moonlight full upon her. "Do I act like a woman in love? Have I shed one tear or gone into a single paroxysm of terror at your threats and the sight of your men. If you carry out your plans to murder a defenseless, wounded man in cold blood—I shall loathe you as I should any other brute, but I can excuse your following me from Paris— excuse your foolish threats of revenge because I believe you are jealous of this Prussian.

Yet, I do not care for him," she whispered;
"so why play opera bouffe?"

He loved her in his tempestuous way—loved
her because she had been unyielding.

"You must think I am very credulous," he
said, "but I have not forgotten that you fled
from Paris on account of this Prussian and
that you have nursed him back to life."

"I did love him," she answered in a tone of
ennui, "but a woman can change her mind,
can't she? *Mon Dieu*, but you are stupid."

He saw the look of the temptress and stood
there enraptured.

"If you understood women," she murmured.

"Marguerite," he cried trembling.

"*Fichtre*, but you are stupid," she laughed.
"It is one thing to love a well Prussian—but
a sick one—*oh, la-la.*"

He saw her eyes so starry bright and
trembled with a throbbing fire.

"I love you, Marguerite," he cried.   "I
love you!"

His words gave her heart beats a tune of joy.
The price! she thought.   Yet she knew she
should give her life gladly.

"Wait, Monsieur," she said when he tried to
take her in his arms.   "Because I don't love
a Prussian it does not follow that I love tigers

—or barytones," she added in a playful way.
"I am exacting, Paul D'Arblay."

"And adorable," he murmured. Her hands
were cold and her heart throbbed, but she
made a bold play of the rôle she was acting.

"Nursing wounded soldiers," she said.
"Very romantic in novels—but when they are
peevish and exacting give me Paris, Paul
D'Arblay, even with a *mauvais sujet* like you,"
and she turned her lips up towards him, but
when he tried to kiss her—a laugh and a slap
of her little hand.

"Not till I'm sure."

"You bewitching creature," he cried.

"Listen," she said, with a glance at the
francs-tireurs in the night beyond, "I can
tolerate a jealous man—but not a brigand.
Send those fellows away."

A hard smile crossed his face.

"Ah, I see; a trick to save your lover's life."

"He will think that I betrayed him. I could
not be so brutal even to a man who bores me."

"I'm not a fool," he sneered, "I'll settle
accounts with him, and then——"

She looked at him straight between the eyes
though her heart stood still.

"You talk to me of love and in the same
breath of murder. The man has done me no
harm. I'm not a Borgia."

"He is a Prussian spy," he said.

"You know better, Paul D'Arblay," she cried, the gleam of a terrible prescience in her eyes.

"He shall have a trial," he growled.

"By you?"

"No, by the authorities."

"Then I must be tried as well," she answered with a shudder.

"You!" he exclaimed.

"I'm his accomplice if he's a spy. I was a hospital nurse. I deserted my post. You must arrest me, too; yet, you talk to me of love. *Allez vous en.*"

He caught both of her hands and peered into her face.

"If I could believe you're not tricking me."

"Have I ever broken my word?" she asked, searching his face for a ray of pity.

He felt the flutter of her hand in his—saw a look which sent the warm blood through his veins.

"You said that some day I should belong to you. Ah, can't you be generous?"

"And if I should be generous?" he said, blind to all but her beauty.

"Anything," she faltered, for his glance made the blood mount to her face.

"To-night?" he asked in a hoarse whisper.

She drew away trembling from head to foot. He stood watching her. She dared not hesitate.

"The Prussians are in the village," she said in a low, measured voice— "A word to them that a wounded officer is here."

"It is treason," he muttered. "My men would denounce me."

"Your men!" she scoffed. "Every rascal in the Ardennes. Brandy and hush-money are better than a dead Prussian."

He looked long and searchingly into her face, but her eyes did not waver from his.

"Ah, Marguerite," he cried, "if I did not love you!"

She turned towards the cottage which stood white and shadowy among the vines.

"To-night when he is gone you shall find me there."

"If I could believe."

"I have given my word," she said, and turned away.

IX

L'AMOUR OBLIGE

She stopped at the door of the cottage to listen. The moon had gone behind a cloud, but through the night she heard a muttered command, then footsteps rustling the dead leaves. For a time she stood very still with a hand upon her breast thinking of her misery. When she could hear no sound she went back to Ludwig's room. It was dark, but she heard his gentle breathing and knew that he lay asleep.

She lighted a candle and drew a chair beside the bed. She was capable of but one wish, and she sobbed, rather than breathed, it again and again—only to die! For a few moments she had lived in paradise; then she had been dragged down to torments, neither seeing why such torture had been hers, nor reasoning, but knowing only that love had lifted her above this world, above the stars. Ah, those few moments! They were her own, for even he should never understand. They had been the only real moments of her life, the only true moments—all the rest had been falsehood, delirium, emptiness.

She gazed at the sleeping soldier and to her he seemed the symbol of her faith. "A man with the courage to wait," she thought. "Yet, if his comrades knew they would turn from him and laugh. But it is the only way; all the rest is contradiction, hypocrisy, misery. Yes, and for the pleasure of men a world of women must suffer."

She bent her head and kissed his forehead, afraid lest he awake.

"Dear," she whispered, "we know that they are wrong."

Trembling, the girl pored over his face, and at last the words she feared to speak dragged out of her. "And because I am not worthy she will have the best the world can offer."

She paused, and in that moment it seemed as if destiny were beside her awaiting an answer.

Within the narrow prison of her heart a pure and glorifying love had been born and lo! the walls had been torn away and for a few short moments she had been free. Now she had been dragged back to the hateful bondage, and again the walls were there to crush her. "Is there no escape?" she cried out in her misery. "Must I live amid the lights and mirrors to the end?"

She was white except her lips. The moon

hung low and its pale glow came through the window and lighted her bowed head.

Motionless and cold she gazed at Ludwig with wide, tearless eyes—it seemed pain was no more for her; she had suffered too much.

"He will go back to the grey château—and the curtain will fall upon the beautiful war play." Suddenly her eyes filled with tears and the huge drops fell unheeded. "And he will never know," she thought.

She could see the garden, the still clouds motionless above the trees, the rifles in the misty light—see the glitter of D'Arblay's eyes —the smile of his thick lips as he whispered: "To-night."

A low cry of pain started from her; she caught at her breast and touched the locket which hung there. Hurriedly she buttoned the dress, afraid that he might awake and understand.

She took the candle and went over to the bureau. In the mirror she saw her pale face, and shuddering she thought of those hateful words, "Sometime, one year, ten years, it matters not, you will belong to me."

"Dear God!" she cried out. "Is it right? Is it just? She bent her head and held out her trembling hands; her heart was like an

aching, open wound, but praying she seemed
to see a dimly-lighted church where black-
gowned women knelt, and pale in the gloom
beyond the blazing altar, Saint Mary Magdalene borne heavenward by angels. "*Venez,
venez, Toi que j'adore*" came the voices singing.
Upon her outstretched arm she saw the cross
of red.

"Ah, what atonement can I make," she
thought, "except in death?"

"Marguerite," she heard him calling from
behind her, for he had awakened and seen her
standing before the mirror with hands out-
stretched.

Startled she turned and went towards him.
She was white as the starshine but she was
smiling.

"The peasant has gone to the village," she
said, fastening her tumbled hair and afraid
that he might ask.

He raised himself upon his sound arm.

"Ah, yes, I remember," he murmured, rub-
bing his eyes vaguely, "the Uhlans."

She came and stood beside him.

"Ludwig," she said when she dared look
into his questioning eyes, "the peasant was a
franc-tireur."

"A franc-tireur," he exclaimed, for her tone
rose menacing on that word. Her thought

was to make him realise the danger, but not for all the world should he know her sacrifice.

"A friend who came to warn me," she went on quickly. "They had watched the house and had seen me at the door when the Doctor came, so the ruse of my illness made them suspect, and to-night— Ah, Ludwig, if those Uhlans had not come."

She felt his gaze fixed upon her.

"Brave francs-tireurs," she said, with a quick little laugh. "A handful of Prussians come, and they scuttle to their holes like rabbits. To-night they are peaceful peasants—to-morrow they will shoot some lone courier from behind a hedge."

"But the friend who warned you?" he asked.

"At the age of seven he was my sweetheart. *Mon Dieu*, he loves me yet, so I sent him to the village."

"Ah, Marguerite," he cried in a voice full of gratitude, "must I owe you one more debt when my heart is already bankrupt?"

The eyes of the two met an instant, yet something she must have looked, for he understood. She turned away lest he divine the truth.

"Ah, would the Prussians never come!" she thought. Beaten out of her senses by the fear that D'Arblay might have tricked her, she went to the door and opened it. She listened until finally though the darkness she heard the steps of horses walking, the tinkle of sabres. She remained a long while in the doorway— until she knew that he stood beside her.

"They are coming, Ludwig,' she said eagerly; "they are coming," and she closed the door.

He felt in that moment that he could not leave her: gratitude, love—though he dared not think the word—all her sweet nature seemed to hold him spellbound.

"And you, Marguerite?"

But his eyes brimmed over he could say nothing more with his dry lips. She raised her white face and smiled.

"I shall play *La Dame aux Caméllias* and Armand will come to Paris and sit in the stalls; when the house applauds my wonderful acting —perhaps he will understand."

He could not leave her without a word—he could not deny the beautiful love he confessed to his inmost self.

"Marguerite," he cried trembling, "though I break a thousand promises——"

The miserable girl turned him a frightened face.

"Don't," she pleaded, "don't spoil the memory of that night."

Then, turning, she went to the bureau and

he saw her open a drawer she had locked and take from among the trinkets hidden there a bow of ribbon she had found next his heart when the surgeons dressed his wound.

She saw nothing with her dim eyes. She could only motion with her lips, but she held out her hand and he took it—a bow of scarlet ribbon stained with blood, and in that moment shame arose, a knight-errant to rescue his love for Marcelle.

His life passed before him with its struggles and pitfalls; he thought of the faith which had guided him from afar—like the single star which shone above the mountains. Was it his own will or an inheritance from that strange sect—his mother's people? He could not answer nor could he understand the mystery of a dual love, distinct, but a part of himself.

Of one thing only was he certain—when he might have wavered Marguerite Clairon pointed the way—so he bestowed willingly the homage of his heart. A poor return it seemed for all she had given him. In his inmost thoughts he seemed to stand alone with all the world arrayed against him. Had his life been a failure? Had he fought in vain for a false ideal? He dared not answer. Marcelle alone could judge.

He heard the steps of the Uhlan horses come nearer in the night and he watched her pathetic beauty, but his dumb lips would not speak.

Deadened by the suffering of her mute love she fingered the trinkets in the open drawer before her, until she touched a chemist's phial and wondered if her heart had the patience to live out its span of misery. Too weak to put aside the thought of peace, she held the pinkish fluid to the light, then, shuddering, she put the phial in the drawer, afraid that he had seen. But a feeling of rest stole over her as it did that night in the silent church, and she gazed steadfastly through the window into the night.

"*Halt*," came a voice from the darkness, then the jingle of steel as the soldiers swung from the saddle.

X

THE RENDEZVOUS

"The Uhlans march at daybreak," whispered a franc-tireur to Paul D'Arblay. "I have it from Yvette."

D'Arblay eyed a Prussian lieutenant holding the hand of a pretty girl beneath a table.

"Yvette would sell her soul to the devil, but not to a Prussian," he laughed.

"Therefore," said the franc-tireur, "it must be true."

The air of the cabaret was dense with smoke. At the tables sat members of D'Arblay's band in the guise of village idlers. Arms and accoutrements lay safely concealed in the forest of Avaux, and where was there a better hiding place, the leader thought, than under the noses of the Uhlans?

"And the wounded Prussian?" he whispered.

"Safe at the Uhlan camp, my captain."

"Sufficient unto the day," mused D'Arblay, as he filled his glass. "I am content to wait. Perhaps my time will come."

"The men are satisfied, I hope," he said after a moment.

The franc-tireur leisurely rolled a cigarette. "A napoleon apiece and brandy," he grinned.

"It's better than a dead Prussian," D'Arblay continued, thinking of Marguerite's words.

"So is a pretty girl, my captain," said the franc-tireur.

He resented the fellow's impudence, but to surrender a prisoner for his own ends was dangerously near treason. The man was the most desperate character in the band, and he knew that he had need of his good will, so, keeping an eye upon the Prussian officer, he quickly opened his purse beneath the table and slipped a few gold pieces into the franc-tireur's hand.

The man glared at the well-filled purse with envious eyes.

"*Sacré,*" he thought, "enough to keep me for a year." Then he raised his glass.

"To the rendezvous," he said with a knowing look.

The thought of Marguerite thrilled D'Arblay's blood. For a time he watched the Uhlan officer and Yvette, the pretty waitress of the cabaret. The Prussian tried to kiss the girl, and when she slapped his face a titter ran round the room. The Uhlan was flushed with drink and he staggered to his feet with a hand upon his sabre. While he stormed and cursed at those who mocked him, D'Arblay improved the moment to steal from the room, as he thought, unobserved.

But the franc-tireur who had sat beside him fingered the gold pieces in his pocket.

"There are more where these came from," he mused, and he felt the sheath-knife beneath his peasant blouse.

"He is going to the rendezvous. I might go, too—then one less rascal in France and the gold pieces for Jacques Tellier."

Pleased with the thought, he drained the absinthe in his glass; while Yvette calmed the angry Prussian with a kiss upon his bearded cheek, he slipped through the door unnoticed and, skulking through the village street in the shadow of the house walls, reached the highway. Hearing D'Arblay's step ahead, he walked upon the grass beside the road and kept behind the trees.

"I don't begrudge him the rendezvous," he thought, "but when it is over a few more louis d'or for Jacques Tellier, sergeant of francs-tireurs and *ci-devant* pickpocket."

He followed D'Arblay until he reached the cottage among the vines. When he saw him enter he crept among the shrubs beside the door to wait, and drew from beneath his blouse a knife.

"*Mon Dieu,*" he thought as he fingered the blade, "there'll be one less rascal in France—so I do her a service."

When D'Arblay left the cabaret he hurried through the village street until he reached the highway stretching pale between two rows of poplars. He stopped to listen, but the man who followed walked noiselessly upon the grass beside the road and kept within the shadow of the trees; reassured, he hastened on.

It was a still night of surpassing radiance with the moon hanging high in the spangled sky above; the crisp air tingled and his coward heart throbbed faster at the thought of Marguerite's beauty, at the thought of triumph.

At last beside the road a cottage stood white in the silver night. He saw a light in the window. His eyes blazed and his face took on a look of fierce gladness, for he knew that she had kept her promise. The door stood partly open and he entered. In the little white room beside the hall a candle burned.

"Marguerite," he whispered, and hearing no answer, crept softly through the door she had left ajar.

In the alcove beside the table where the taper burned he saw the bed. A flicker of moonlight came through the window and beneath the glistening folds of her reddish hair he saw her white face upon the pillow with a smile supremely sweet—a look of happiness in the motionless open eyes.

"Marguerite," he called — she did not answer. He ran to the bedside with out-stretched arms and a face eagerly flushed, but a cry of horror started from his lips and he drew back shuddering. In the light which flowed through the window he saw that she was dead. Upon the table beside the bed he saw a chemist's phial with blood-red label and near it lay a gold locket. Clasped in the death-white hands pressed tight upon her breast was a faded rose.